the liar,
the bitch
and the wardrobe

the Liar,
the Bitch
and the Wardrobe

allie kingsley

BERKLEY BOOKS, NEW YORK

BERKLEY BOOKS
Published by the Penguin Group
Penguin Group (USA) Inc.
375 Hudson Street, New York, New York 10014, USA
Penguin Group (Canada), 90 Eglinton Avenue East, Suite 700, Toronto, Ontario M4P 2Y3, Canada
(a division of Pearson Penguin Canada Inc.) • Penguin Books Ltd., 80 Strand, London WC2R 0RL,
England • Penguin Group Ireland, 25 St. Stephen's Green, Dublin 2, Ireland (a division of Penguin
Books Ltd.) • Penguin Group (Australia), 250 Camberwell Road, Camberwell, Victoria 3124, Australia
(a division of Pearson Australia Group Pty. Ltd.) • Penguin Books India Pvt. Ltd., 11 Community
Centre, Panchsheel Park, New Delhi—110 017, India • Penguin Group (NZ), 67 Apollo Drive,
Rosedale, Auckland 0632, New Zealand (a division of Pearson New Zealand Ltd.) • Penguin Books
(South Africa) (Pty.) Ltd., 24 Sturdee Avenue, Rosebank, Johannesburg 2196, South Africa

Penguin Books Ltd., Registered Offices: 80 Strand, London WC2R 0RL, England

This is entirely a work of fiction. In those instances where celebrities are named,
and make cameo appearances, the use of the celebrity's real name should not be understood
as suggesting that the occurrence described actually took place, much less that the celebrity was
involved in any way. As for the rest of the characters and events in this novel, they are all fictional.
Thus, although some of them are inspired by real-life personalities and events, that should not
be understood as suggesting that any character is meant to accurately depict a real person
(none are), or that any event actually happened as described (none did).

This book is an original publication of The Berkley Publishing Group.

Copyright © 2012 by Allie Kingsley.
Cover design by Diana Kolsky.
Cover photographer: Ashley Barrett.
Hair stylist: Stephanie Hobgood.
Makeup artist: Alexis Swain.
Book design by Kristin del Rosario.

PUBLISHING HISTORY
Berkley trade paperback edition / September 2012

Library of Congress Cataloging-in-Publication Data

Kingsley, Allie.
The liar, the bitch and the wardrobe / Allie Kingsley.
p.   cm.
ISBN 978-0-425-25539-1
1. Women photographers—Fiction.   2. Fame—Fiction.   3. Celebrities—Fiction.
4. Hollywood (California)—Fiction.   I. Title.
PS3611.I63256L53   2012
813'.6—dc23
2012017074

PRINTED IN THE UNITED STATES OF AMERICA

10   9   8   7   6   5   4   3   2   1

"Don't count on this book thing happening.
Please get a real job."

—MY MOTHER (I LOVE YOU, TOO.)

Preface

A series of flashes exploded from multiple strobe lights, setting off a popping sound each time. I lifted a folded tripod, kicked out its legs, then knelt down to secure it in place. I felt a hand on my shoulder and turned to the two women standing over me.

The shorter of the two wore a half apron packed with makeup brushes of every size. She had smudges of eyeliner and shadow on the back of her hands from testing colors out on herself. "Hey, Lucy . . . what do you think of this?"

I stood up and did an about-face. I folded my arms and put one hand under my chin as I did whenever I was giving something my full attention. I tilted my head while carefully studying the model's face. Her porcelain skin was painted to near perfection. "I think that she needs a darker, pinker lip."

The artist exhaled a sigh of relief and exclaimed, "Thanks

Lucy! I thought so too!" The women strutted off into the flashing lights.

"There's my girl!" The photographer, world-famous Stefano Lepres, skipped over and handed me a medium-format camera. "Let's set this up for the next shot, shall we?" I smiled at him as he patted me on the back before walking away to discuss lighting with two other photo assistants. I flipped the Hasselblad over and began tinkering with the aperture. The flashing lights continued to pop off toward a fog that flooded the ethereal-looking set. The makeup artist was putting finishing touches on the models who were practicing preening in the direction of the lights as we, the crew, prepped for the shot.

Abruptly, the camera I was holding began beeping wildly. I turned the dial from auto to manual but the nagging sound persisted. People were staring, some glaring at me. What was happening? Why couldn't I silence the annoying sounds interrupting the shoot? I frantically wrapped my cardigan around the camera, trying to muffle the incessant *beep beep beep*ing, but it seemed to be getting louder by the second. I started to really panic, when—

I stretched my arm out from under the cozy comforter. The cold air tingled across my skin as I blindly located the largest button on the little black box next to my twin-sized bed. I slammed my fist down on it and the beeping ceased. I peeked out from my tangled sheets to look at my alarm clock. It was 8:00 a.m. Time to start the first day of the rest of my life.

chapter one

Don't You Know Who (I Think) I Am?

I couldn't tell if the wetness dripping down the sides of my face was sweat or rain drizzling from the gray sky. As I held the creased *Los Angeles Times* directly above my head so as not to drench my coveted portfolio or smear my mascara, I leaned my body in toward the forbidding steel door. My voice became frantic. "What do you mean, you have no idea who I am? Dan is expecting me."

"Who?" An exotic-looking Asian girl with smoky pink eye shadow backed up slightly, keeping the door open only a fraction.

"Dan . . . DAN! I interviewed him for my 'Working in the Arts' article for the Art Institute of Seattle . . . because he works here . . . for Stefano Lepres." At the mere mention of His name, the young woman closed the door even more. "My name is Lucy . . . Lucy Butler." Desperation shook me to the core.

"Look, I don't know who you are and we're in the middle of shooting. You're going to have to leave, sorry." SLAM. LOCK. LOCK. LOCK. An evil bolt of lightning flashed briefly across the sky, followed by a jolting pound of thunder that roared across the palm-tree-lined streets.

I could actually feel the color leave my face. My heart barreled down into my stomach as I stood on the step of a Spanish-named street in an unfamiliar area. The rain continued to pour down on the City of Angels as if heaven were attempting to submerge it completely.

I dragged my feet across the quiet, slick road in disbelief. This was not how I had imagined the first day of my internship. I paused mid-road and pivoted to take another look at the studio. It appeared to be a deserted and ordinary garage from the outside, but I knew what could only be described as magic was happening beyond the fortress façade—and I was supposed to be in there. Raindrops trickled down my ponytail and into the neck of my oxford shirt. I blinked away a blend of rain and tears while reciting the conversation that had brought me here.

I was ecstatic to be speaking to an actual employee of Stefano Lepres! He had called me, in response to my numerous phone calls to the studio and e-mails to the generic address on Lepres' website, pleading to interview anyone from the studio for a school assignment. It was one of the highlights of my life, so of course I vividly remember every word that he said. Plus, I took notes. There is no way that I misunderstood what he meant when he said, "You sound like a cool chick. We're always hiring interns. Come to LA! I'll get you in!" A cool chick I was not, but possibly he felt some kindred spirit with me, since he had probably once been in my shoes. Why not pay it forward? I certainly would. I recall beaming. "You'd help me get a job with Stefano? That would be amazing!" His friendliness and open-arms attitude was starkly contrasted with my encounter with the mean door girl and her stupid conjunctivitis-esque eye shadow.

My posture fell into a defeated slump after I climbed into my Jeep and started the engine. As I sat there, gripping the steering wheel with my wet hands, I dared to glance back once again at the building. The one ounce of optimism left in me hoped that Dan had heard that I'd arrived and was mistakenly turned away. He would rush out the door in search of me, apologetically escort me in, and introduce me as the new intern for the greatest photographer in the world, the one and only Stefano Lepres. I stared at the building, willing Dan to appear, but the steel door remained shut.

Navigating my ancient Jeep Wrangler through a sea of stalled luxury cars, I headed north on Sunset Boulevard. "It's just rain, people!" I yelled through the zipped-up plastic windows. I hoped that I was going in the right direction. I had only driven up the famous strip a few times. Fortunately the iconic landmarks assisted me like breadcrumbs on a trail. Chateau Marmont. The Sunset Plaza. The Roxy. And . . . turn.

Infiltrating the "cool crowd" was not an unfamiliar challenge for me. Unfortunately, this was not the first time a mean girl shut a door in my face. Natalia B. was having the slumber party to end all slumber parties. The crème de la crème of the ninth grade was in attendance. I could only imagine what actually happened at a "cool girl" sleepover. Luckily I would soon know, since Julie K. passed me her Bedazzled invite during biology class and said, "You should come! Natalia's mom told my mom everyone is invited!"

From the porch I clutched my *NSYNC sleeping bag and glittered retainer case tightly. I motioned quickly behind my back, waving my parents off so they and their minivan didn't embarrass me. The giant front door opened halfway, much like it did today, although this time, Katie G. answered the door and quipped, "No nerds allowed. Sorry, Lucy, but this party is by invite only." The door shut and I could see her shadow walk away from the frosted glass entrance as another came forward. Julie K. slipped through the door and put her hands on my shoulders. "I am so sorry, Lucy! I guess that I was wrong about everyone being invited." It was hard to be mad at Julie even then because she was so beautiful and angelic looking, with her almost white hair and luminous blue eyes. Julie was the only nice popular girl in school. I shrugged my shoulders and began to walk down the driveway before any of the girls, now piled up along the living room window to watch the scene unfold, could see me cry. "Wait!" Julie bellowed as she skipped down the driveway. "I'll walk you home!" Perhaps it was this twinkle in my childhood that gave me a glimmer of hope that Dan would appear and turn things around.

The Los Batres apartment complex was a tiny Spanish-style building with a minute kidney-bean-shaped pool located just off Melrose Avenue. I dropped my soaked trench coat, shoes and bag in the tiny den of my apartment. "Julie? Sebastian?" I called out toward the two bedrooms. There was no response. I had figured when I moved into the converted two-bedroom apartment with two other roommates that any alone time would be few and far between, so I decided to take advantage of this current solitude.

I entered the bedroom that I now shared with my best friend since ninth grade, Julie Kaplan. You see, when Julie walked me home after being rejected from the house of awesome, my life was forever changed. I offered to show her the photographs I had been editing for our class yearbook. It was then that I became aware of the power of photography. Naturally, she wanted to take the pictures of her friends back to the party, but as an official yearbook photographer, I could never let them out of my sight. So with one phone call, I was re-invited back to Natalia B's. "Bring your camera!" they urged. Thereafter, I wasn't just invited to the cool kids' parties; they insisted I attend. Photography was my "in." I became an even hotter commodity once I learned how to use Photoshop. According to photographic evidence, there was not a single pimple or flyaway hair to pester the populars all through high school.

What drew me to photography in the beginning was its honesty. The camera does not lie. Film records truth, delivering experiences exactly as they occur. It is the photographer's job to capture the emotion in the best light by way of composition and timing. It is a very simple, honest concept. The more that I compromised this honest documentation, the easier it was to get caught up and lose sight of what it—and I—was all about. By staging shots and retouching the images to the girls' liking, together we created a false reality, much like the pros do in fashion photography. Digital manipulation granted the girls fuller lips, bigger breasts and clearer skin, and I was the one who could deliver such luxuries with just a few clicks of a mouse. The camera may not lie, but we sure do.

I constantly reminded myself that my presence was not to be confused with their acceptance. Although I received a VIP pass to popularity, I was still the outsider, a gawky girl who knew how to make everyone else look spectacular. The alternative was to remain a nobody, and being around those girls made me feel like a somebody. I wasn't in any of the pictures, so it didn't matter that I didn't look like one of them. Why even try? It was the same way that I viewed my relationship with fashion. Upon inspection, one would never assume that I know fashion. And I don't mean that in an I-know-better-than-to-wear-stripes-with-plaid kind of way, which you can actually do—but that's another story. What I mean is, I know the difference between Proenza and Prada. I can spot a stiletto and tell you who made it and what season. Well, when I spot it in a magazine, that is. But just because I devour dailies and watch *Fashion Week* on YouTube, it doesn't mean that it has a place in my real life. I often wonder who actually wears those clothes, and where are they going? True, of course those people exist—just not in my world. Besides, I would rather spend my money on a new Nikon. I was forever going to be a little chubby, a little frizzy and a lot less fashion forward than my peers—and I have always been cool with that. That's who I am and it's worked for me. Up until now.

Julie and I had always enjoyed slumber parties, but sleeping in twin-sized beds at twenty-two seemed absurd. I collapsed backward onto my mini-mattress and pushed hard on my tired eyes. I refused to get upset so easily and promised to daydream of the happy, hopeful place I had been just one week ago . . .

It had been another rainy day much like today, however in Seattle where it is expected and accepted. I waited impatiently in my career counselor's office for our final meeting. James Braves was young, only ten years my senior, and enthusiastic about helping "his" students. His perfect smile and winning personality caused quite a few girls at the Art Institute to scrutinize his hand for a wedding band and hope for a chance at a post-graduation date. I'll admit that I too wondered about his relationship status, but mostly because I was curious to know who the luckiest-girl-ever would be. I imagined her to be a sun-kissed, willowy blonde with a toned body and blinding smile, just like James. Fantasizing about him being with me would be a waste of time because there was no way a girl like me stood a chance with a guy like him. But he was always nice to me. He often e-mailed me industry news and notified me of local photography assistance work. In fact, I suspected that he sometimes sent me job postings before placing them on the student bulletin board. Fortunately, since he was a huge supporter of my work, it gave me plenty of face-time where I'd pretend that we were at a Parisian bistro table for two and not a particleboard desk for too many. Okay, fine. Yes, I did fantasize about James Braves—but who didn't? As I waited in his office, my eyes fell on a photo of James and his golden retriever on a river raft. My heart felt like it was thumping and flashing from inside me like a strobe light gone awry. He had the kind of long, curly brown hair that fell just where it should, and his natural smile showcased the kind of teeth that people paid top dollar for.

"Good morning, future star shooter," James said with that mesmerizing smile as he entered his office. He put his hand on the shoulder of my faded zip-up hoodie as he walked by. Could he hear my heart being catapulted across my chest? I sure did. "You must be pretty stoked about being this close to the end." He sat down in his chair.

"As my guidance counselor, shouldn't you be saying 'close to the beginning'?" I studied him as he got up, retrieved a file with my name scribbled across the top and quickly shuffled through the papers before tossing it on the desk between us.

"Touché . . . got me there. Tell me, what are you thinking? Wait, let me guess: Stefano Lepres or bust?"

I smiled and nodded. "Yup."

"Hollywood is a tough place, Lucy. You might want to get a few years in working for some local photographers, perfect your craft with the small fish before taking on the big sharks . . . You're such a sweet girl, Luce. I'd rather see you stay in Seattle and let me continue to work with you on shaping your career and . . ."

He continued speaking, but he'd lost me at "sweet." He thinks I'm a sweet girl? Did he just call me "Luce"! Only my closest friends and family call me Luce! He thinks I am a sweet girl and he called me Luce! Briefly, I wondered if he saw me as I saw myself, a slightly frazzled art student geek with grease pencils holding up my ponytail. Or was it possible that I had some undiagnosed case of dysmorphia and was unknowingly a smoking-hot Victoria's Secret supermodel doppelganger?

"Lucy . . . Do you get what I am saying?" I mentally snapped back to earth. Reality check to self! I am in fact the frazzled art student geek with grease pencils holding up my ponytail, and I should be focusing on the one and only thing James . . . err . . . um, Mr. Braves would ever be interested in when it comes to me: my career.

"Look, there is no way I am going to turn down a once-in-a-lifetime internship for the photographer who inspired me to get into photography in the first place. I'd be crazy!" I exclaimed. "Besides, I'm moving there with my best friend, Julie, and we have already committed to an apartment and everything . . . Sure, it's Hollywood and I'm still not certain as an adjective what that means exactly but I'm ready to find out."

James sat up and turned away to tap his pencil on the desk a few times before tossing it to the side and facing me. "Okay, I admire your determination and I do believe you will get a job with him . . . eventually. But, don't put all your eggs in one basket. Have a backup plan before you leave. You know what I mean? This internship sounds a little . . . sketchy."

"Sketchy? Dan offered me an internship! He said that it was 'no problem.' What else did he need to say? I'm sure that he wouldn't just invite me down if he wasn't positive that I'd be hired. He knew that I'd be coming all the way from Seattle . . ."

"Based on what, Lucy?" James said, sternly. "You were interviewing him for a paper, correct? Did he interview you?

Did he ask about your capabilities or experience on a set? At any point did Dan Whatever-His-Last-Name-Is request a resume or references even?"

It was kind of cute how heated up he got over my well-being, and it excited me a little bit. James's concerns were valid, and I had considered them myself, but they were overshadowed by the opportunity. I reasoned that it could be possible Dan just had a gut feeling that I was a hardworking, honest girl and he simply wanted to help me out. Instead of addressing every detail of the situation, I silently agreed to disagree.

"I understand and will have a backup plan."

"What about your parents? Any help from them?" The mention of my folks brought me back to earth.

"From Dr. and Mrs. Butler? To support me moving over a thousand miles away? Oh sure, they're stuffing hundred-dollar bills in my pockets every time I visit. It's getting out of control really . . . In fact they . . ."

"Okay, I get it! They still haven't gotten over the fact that you went the 'alternative route.'" James used his hands to gesture quotation marks around the words "alternative route" and flashed his irresistible smile.

"Well, it's my father who doesn't agree with my choosing art over science, being a doctor and having great connections and all. He'd rather see me take a safer, more conservative route. My mom, on the other hand, loves that I am getting involved with photography, since it has always been my thing, but hates the idea of me having anything to do with Holly-wood. She reads those trashy tabloids and thinks that it is all sex, drugs and silicone." I laughed at the thought.

James's eyes drifted to an actual smoking-hot Victoria's Secret supermodel doppelganger as she strutted past the glass partition. I glanced at her too, my eyes momentarily transfixed on the back of her perfect thighs as she walked away. I subconsciously tugged at the bottom of my sweatshirt to cover the top of my own thunder thighs. Late nights in the darkroom had led to many visits to the vending machine and drive-thru dinners—and neither had been kind.

I continued my ramblings. "So . . . I guess they're worried that I am making a huge mistake. But I love photography, and it's not about Hollywood; it's about Lepres! Plus, yes, Stefano is my idol, but he is also the greatest photographer in the world. He is a genius!"

James refocused, tugged at the collar of his shirt and leaned forward, resting his elbows on top of his knees. "Listen, your portfolio is exceptional. But I've heard some crazy stories about this Stefano Lepres character . . . I gotta tell you, Butler, he seems a little out there . . . Even his work is a little . . . out there." He opened the top drawer and pulled out the latest issue of *American Photo,* sliding it across the desk.

I turned to a page marked by a yellow sticky note. The headline read, "Inside the Mad Mind of This Generation's Fellini: The Great Stefano Lepres." Of course, I had already read this issue. In fact, I had two copies because the newsstand had it before my subscribed edition arrived in the mail. A portrait of Lepres was displayed on the first page of the article. His smile was inviting, his dark chocolate eyes alluring. A model once-upon-a-time, he knew how to work with his chiseled cheekbones and square jaw. Another photo of him on a red carpet accompanied the article. He flashed a peace sign and appeared as if he had just stepped out of the Salvation Army based on his androgynous ensemble. His standard look consisted of muddy and muted oatmeal hues layered loosely over his lanky frame. He appeared very thrown together, but judging by his work, one could only assume that it was a thoughtfully planned-out appeal. Regardless, I appreciated that he dressed down and figured that this meant he was low-key, just another photographer who knew his purpose was to make others look spectacular.

"He looks like a nice guy to me," I defended.

James took the magazine from my hands and thumbed to page three. He read aloud, "'Lepres declined to comment on the rumor of his on-set meltdown resulting in setting superstar Beyonce's hair on fire.'" He looked up at me with a smile that said *Are you nuts?*

"I know. I've read stuff too," I admitted. "But I mean, really? You can't believe everything that you read. I'm sure that is part of some silly rumor started by a jealous industry person. Clearly you missed this part of the article . . ." I took the magazine back and flipped back to page two. A portrait of a dozen colorful people took over most of the third page. They all posed and preened into the camera. None of them had model looks but they all exuded confidence and artistic know-how. Surely they were once frazzled art geeks themselves. I read aloud, "'We consider ourselves the Lepres Family; consisting of dreamers, visionaries and trendsetters, each hand-picked by Stefano. He not only captains the ship but encourages us to be better as artists and grow in our field,' says Elizabeth Rich, a former intern turned lead producer." I continued reading: "'My designs would never have seen the light of day if Stefano hadn't come along. Now you can't open any magazine further than five pages without seeing one of my creations. I am forever grateful for his ability to turn anything that he touches to gold!' says former assistant stylist turned fashion maven Frankie Fredo."

James remained unimpressed. "And . . . ?"

"And? Anyone that works for him goes somewhere—fast! Could you imagine the possibilities? A few years with Lepres and I could be the next Ellen von Unwerth! Who knows? And besides that, they are the type of artsy family that I've always wanted to be part of. I want to be one of them so badly. I think that I belong there. Actually, no—I know that I belong there. Does this make sense?"

James exhaled deeply as he spun his chair around to a file cabinet. He removed a heavy paper bag from a metal drawer and put it on my lap. "Perfect sense."

"What's this?" I unfolded the sack and stared inside. Peeking right back at me was an old Nikon camera.

"I found it at a vintage shop a few years ago and never got around to using it. It is basically worth nothing and I know it's not as glitzy as the flashy digital ones . . . but there is something honest and real about its simplicity. It's authenticity made me think of you." My jaw fell. I never in my wildest dreams expected a gift from James Braves. He was thinking of me outside of school? Maybe I'm not clinically insane. Perhaps there is an Otter Pops chance in hell that he . . . Stop, Lucy! Just stop! I had to pull myself back to reality yet again. It's an old camera in a paper bag, not a Tiffany ring in a blue box! Get a hold of yourself! I picked up the camera and gave it a closer inspection. As hokey as it sounds, I felt a real connection to the clunker. I imagined that we, the camera and I, would go on our own adventure, becoming better than anyone expected.

"Wow, Mr. Braves . . . err . . . um, James. I really don't know what to say! Thank you . . . so much!" I stood up and surprised myself by giving him a full-on hug.

"Hey, you'll be great—and remember, I'm always here for you!" Probably realizing the questionable appropriateness of his embrace with a student, James put his hands on my shoulders to put some distance between us. I briefly wondered if he would have done the same with the supermodel doppelganger. "When you're a famous photographer, don't forget about your first fan."

chapter two

What's Your Dream?

Balancing on the tips of my toes over the bed frame, I held up a giant poster of two fashionable girls wrestling over a sleeping jaguar. The vibrant colors jumped off the drab wall. A final thumbtack secured the lower left corner as I smoothed my hand across the poster before leaning back and allowing my eyes to feast on the image.

"Are you going to ask him to sign it?" Julie forced through a yawn as she entered the room with two steaming coffee mugs. I took one of the mugs with both hands.

"Probably. Definitely going to try to get those signed first." I nodded to the bookshelf showcasing Lepres' last three art books.

"You are totally obsessed!" Julie teased as she curled up on her bed, tucking her knees into her oversized T-shirt.

"I'm sorry—how many times have you made me watch

Lost in Translation? Just because Scarlett Johansson hasn't called you to be her next understudy doesn't mean that you can get on me for . . ." Julie sank farther into a sea of mismatched blankets and stared into her coffee. It seemed impossible for someone who had been told her whole life that she was perfect to have an ounce of self-doubt, but deep down Julie did have her insecurities. Something even I, her best friend, sometimes forgot.

"Yet," I amended quickly. "She hasn't called you *yet*, is what I meant to say. You are going to be one of the greatest actresses of our time, Jules!" Julie half smiled. "I can see it now!" I pulled my friend up from the bed by her arm before putting my arm around her shoulders. We turned toward the door, which I swiftly shut using my right foot. The opposing side of the door faced us, displaying a glamorous photo of Angelina Jolie, also shot by Lepres. "That is going to be you and I am going to be the one behind the camera! Together all the way! Just like we've been saying since we were fourteen! Remember the day we decided that we'd move to LA and follow our dreams?"

"Yeah, the day that I didn't get cast for any of the lead parts in *Rent*. I hated that day."

"Yeah, but then we ditched school and snuck into the movie theater with two pints of ice cream! I loved that day!"

"That's right! We tapped our spoons together and swore on Ben and Jerry that one day you'd make it as a famous photographer and I'd make it as a movie star. We were such dorks."

"Jules, it's all happening now! We're here, and we are going to make it. We just need to make it happen! I mean, if only for Ben and Jerry . . ." I held my mug out.

Julie tapped her coffee mug to mine as we both took a sip, still eye to eye with Angelina. "You'd better *make it* to the studio soon. It's already late into the morning. I'd want to be there early just in case they are shooting again . . ." Realizing the time, I bolted for the bathroom and immediately turned the shower on. Over the crushing sounds pouring from the faucets, Julie yelled, "And take it easy in here! It's starting to look like a stalker's shrine!"

Once again, I followed the boulevard breadcrumbs in reverse to the studio. The Roxy. Sunset Plaza. The Chateau Marmont and . . . turn!

Eyeing myself in the reflection of a window around the corner from Stefano's studio, I tried to pump myself up. "You got this. This is your destiny," I whispered aloud. I stepped back and adjusted my sensible black slacks, beige button-down blouse and business casual flats. I had purchased a few interchangeable work-appropriate pieces from Ann Taylor Loft before leaving Seattle just in case they had me start right away. I pulled my ponytail apart tightly to secure it. My red hair was still slightly damp but I didn't want to waste time with heated tools. I was on a mission and time was of the essence. Once again, I marched right up to the familiar door and rang the buzzer.

"SLS," a male voice crackled out of the speaker box. Not so shockingly, I lost my voice and my nerve, as well as any ability to put words together. "Hellooooo? . . . Stefano Lepres Stuuuuudiossss . . . Wait, are you selling Bibles?"

Bibles? I looked up and acknowledged the small but obvious CCTV camera above the door. I spoke to it and said, "Am I . . . what? No . . . My name is Lucy Butler and"—deep breath—"I am here to intern." I pulled my head up high and took a dry gulp.

The door swung open and the human equivalent of a peacock emerged. A femme man wearing a rhinestone-encrusted, leopard-print, cropped Jeremy Scott T-shirt folded his arms and rested his fisted hand under his chin. "Are you sure? Because, quite frankly, you look like you're selling Bibles." He batted his faux eyelashes.

"No . . . I . . . I'm here to work. Is Dan here?"

"Who?" The peacock lifted his penciled eyebrows.

"Look, I came here to intern. Dan said to come to LA. I have a paid internship working for Mr. Lepres and . . ."

"A *paid internship*? Ha . . . darling, that is adorable! Tell me more!" He twirled his blinged-out Patricia Field grenade necklace in fascination.

"Yes, a paid internship . . . Is there a manager here? Or someone that I can talk to?" My face burned red with embarrassment and frustration.

"Yes and no. There is a manager; however, she is currently . . . indisposed. Now about those Bibles . . ."

For the next three weeks I diligently tried gaining access to Stefano's studio. It seemed like new people rotated there daily, because I never met the same person twice. Nobody knew who Dan was, so I stopped dropping his name after the third attempt. Not once did the steel entryway open farther than five inches as one exotic creature or another would scrutinize me up and down, then raise an eyebrow as if to say, *What can you possibly contribute here?* One day someone kindly let me slide my resume through the crack under the door. Still, every visit ended with a sassy studio worker cutting me off mid-sentence and slamming the door just inches from my reddened face. I was determined to keep trying because, while the door was barely being answered, I just knew that one day it would swing wide open. All I had to do was keep showing up. Besides, I told practically everyone in my life that I had this internship, and returning home to Seattle to say "I was wrong" was not an option.

Following the last rejection, I huffed all the way home and steamrolled into the apartment. Slamming the door behind me caused both roommates to look up from the couch in unison. I dropped my bags and portfolio to the floor and stomped into the bedroom, closing the door with my back and sliding down Angelina's pouting face before sobbing into my hands.

After a few quiet knocks on the door, I opened it to find Julie looking down at me. I rose to my feet and wiped away tears with my sleeve after accepting a much-needed hug.

"Don't worry, Luce. If you're stressed about money, I got a job at GiGi's today, and from what I understand that is a really good thing! Apparently, being a waitress is this town's secret gateway to everyone that you need to know. Maybe I'll meet a casting director on his lunch break . . . or a photographer looking for an assistant . . ." I nodded as she consoled me, but the thought of giving up on my dream was devastating, especially since I had come so close to making it happen. Or had I? Maybe I just wasn't cut out for this place.

Our third roommate entered the hallway with three color-ful margaritas in hand. Just like the flamboyant concoction, Sebastian was large, loud and proud. Although he was African-American, he was obsessed with all things Latin due to his unwavering crush on Ricky Martin, who he insisted he "had a moment with" at a bar once. He even had a Puerto Rican flag tattooed on his shoulder. Bas was never seen with-out a signature silky scarf worked into his wardrobe. He'd collected them for years, finding most of them on eBay where, he admitted, "It may not be real, honey, but it looks real good." Today he was wearing a navy one decorated with tiny "LV"s all over. It loosely hugged his neck and really brought out the blue in his colored contacts. Julie and I found his room for rent online and fell in love with him immediately. He was a self-described "slashie" (fashion stylist "slash" actor), although he never actually spoke of work or went on auditions. Julie had seen an unemployment check once, and he had mentioned being laid off from a "major film agency," which explained his ability to maintain. With his confident demeanor and fabu-lous presentation, Bas defined the phrase "fake it till you make it."

He beamed, "Girl, there isn't any sense in crying over not becoming America's Next Top Intern. You only just got here! Did Julia Roberts become a wifey one week after whoring her-self out to that financial fox? HALE no!"

"Um, actually, it *was* one week," I corrected.

"For the bargain rate of *three thousand dollars* . . ." Julie dra-matically quoted between sips of the potent drink.

"But nice try, Bas." I giggled through my tears.

Sebastian snapped his fingers and pointed at me. "Well,

there's your problem, honey! You put the wrong bait on the fishing wire! You should have sent me to Mr. Lepres—I'd have hooked that fine man just like Miss Roberts did!" He turned to walk away, slapped his derriere with his left hand, raised his glass high above his head with his right and let out a "Cinda-fuckin-rella! Welcome to Hollywood! What's your dream?"

chapter three

The G-Spot

The GiGi Spot (G-Spot, to those in-the-know) was a Spanish-Italian-French fusion restaurant that had been the most happening place to see and be seen at for the past year—a lifetime in LA, where attention spans are short and diners fickle. Rather than the standard chairs and barstools, the interior was adorned with wine-colored velvet chaise lounges. Seven gigantic gaudy chandeliers hung from the mirrored ceiling. It was alluring and overdone—much like its owner, Gi Gi Ramone, heiress to the Ramone Records family, a socialite known mostly for her late-night antics and appetite for infamous men. All those men must have kept her appetite at bay since, according to staff, she hadn't been seen in her own bistro for at least six months. I don't know if it was her absence or just the typical life cycle of an LA restaurant, but the G-Spot's glory was starting to fade. Although still busy, the crowds were beginning to thin and star sightings were less frequent. Still, I had to admit, I had read so much about the G-Spot in the tabloids that I was excited that Julie had an in where my favorite stars drank and dined.

Julie had become an excellent server, relishing her conversations with the rich and sometimes famous, even if it was limited to, "Shall we cook that rare, medium or well-done?" After five weeks of delivering minuscule servings of nouvelle cuisine on unnecessarily large plates, Julie was quite pleased with her finances and didn't even mind paying for both our parts of the rent and groceries, as long as I cooked, cleaned and did our laundry.

It was around this time that Gi Gi Ramone got caught in a sex tape scandal with her boyfriend of the minute—a rock-musician—and, thanks to the media, the G-Spot underwent a renaissance. Once again it was hot and business was booming. Famous people were making the scene and hordes of paparazzi lingered outside, hoping to get the "money shot." When the action outside was slow, Benny, the manager, provided the shutterbugs sandwiches and pasta to keep them close by. Yet when escorting a celebrity out of the club to a waiting car, Benny yelled at the paparazzi and called them "rats," only to wink and nod at them on his way back in.

Tonight had been an average night for the G-Spot, which was far above average for any other place in town. At eleven thirty in the evening the place was still buzzing with the A- and B-list.

"You waiting for Julie?" a bartender with movie-star looks questioned me as he flipped a short glass behind his back, caught it and filled it up with water, adding a sliver of lemon before placing it on a napkin in front of me. I pretended to be impressed even though he did this every time I came by to pick up Julie from work.

"Wow! Thank you! Yes, just waiting as usual." I knew why he was flirting with me. It was for the same reason that any guy had flirted with me since I was fifteen: Julie. Guys would do nearly anything to get closer to her. I had more dates with wingmen than I care to admit. Or dare to count.

"You want a cocktail?" he further inquired. I have never been much of a drinker. Even at parties in high school, I would sneak off to the bathroom, pour the beer out of a bottle and fill it with water. I had held the hair back for one too many of the populars puking their Pabst out at a house party. I swore that I would never be "that girl." I politely declined the beverage and zipped among the crowd in hopes of finding Julie. I stopped and looked around, eyes darting from famous face to famous face, when I felt my feet start to slide and, horrified, realized that I was stepping on the train of Jennifer Lopez's white silk Marchesa gown! Terrified, I leaped off the fabric. Like a cartoon, I imagined my eyes popping out from my head as they met the black imprint from my filthy footwear soiling the white train. I turned quickly and found myself eye to eye with an amused George Clooney. He raised his cocktail with one hand and put the pointer finger of his other hand to his lips, making a silent *shhh* motion. I gave him a nervous thumbs-up and immediately made my way to the front. That's right: a thumbs-up. Why was I acting like such an idiot? How did Julie manage to keep her cool around famous people?

"Julie! There you are! I have to get out of here. I'm an accident waiting to happen . . ."

"Yeah, me too. My feet are killing me." Julie rotated her left ankle. I also couldn't comprehend how the girls at GiGi's worked in their required sky-high heels. "Oh my God, I waited on Ryan Reynold's table tonight, and I have to tell you what he said! . . ." Julie always had the craziest celebrity encounters, which she excitedly shared with me after every shift.

We pushed open the tall double glass doors and took in a soft breeze. We were barely paying attention, as we almost walked right into two men.

The first man entered the restaurant, brushing past us without making eye contact, but then the second man opened the door the rest of the way and waited for us to walk out. I looked up to thank him for being so kind, and at that moment everything seemed to go into slow motion. In that split second, that face, *his* face, only inches from my own, registered in my mind. I couldn't breathe! As he headed inside and disap peared into the restaurant, I turned to an equally stunned Julie and we both mouthed in unison, *"Stefano Lepres!"* My knees went weak and I am still not sure if I was breathing at this point. I watched him make his way through the crowd and up the stairs to a table for two overlooking the scene.

"Go on. Go back in there and talk to him! This is your big chance . . . *Go!*" commanded Julie.

"I can't. I physically can't move. I can't do it," I told her as I started to shake.

"If you can't, then I will." Julie pushed past me and headed back into the restaurant. She slid her purse behind the hostess stand and picked up a cocktail tray from behind the bar.

I followed behind her, worried about what she might do. "Wait! Julie, stop! What are you doing?" I gasped.

Without a moment's hesitation, Julie marched right up to table thirteen and took his drink order. I was dying inside, watching her lean over Stefano Lepres. I could see her mouth forming the words, "See that girl over there?" and pointing right at me, frozen like an idiot standing in the entryway. "She's your biggest fan!" Stefano smiled politely. I remained rooted as Julie headed to the bar. Returning with drinks in hand, she simultaneously removed my purse from my tight grip and replaced it with a serving tray showcasing two dirty martinis, all while literally pushing me toward table thirteen, even as my head was shaking no. *"Go!"* she commanded.

I knew damn well that if I didn't drop the tray, it would only be by the grace of God. Somehow, with one foot following the other, I made my way through the sea of people and toward the man I had only dreamed about. All was going well. At least I hadn't fainted. Now if only I could find my voice.

"So, I hear you are my biggest fan." Nodding, I placed the drinks on the table with shaky hands. "Well, it's nice to meet you." Pointing to the man seated next to him he said, "This is my boyfriend, Mathieu."

"It's nice to meet you both. I'm Lucy."

Now, I don't exactly remember this, but I fear that I might have curtsied at this point.

"Have a seat!" He pulled a vacant chair from the table behind him and swung it over beside him. I sat down and uncomfortably shifted positions several times. Where had my voice gone?

"Are you an actress?"

An actress? Me? Oh yeah, sure!

"Actually, I am a photographer . . . I majored in fashion photography."

"That's what I majored in!"

He was talking to me. *He* was talking to *me*! I could have peed in my pants. I mean, I might have—but just a little.

"Yeah, I know," I responded, smiling down at the table, unable to make eye contact with Him.

"Have you found any work in LA? Why aren't you going to New York? That's where the fashion is at."

"Well . . ." I swallowed, noticing that my throat was abnormally dry. Finally, I looked Lepres in the eyes. This was the encounter I had dreamed about. I'd even prepared a speech for when I would meet him. Of course, after years of practice, somehow the words now escaped me. Alas, I continued, "Because you're here. I've been dreaming of working for you basically my whole life."

"Get out of here. Work for me?" Lepres started to laugh. Mathieu seemed bored with the entire conversation.

"Actually, I've been to your studio. Your assistant, Dan, promised me an internship. When I got there, he was gone. I thought I . . ."

"Dan? That guy was a drunk and an idiot. He was probably wasted when he said you could intern . . . He was always doing things like that." Turning to Mathieu, "Glad he's long gone. That's so typical of Dan, don't you think?" Mathieu shrugged his shoulders and looked away. Pointing to the martini glass, Stefano directed, "We'll have another couple of these." It appeared that polite chitchat with the fan was over, and I feared I was blowing my big opportunity.

In a last-ditch effort to make him understand what he

meant to me, I grabbed Lepres' arm as my eyes welled up with tears. "Mr. Lepres, it is my lifelong dream to work for you . . . I swear, I will work so hard for you. You won't regret it! Please give me a chance. I'll do anything to prove myself. I *have* to work for you."

Stefano seemed humbled. "Sweetheart, relax. You really should be going to New York." Picking up his boyfriend's martini and washing it down with one gulp, he placed the empty glass on my tray. I felt my heart sink to the bottom of my chest as I released my clammy hands from his biceps. I began to tell myself that the fantasy would stop there and rationalized that it's okay, at least I got to meet my idol. Not everyone can say that, right? He continued, "But . . . my studio is here in LA. And you start Monday."

chapter four

One Foot in the Dior

Sebastian and Julie had given me a complete makeover that morning. They flat-ironed my hair and expertly applied neutral makeup. I stepped out of my Jeep where I had parked time and time again. I adjusted the low waist of Julie's Abercrombie jeans and pressed down on the sides of the flowing light pink Juicy Couture peasant top that I had previously only worn for special occasions. Julie and Sebastian had woken up early with me and put in their best efforts to ensure that I, their dorkiest friend, would fit in with the fashionistas at Lepres' studio this time around. What would I have done without those two?

I couldn't help but be flabbergasted when the buzzer actually granted my entrance. I timidly entered the studio and was immediately blown away. The massive interior was ultra modern. Enormous prints were suspended from the walls and ceiling. In the center of the room was a large, industrial-looking steel table that could easily seat thirty. To the left was a kitchen that would make Wolfgang Puck proud. As I observed the incredible space, I couldn't help but think, *I'm inside . . . I'm actually here.* I followed a quiet rumble of commotion to a small office set off to the side.

A woman was lying facedown on the concrete floor, moaning, "Oooh God, whyyy?" Her teased and tousled black hair extensions obscured her face.

"Um, hello? I'm here to work for Mr. Lepres?" The woman did not respond. Instead, a pretentious-looking man peeked out from behind a giant MAC screen.

"Yeah, Lucy, is it? I'm Roman. This is Marc, Ebony and Rio." A few hands waved in the air, although no one made eye contact with me. I wondered if those were their actual birth names. "The hot mess on the floor is Liz. We call her 'Lushy Liz,' and I guess you can see why." It was Elizabeth from the *American Photo* article! At the time, I considered her a celebrity. She had, after all, been in a national magazine.

"Fuck off, Roman." The woman picked herself up, barely able to make it to her feet. She wrapped her arms around my shoulder and leaned on me. I studied her heavily painted face and tried not to stare at the false eyelash barely hanging on to her left eye. She smelled like she might have taken a bath in perfume. "Hi, darl, I'm Liz. I haven't slept in four days and, well, if you're going to work here, you'd better get used to it." I wasn't expecting her to have an Australian accent.

I guessed, "It's been pretty busy around here, then?" The others let out a chuckle.

"No, babe. Get used to walking in on me ass up on the linoleum, still legless from the night before." Everyone laughed and I tried to conceal my astonishment. This isn't exactly how I imagined Stefano Lepres' lead producer. She was a curvaceous woman, filling out every inch of the fabric in her Pucci-printed caftan. Liz managed to stand on her own and wobbled toward her desk in a pair of oddly matched Stuart Weitzman Highline boots. Once she had collapsed into her chair, she rested her head on her crossed arms and returned to a comatose state.

Roman admonished Liz, "Oh that's great. Scare away the tenth intern this week." He pulled me out of the office by my elbow. "We have a lot to do today before the chic hits the fan." Roman was like no other man I had ever seen. His hair was neatly and perfectly parted to the side. He was wearing thick horn rimmed glasses and an argyle-patterned Thom Browne suit. His loud three-button blazer, bow tie and coordinating trousers screamed for attention and respect both at once. His eyes were lined with a rich reddish-chocolate brown liner, and his nails were painted a similar shade. He caught me studying his hands and proudly held them out. "It's called 'Bitter Bitch' and Tom Ford has a waiting list for it longer than Betty Ford, post Emmys." I didn't know what he was talking about, and it must have shown in my doe eyes because he just shook his head and continued, "This just happens to be the beginning of an insane week. In just nine days' time we have eight photo shoots and a music video. But, when you're hot, you're hot! Liz and I produce all of Stefano's shoots, so you report to us. Still, if anyone asks you to do anything, just do it. Stefano is crazy. He knows what he likes and he demands it immediately. Are you following me?" I tried to appear as if I was soaking in all of this knowledge as I eagerly nodded.

"Okay now. I suppose the most important thing to know is that Stefano is *always* right. Got that? Even when you know he's wrong. Say, for example, he says that hideous pink shirt you have on is green. You know it's puke pink. In fact, it has the word 'pink' written across your . . ." He glanced down at my modest breasts and raised an eyebrow. "Chest. But if *he* says it's green, it's green. Got it? Stick with this simple rule and you should last a few weeks. But really . . . you got it?" I nodded again, while wondering if he was insulting me or actually trying to help. "I mean, that's just a tip from me to you."

"Thanks, I appreciate that." Best to just nod and smile, I figured.

"Okay. So, let's see . . . Oh, a perfect job for you. Stay right here." Roman buzzed in then out of the office, returning with a half sheet of paper. "Here's the coffee order and some petty cash. Starbucks is two blocks left, two blocks right, and the Coffee Bean is across the street. I wrote down who gets what and from where." And with that, he was gone.

After picking up the insanely complicated order during the morning rush at each coffee shop, I balanced three carry-out cartons of beverages and two bags of scones and low-carb muffins as I eagerly made my way back. Outside the studio, there were three trucks being unloaded of all sorts of crates and equipment. Pop music was pumping out through the walls of the compound. I got a sudden chill, realizing again that I was entering Stefano Lepres' set, this time with granted access. The men who were unloading the trucks looked about my age, and most of them were very cute. I pushed my shoulders back and dared to grin at them as I passed. I was an employee of Stefano Lepres too, and I felt that it gave me an edge.

I had just caught the eye of one of the gorgeous grip guys when my entire body flung forward as my foot caught itself under the leg of a tripod. If the mochas and chai teas beneath me had been red, it would have looked like a murder had just occurred. I pushed my torso up and peeled a banana nut muffin from my chest. It took a few seconds to register that this had, in fact, just happened. I could not look up to see the reaction of the crew, mostly because I knew that Rio's whipped cream frappucino had given me a facial. Instead of looking up, I just took off running back down the street. Mortified.

I stood last in line at Starbucks and pressed away tears with my dampened sleeve. I knew that everyone was gawking at me because I looked like a disaster, but that was not why I was crying. Why would this shit happen to me   today of all days? I tearfully waited in line but was able to not cause a complete scene—that is, until I reached the counter.

The list. I had lost the fucking list! I emptied every pocket and begged every barista to recall any part of my order without success. My only hope was in the trash, literally. I dove both of my arms into the wastebasket near the counter where I had added "a touch of cream" and "a splash of skim milk" and half a raw sugar and a dash of cinnamon and so on, but all that I could find were wet napkins and pastry wrappers. I continued to the Coffee Bean with the same results.

"Girl, you have one foot in the Dior—this is no time to fuck around," Roman reprimanded me upon my failed empty-handed arrival.

"I am so sorry. I am not usually this klutzy—I don't know what happened." I have never felt like a bigger idiot.

"The intern fucked up our coffee order—tell her what

you want. Again," Roman shouted into the office. A collective groan echoed through the space.

I went to the bathroom so I could clean up and allowed myself to cry, but only for a few minutes. That's when I heard Him arrive. The music was hushed and several people called out to him, "Good morning, Stef" or "Great shoot last night, Stefano!" I pushed my ear up against the door and tried to decipher whether or not they were directly on the other side of the bathroom wall. When the distinct greetings turned to soft mumbles, I cracked the door, confirmed the coast was clear and hopped back to the office. I was not avoiding Lepres per se—however, I was not exactly ready to see him either, seeing that I looked like the victim of death by decaf.

I diligently made my way to each staff member to re-take their coffee order. A giant black velvet curtain had been erected and it obstructed an area that people were buzzing in and out of. Each time someone stepped out, I took their order. I really wanted everyone to like me, and they seemed to once I told them that I was going to get their coffee.

Since I had taken a grand total of twenty-seven orders, I needed to make several trips back and forth to each café. With the final order in tow, I returned to the studio at last. I had my eye on the curtain opening, hoping for a glimpse of what was going on behind it, should someone exit and hold the curtain open just enough. Flashes from the strobe lights peeked their way out along the top and bottom of the blocked area. Stefano was shouting, "That's it . . . yeah, right there . . . amazing . . . fucking hot bitch . . . I love it!" and I can't even tell you how badly I wanted to know what was going on behind that curtain.

"Hey, are you the coffee girl?" a witchy-looking woman

said in a strong New York accent. I nodded my head while thinking, *Oh my God, I am the coffee girl.* "I'll take a skinny vanilla latte, extra hot and—hold on . . . Joyce! She's over here!" An even stronger New York accent from behind the curtain yelled out, "The caw-fey girl? Large black!" And, faster than you can say venti skinny mocha latte, an avalanche of orders ensued. Medium Earl Grey. Steamed soy cap. Hazelnut with half-and-half . . . The coffee girl? I thought that I was here to work for Stefano! I hadn't even seen him or the set or anything. The closest I had gotten to a photo shoot all day was at the yellow traffic light I ran earlier in fear that I would be late. Late to fetch lattes for seven hours straight.

On what was my last run for the day, six, seven, eight people buzzed in and out of the giant door, but no one offered to hold it for me. As I struggled with the deliveries, I pried the door with my foot, caught it with my hip, and squeezed in the rest of the way. The door slammed shut on me, causing me to bounce forward. The drinks splish-splashed but I cradled them like a newborn and safely delivered each beverage like a dumb stork. I felt like such a loser as I walked into the office and announced, "One tall double shot no fat no foam sugar free soy vanilla latte." Without a word of gratitude, the final cup was claimed as I collapsed into a chair. The photo shoot was over and Stefano had left the building. The crew had left the building. My dignity had left the building.

"Same time tomorrow?" Liz called out from behind her desk. She was applying an alarming cherry red lipstick and using the webcam and monitor as a vanity.

"Oh, yes. Of course," I responded, and then I too left the building.

chapter five

Something Old, Something BMW

"Today, I will make it onto the set." For the sixth day in a row, I repeated this mantra to myself as I got ready for another long day at the studio. Although I had not yet directly dealt with anything remotely related to photography, let alone set foot near the action, I knew that all it took was one opportunity to show them that I was worthy. "Today . . . I will make it . . . onto the . . . set." I zipped up my nicest pair of khaki pants and pulled my ponytail tighter. This would be the day. It just had to be.

"You just got in four hours ago and already you're going back?" Julie yawned as she stumbled to the bathroom.

"Yup! I am the coffee wench, which means I'm the first one in and the last one out, every day." I stepped into the heap of clothes that had taken over the bedroom floor. I reached into a pile and pulled out a crumpled light blue cardigan. I stuffed it into my messenger bag, which I swung across my body. I removed my camera strap from the bedpost and swung it across as well. I must have looked as if I was about to go on some sort of safari, but like a true photographer, wherever I went, my camera did too.

Julie leaped across the clothes and snuggled back into her bed. "What are you guys shooting today?"

"Well, *they* are shooting Christina Aguilera's music video. *I* am shooting myself if I have to go through another day like yesterday." I picked up two sets of earrings from the nightstand, showcasing them to my friend. Julie pointed to the pair on the left.

"No offense, but how difficult could it be to order and pick up lunch?"

While putting in the earrings I thought back to the previous afternoon. How was I supposed to know that the vegan meals couldn't be in the same bag as the kosher meats, which couldn't be served on the same plates that non-kosher fish might have once been on? "It doesn't matter because today I am going to . . ."

". . . make it onto the set," we said in unison.

"Good luck, Lucy! Go get 'em . . ." Julie encouraged.

We whispered our good-byes, careful not to wake Sebastian, and waved as Julie went back to bed and I made my way back to the studio.

Just as I arrived and put my car into park, my cell phone began buzzing. James Braves. It was my second missed call from him this week, but I wasn't ready to talk to him. He was likely calling to congratulate me and hear all about my dream job. I e-mailed him the incredible news that I had in fact

attained the unimaginable, however I wanted to wait until I
had an actual hand in the photography before filling him in
with the details. I would much rather tell James that I was
adjusting the lights, changing film or editing contact sheets
instead of ordering lunch and taking out the trash. I'd only
been working for Stefano for one week, so I figured any day
now I'd have responsibilities that I would be proud to discuss.
So I let it go to voice mail. Soon after, my phone began to buzz
again, but this time I answered it.

"G'day, darl, it's Liz. We had an issue last night and had to
get rid of Ebony, Stefano's assistant. I'm running behind so
you all are going to have to go up there and help Stefano.
By you all I mean you."

"Go up where? What do I do?" I wasn't sure if I should be
excited or nervous.

"Go to his house in the Hollywood Hills. The Bible's on my
desk with all you need to know. Just follow the instructions,
fix him up a good brekkie and you should be fine. Call Roman
if you need anything."

"The Bible" was an enormous binder filled with laminated
pages of lists. It contained the most meticulous instructions
for everything from Stefano's preferred groceries to alarm
codes to his grandmother's renowned banana pancake recipe.
It also contained Stefano's social security information and
emergency numbers to close friends such as Elton John and
Madonna. The overwhelming honor of being able to enter Stefano's studio was one thing, but going to his house was a
whole new level of holy shit. Even in Oz all of the munchkins
got to hang out in Emerald City, but only Dorothy and a select
few were invited to the wizard's lair—let alone able to see the

man behind the curtain. I toted the Bible like Toto and took off for the Hills.

The house commanded views of all of Los Angeles. I wondered if it was too early to just walk into my boss's house but decided to after remembering we had to be on the set soon. I used the spare key tied to the Bible to unlock the front door. I took several steps into the bright foyer and closed the door behind me. Holy shit, I mouthed. I was in Stefano Lepres' house. The directions instructed me to wake Stefano up with an array of items, including a Pressed Juicery detox drink, a freshly made shot of wheatgrass and two medium-sized strawberry guavas. The Bible instructions were complete to the last detail, even stipulating which glass to use for which drink.

I looked around the house in fascination. It was very modern and simple, even stark, classically decorated in rich cocoas and clean taste. There was no clutter or hint of artistic expression, which was in sharp contrast to Stefano's photographs, which were garish and colorful.

Back to the task at hand . . . the kitchen was decked out with the finest of culinary equipment. I walked to the stainless steel Sub-Zero refrigerator and opened it. There was a labeled assortment of colored Pressed juices, numbered one through eight, perfectly lined up inside. I removed a number one and poured it into a tall frosted glass. The guavas were to be freshly picked from a small orchard in the backyard. I dragged a lawn chair underneath a small tree and began selecting what I could only guess was ripe guava. White sap oozed from the branches each time I pulled off one of the ruby-colored fruits. I tried twisting them off, pulling them straight down, and pulling them to the side, but every time I attempted to retrieve one , the juice ran down my arm, soaking my sleeve.

Once I had semi-mastered the manual wheatgrass grinder and managed to crank out enough liquid green to almost fill a small shot glass, I placed the beverages and guavas on a tray and began to climb the banister-less staircase. Halfway to the second floor, I was greeted by thunderous snoring. The sounds of Stefano swallowing air through his nasal passages shocked me into reality. I swiftly tiptoed back downstairs and phoned Roman. "Am I really supposed to just walk into his bedroom and wake him up? I mean, this is kind of weird! I haven't even really seen him at the studio yet—and here I am waking him up in his home?"

"Yes! And hurry! You're like fifteen minutes behind! Now, listen, he is going to get in the shower, and while he's in there, pick out his outfit for today. His closet is basically an Atelier New York pop-up shop, so everything goes together. Just grab a few layers and you'll be fine. Got it? Oh, and don't forget to pack his backpack and his wallet and his cell phone." My head was spinning.

"Wait . . . what?" I was beginning to question whether or not this was some sort of hazing they played on new interns.

"I know it's a bit much, but hello! He trusts you enough to do this. You're very lucky. He specifically asked for you."

I wasn't even sure that he knew I had showed up to work for him until this point, yet here he was trusting me with . . . everything. "He did? Me? Okay, well, we'll see you soon!"

Still unsure of the legitimacy of the request, I made my way back up the stairs and slowly opened the bedroom door.

There I found my idol sleeping in a fetal position, wearing white Fruit of the Loom briefs.

"Um, good morning . . . Stefano. Good . . . morning." I lightly touched his arm.

"Heeey, Laurie, good morning. Mmm, yum. Fruit, thanks." He rolled over onto his back, plucked a guava off the tray, tossed it upward and caught it, while still lying there as if I had seen him nearly naked a thousand times before.

Now, I am no prude, but I mean—we had only just met a few weeks ago, and since then I had been the coffee girl to everyone else. I hadn't even been trusted to get his coffee yet! To see his package seemed so unnatural and awkward and, well, he still hadn't even gotten my name straight. I second-guessed myself before correcting him on my name. I wanted to say, "Actually, it's Lucy," but remembered what Roman had said about him always being right. Besides, at this point I was so elated to be there that I kind of didn't care if he called me Lacey or Leslie or whatever. He is Stefano Lepres! And I am in his house!

Stefano stood up to stretch and bask in the sunlight pouring in from the double French doors off his balcony. He then slid out of the tighty whities, picked up a towel from the floor and nonchalantly breezed out of the room. "Going for a swim," he mentioned. I thought that I was going to implode from the amount of freaking out that I was somehow containing.

As soon as Stefano and his bare ass were out of sight, my phone began vibrating.

"It's Roman. How did it go? Is he in the shower?"

"Well, he umm . . . went for a swim."

"A swim? Lucy! No, no, no! Christina is here . . . in hair and makeup. We're ready to shoot in one hour! It's your job to get him here on time! I told you what to do and you totally failed me! Please, get him out of the fucking pool and dressed! Get him here . . . *Now!*"

Shaken out of my stupor, I walked into Stefano's massive closet to find row upon row of meticulously displayed muted and murky but expensive looking clothes. If anything was for sure, it was that this fashion monogamist didn't stray. I selected a Rick Owens jersey T-shirt, a frayed, draped cardigan and a pair of distressed jeans and folded them on top of a chair, placing a pair of military-style A Diciannoveventitre boots underneath. I had seen him wear something similar in numerous tabloid photos before, so I figured it was a safe bet.

From the balcony atop the lavishly landscaped backyard, I found him floating around the lagoon-style pool. "Stefano, the studio called and they want you to know they'll be ready to shoot soon. Your clothes are upstairs and I'll have your backpack by the front door."

"Okay, thanks," he chirped.

What did Roman expect of me? I couldn't simply yank Stefano out of this peaceful haven and tell him what to do! He was Stefano Lepres, for crying out loud! We all worked for him! I decided to take a seat on the couch and wait for him to get ready. Forty-five minutes later, Stefano finally made his way downstairs, dressed and ready for work. He seemed in no particular hurry.

"Are you old enough to drive?" he asked me.

"Sure, I'm twenty-two . . . Do you want me to drive?"

"I don't drive. I'm from New York," he stated matter-of-factly. We walked out onto the driveway and I swung open the driver's side door of my less-than-impressive Jeep Wrangler.

"Oh no . . . no way I'm getting in that death trap. No way, no how." Stefano dramatically grasped his chest and stepped away from the vehicle. I felt my cell phone vibrating in my back pocket but didn't dare answer it.

"Death trap? Hardly. A tornado couldn't destroy this beast! I actually drove it through a minor one last year and . . ."

"We're taking my car. Pick one. Let's go." With the flip of a button, the garage door opened to reveal three incredible cars. I eyed a vintage Mercedes, a Karmann Ghia and a BMW. All three were black and in mint condition. I chose the BMW since it was the least intimidating of the three. As I settled into the deluxe leather driver's seat, I imagined the car's interior was similar to a NASA rocket.

It was only 9:00 a.m. and already I was noticeably sweating through my shirt. I decided to break the silence by taking the opportunity to let Stefano know I was capable of more than cappuccinos.

"Stefano, I was wondering if I could maybe get to assist you on the set today? I'm not sure if you remember our first conversation when I told you that I studied photography in school where I was trained on how to use the . . ."

"Sure," he blurted out. I waited for him to continue, but he didn't. "Sure" meant yes, and that was good enough for me!

As we strolled into the studio—Stefano still in no hurry—everyone bid him a congenial "Good morning." I felt important walking alongside him, ignoring the fact that everyone was reacting to his arrival, not mine—also ignoring the fact that I was carrying his leather Julius backpack like a mule.

He vanished behind closed doors and I was instantly put in check as the crew pounced on me like a team of vultures. "Do you have any idea how important this shoot is?" . . . "Christina's been waiting for over an hour." . . . "So unprofessional!"

Liz came to my rescue. She wrapped her arm around my shoulders, using me to help her stand but, regardless, standing up for me. "Hey, hey . . . Leave her alone! It's her first time and he seems relatively happy. I'd say you did a rippa job, darling." Kissing me on the forehead, Liz held up a sparkling flute. "Mimosa?"

"Laurie! My coffee!" Stefano boomed. Up until now, I had been fetching coffee for the staff and crew but never for Stefano. He only let Roman or Ebony, maybe Liz, get his coffee. This was a very big deal. I returned to the set with a venti plain iced coffee. Roman gave me a head nod and I felt like everyone was watching me return from my mission à la *Apollo 13*. What was the big deal? It's plain coffee, right? And I had been doing it all day, every day, under worse circumstances. What was with everyone?

Little did I know.

And then it happened: I made it onto the actual set! Cue the sounds of crowds cheering! Who would have thought that a plain iced coffee would have been the golden ticket? Even though I hoped this wasn't what Stefano had in mind when I asked to assist on the set, I felt a sense of accomplishment in getting there. Christina was surrounded by her dancers, all wearing black satin lace-up corsets. They were practicing a provocative burlesque dance on top of a gigantic dining room table. An enormous chandelier swung above with two male dancers dangling from its base. It was something out of a dream. Stefano was perched atop his stool, arms folded, as he studied the scene. I handed him the beverage.

He took a sip and instantly spit it onto the floor. "Fucking sweetener! Disgusting! Do you know how horrible that is for my body?" I used all of my willpower not to glance at the cigarette resting behind his ear. Knowing for certain his coffee was unsweetened, I looked at Roman, who was nodding his head up and down like a bobblehead to remind me that He is always right. With a shrug and an apology, I returned to Starbucks and watched as the barista put unsweetened coffee into the cup. Tasting it for good measure, I confidently returned to the set, handing him the coffee once again. One sip and he was in a rage. Stefano catapulted the plastic cup to the floor, soaking my khakis and shoes in the process. I felt the cold brown beverage saturate through to my skin from the knees down. He roared, "Can somebody competent please get me my fucking coffee! For fuck's sake!"

I lowered my head and walked out of sight, feeling like a chastised puppy who had messed on the living room carpet. Everyone on set stared. I could feel their eyes follow me. What I couldn't feel was sympathy since they'd all been brainwashed to believe that He was *always* right. I made my way into the kitchen. The chef handed me a towel, asking, "Sweetener?" I nodded my head.

Liz pulled me into the hallway. "You okay, darl? Keep your chin up. In a few minutes, he'll forget what happened. You're doing a great job!"

"It sure doesn't feel that way," I pouted while wringing out my pant leg.

Liz pulled a file from the cabinet and removed a document. "This always gives me a laugh. Check it out."

It was a copy of Stefano's passport. "Steven Leper? His last name is a flesh-eating disease?"

"That's right, darl. Stefano is off his rocker, but deep down inside he's just trying to forget where he came from and make something of his life. So, don't take it personally."

"Okay, thanks, Liz." I gave her a half smile.

"Change your mind about that mimosa?" she teased.

"No, thanks."

After a twelve-hour shoot, I was exhausted and couldn't wait to go home and take a bath. True, I had made it on the set, but I didn't contribute anything. I tried to remain optimistic, seeing that I had made it into the studio and technically onto the set—the natural progression would be in the direction of where I wanted to be. Patience and baby steps, I figured.

I started up the BMW as Stefano climbed in and we headed back toward the Hills. "What a great shoot! Christina is the best! I love her! Turn right at the next street. We're meeting her here."

"Chateau Marmont? Am I dropping you off?"

"No. Christina wants to have a late dinner and talk about some ideas for the next video. You have to be there to take notes." I looked down at my disgusting duds. How could I go anywhere public looking like I did? I wondered if I could run home and change. I didn't live very far.

As if reading my mind, he went on. "No time to change. Besides, maybe this will help you remember never to put that poison anywhere near my body. Are you trying to slowly kill me?" He pulled a cigarette from behind his ear and lit up.

As I pulled up to the valet, the BMW's custom rims roughly scraped along the curb of the sidewalk. The grinding sound of metal on cement crunched below our feet. I knew that I was done. Dead. He'd had a meltdown when he thought I put artificial sugar in his coffee. He would sure enough tear me to shreds for damaging the $40,000 rims on his brand-new car. I gripped the steering wheel with my clammy, shaking hands, briefly closed my eyes and braced myself for the explosion.

"Ouch, that's going to leave a mark. Come on, inside we go." I opened my eyes as the passenger door shut behind him. That's it? No explosion? I looked down at the muddied pants and shoes, comparing my attire to that of the glamorous patrons now entering the trendiest hotel in Los Angeles. Talk about humiliation. He was right: I never again forgot to hold the sweetener. Even now I can't look at a little pink packet without wincing.

chapter six

Is There a Cloud Ten?

"Okay, kids! Presley is pulling up. Is her room ready? Are we ready for her?" Visibly flustered, Roman pushed me out of the office and into the madness. He was decked out to the nines in another colorfully checkered three-piece suit. "Okay, intern, it's go time. Be sure the makeup room is set up. Presley Dalton is on her way! She's only an hour late. Usually it's two, so this is ahead of schedule for her! And we're not ready!"

"Ready?" I awaited further instruction.

A frazzled fairy, Roman threw his arms up in the air, his Bitter Bitch spirit fingers flailing. "As in candles, champagne on ice, magazines, snacks. Whatever! Use your head, intern!" I wondered why he kept using the word "intern" instead of my name, which he undeniably knew after three weeks.

Liz placed a typed sheet of paper atop the crate of beverages cradled in my arms, never looking up from the phone, where she was engaged in an intense-looking conversation.

PRESLEY DALTON REQUESTS

Soy wax–based candles, votives only, gardenia or rose scented
Dom Perignon champagne
Premium top-shelf drinking water, room temperature
Marlboro Lights
Two white lighters—no matches!
Cashmere blanket
Pink roses or white lilies or both—but not mixed!
Cheetos—in a glass bowl, not bag
Diet Pepsi
Skittles—remove all green and yellow

With my left hand, I studied the ridiculous list in awe. Roman removed the tray of coffee from my right hand and tossed it into the garbage. I took off to inspect the cabinets and closets, where I surprisingly found everything required and displayed it as attractively as I could.

"Darling! So good to see you again!" Roman's voice echoed through the studio. An entourage of five followed Presley into the makeup room, knocking me against the wall as they passed. Only then did it hit me that I was sharing air with Presley freaking Dalton! Presley Dalton is one of the most famous women in the world . . . for no apparent reason. She's famous for being famous. At twenty-two years old—my age—

she hasn't accomplished much of anything. Yet she graces the covers of every fashion magazine and tabloid on the news-stand, and paparazzi follow her every move. Her first album was about to be released and today's shoot was for its cover. For a second, I considered texting Julie to recount the encoun-ter I had just had—but then I remembered what Sebastian had explained to us when we'd moved to LA. The golden rule of working with celebrities: to act as if completely unfazed. This meant that under no circumstance was I to appear excited or impressed by anyone around me. So, although I was honestly freaking out on the inside, on the exterior all was cool, calm and collected.

The set was just about ready. A faux prison cell had been built out of fake gold bricks and rolled rows of gold coins for prison bars. Glitter and gems spilled out from money bags strategically placed around the inside of the cell. Photographic kickstands, lights and a tripod were ready. And in the kitchen, a chef and his assistant were setting up a spread fit for a wedding.

"Put this in there and don't speak unless spoken to." Roman handed me an enormous assortment of pink roses in a glass vase. I tiptoed my way into the makeup room, placed the vase in a corner and looked up to find Presley in a plush pink terrycloth robe. I could not help but pause to examine her in the flesh. Her famously long limbs were casually crossed and rested over the makeup counter as she reclined in the chair and chatted on her phone. One woman expertly painted on Presley's face as another unpacked dozens of shades of powders and creams while a man twirled her golden silk-like hair into hot curlers. Another young man separated the Skittles by color. Presley put one hand over the phone, tilting her head toward me, "Thanks, gorgeous."

Presley Dalton is talking . . . to me? I could hardly believe it! Did she just call me "gorgeous"? Did she mean it? I've never been called gorgeous before. As strange as it sounds, she wasn't "real" to me up until that point. I didn't know what to do or how to react but the words, "You're welcome, thank you," spilled out of my stupid mouth. Why had I thanked Presley Dalton for thanking me? What was that?

I closed the door behind me and smacked my hand to my forehead when, as if on cue, the music stopped and Roman's voice echoed through the studio. "Quick! Stefano is a block away. Get ready! Intern, come see me *immediately!*" I had not seen any other interns so I could only assume that he was referring to me. All the workers rushed around the set to perfect everything before He got there. The chefs stashed anything unsightly under the sink while the photo assistants shot several Polaroids and carefully lined them up on a table.

I hurried back to the office where Roman handed me Stefano's iced coffee. I was stunned. Wasn't *I* the coffee girl? It then occurred to me that Roman was being nasty because he was back to fetching Stefano's coffee since I couldn't be trusted with such a vital task. I had been demoted from Senior Coffee Wench back to Junior Coffee Wench.

Like a quiet storm, Stefano blew into the studio, followed by Liz. You could feel the mood completely shift every time he entered the room. It was a combination of tension and fear, but at the same time everyone seemed delighted to see him. I too felt all of those things at once. He warily accepted the coffee from me. "This isn't . . . ?"

Before I could respond, Roman hollered, "Of course—no sweetener! We know better! Presley's in the chair . . ." Stefano disappeared into the makeup room as the entourage exited, making a beeline for the culinary creations like they hadn't eaten in weeks.

Stefano and Presley holed up in the makeup room for hours. Several times Stefano emerged to critique the set. Resting his hand under his chin, squinting, Stefano said, "The gold is too gold and the pink padlock needs to be pinker," before disappearing again. I was amused and taken aback by the degree of urgency everyone reacted with after Stefano would make one of these vague, general claims. How did they know how much pinker the pink needed to be? Yet they didn't question any of his remarks. They just responded by adjusting whatever needed to be adjusted. I paid close attention, taking mental notes because one day that would hopefully be me making the gold "less gold."

At 7:00 p.m., an obviously drunk Presley Dalton dramatically entered the set wearing a stunning Alice & Olivia gold sequin dress. She dangerously wobbled in a pair of leopard printed Christian Louboutins. My eyes were transfixed on the striking shoes. Just that morning, I had seen an entire two-page story in *InStyle* magazine dedicated to the coveted "Maggie" shoes. They listed the names of celebrities who had been waitlisted and showed pictures of the lucky few who had scored. I'd never imagined that I'd be in such close proximity to a pair of shoes that alone could pay my rent. And car insurance. Plus my cell phone bill. They were like a celebrity in their own right. When she raised her arm and pointed at the set, dozens of Noir pyramid bracelets stacked wrist to elbow clanged together. She exclaimed, "That is fucking gorgeous."

Stefano clapped his hands and belted out, "Where are the extras? Where are the cops? Come on, people. I don't have all day and night." He was oblivious to the fact that he had just kept the crew waiting for more than three hours while he and Ms. Dalton boozed it up in the makeup room.

"Yeah, and I have this thing in an hour . . ." said the starlet nonchalantly.

"Are you kidding, Presley? Say you're kidding." Stefano whined.

Presley swung her long blonde curls from her shoulder to her back and laughed, shaking her head from side to side. Giggling, she snorted, "No, really, I have to go soon."

Stefano turned around, mouthing "Fucking idiot" to Liz. He then clapped his hands and belted, "Alright! Showtime! I need our cops and one last touch-up on Presley. Lushy, let's get this party started!"

The plan for the shoot was to take a photo of Presley looking like she had been arrested and thrown in jail, mocking the lyrics in the title song of her upcoming CD, "Arrest Me Sexy." Two extras climbed out from behind the dessert table. Wearing blue policemen uniforms and carrying batons, they posed beside Presley and pretended to guard her cell. Presley held the bars and erotically caved her shoulders over her chest, elongating her neck and pouting into the lens from behind the prison bars. It was a moment that I had fantasized about. There I was, standing behind Him—photographing Her— surrounded by these people that I had only dreamed would be my peers, and there they all were. I was jolted back to reality when I bolted to the side to avoid a stool flying right at me. Out of nowhere, Stefano had gone ballistic and kicked his stool backwards. "Why do our police officers look like God-damn mailmen? Can somebody tell me where the badges are? And where are the handcuffs? Hello? Wardrobe!" Stefano jumped up and down in a childlike tantrum.

A brave but shaken woman—the stylist—stepped in front of the lights and explained, "We thought the art director would be on that . . ."

Another man stepped forward. "Are you out of your mind? We build sets, not costumes!"

"I mean, those are technically props," she defended.

"Well, technically you're retarded," he blasted back.

Stefano roared, "Somebody better figure something out. If I have to add it digitally, believe me, it's both your asses . . . Fuck it. Let's go . . ." By then, someone had replaced the stool, something Stefano must have expected because he didn't even check to see that it was there before returning to sit down behind the camera.

The shoot continued while the art director and stylist stormed off behind closed doors to continue their fight. What could I do to solve this situation? I had to do something. I prayed for divine intervention, an idea that would save the day. I remembered a drugstore near the Starbucks and took off running. It was now late at night but maybe the store was open. My tired feet pounded the pavement as fast as they could. I was hoping the store had a toy policeman set or something. I didn't have a plan but I just had this instinct that I could solve this and I couldn't just stand there and observe. I figured it was worth a chance. As I approached the store and noticed the lights were still on inside, I felt a glimmer of hope. But when I made it to the electronic door, I crashed into it at full force. Closed. "Damn!" I screamed aloud.

As I walked away from the drugstore, I saw two of LA's Finest sitting at an outdoor table at Starbucks. Without hesitation, I dashed up to the policemen and frantically implored them to help me save the day.

"Officers, I'm working for Stefano Lepres, the famous photographer. His studio is just up the street. We're shooting an album cover and forgot to get police badges for our actors. Can you please come with me and let us use yours? Just for thirty minutes? Please, you have no idea what it will do for my career if I save this photo shoot!"

The officers looked at each other, obviously thinking this was a crazy idea and positively against law enforcement policy.

"Here's my bank card and my driver's license. If you let me borrow your handcuffs and badges, I swear, I'll return them safely! Or no! Come with me! We have lots of great food and coffee, and you'll get to see Presley Dalton in person! Please! Please—I beg of you!" I pushed my trembling hands together and gave the officers the best puppy dog eyes that I had in me. The policemen knew they had met their match. How could they say no to my desperate plea? All three of us sprinted back to the set.

Panting and sweaty, I practically collapsed onto the set, stumbling into the flashing strobe lights and holding up my findings. "Official badges . . . and handcuffs!" It was a risk to step between Stefano and Presley—to disrupt the shoot so dramatically—but it seemed right at the time. Everyone stared at me with wide eyes and waited to see how he would react.

"What the . . . ? Where did those come from?" Stefano looked at me, shocked, as I pointed across the room to the two cops digging into the chicken parmesan. Stefano jumped up, once again knocking over his stool, and smiled, "Well, throw them up there, Momma!" The crew cheered and patted me on the back. The stylist took the items from me and whispered "thank you" before expertly applying the police paraphernalia to the actors. Stefano hopped over and pulled me into a full bear hug while screaming, "I'm not shooting without this girl ever again!"

Those words echoed in my mind over and over again. Clinging to my idol, I was elated, shocked and ecstatic. My dream had officially come true.

chapter seven

Swimming with . . . Shark?

Being promoted to Stefano's personal assistant was no easy feat. I was no longer just picking up coffee and ordering lunch. It had become my responsibility to pick Stefano up in the morning and take him home at the end of the day or, more often, very late at night. Although most of my twenty-four/seven job consisted of personal slave work, I was steadily being given more opportunities to be part of the photo shoots as well. When a shot required wind being blown through the supermodel's hair, it was I who got to direct the giant fan. Another shot called for leaves to be falling from the tree above, and it was I who was suspended from the top branch, expertly dropping the foliage. If the structure of our company's totem pole reached the basement, that's where I was, but I was slowly making my way up the pole and being promoted again into the photo team had to be only a few notches away. I'd do whatever it took to get there.

"Hey girl, your suit is in the trailer," the wardrobe stylist's pretty assistant told me as she hurried past, both arms full of bikini bottoms. Zuma Beach was especially hot that day.

"Oh, I'm not . . . I'm Stefano's assistant . . ." I was flattered to be mistaken for an actual model.

"Yeah I know—he wants you in the shot," the assistant insisted, smiling.

Me? In the shot? In a Stefano Lepres photo shoot?! True, I had hoped to do something more technical and photo related on this job, but to be in the shot would be an opportunity of a lifetime! I considered how awesome it was that people would likely hang the finished image on their walls, much like I had with some of my favorites. I would definitely frame it. I didn't hold back my excitement, skipping into the wardrobe trailer and proudly proclaiming, "I'm Lucy . . . and I'm supposed to find my suit in here?"

A dozen models dressed in brightly colored bikinis were being prepped. They were each at least six inches taller than me. And tan. And skinny. Just as I considered that maybe there was an element of miscommunication between Stefano and the stylist's assistant, she reappeared and pushed me past the models and toward the back. Suddenly, it all made sense. Hanging across the rolling rack like an award-winning marlin was a blubbery, rubbery shark suit. "Oh . . . my God," I uttered. I was prepared to do whatever it took but . . . a shark? A shark suit? I took a deep breath and began disrobing.

Hobbling like a penguin toward the set was nearly impossible. I had to work extra hard because the flippers kept getting stuck in the sand. Liz and Roman just about fell over laughing when they saw me. Stefano was equally as amused. *"Dun nun . . . dun nun . . . da nun da nun da nun . . ."* He sang out the *Jaws* theme over a megaphone and everyone on set burst into hysterics.

Once Roman was able to collect himself, he justified, "Don't worry about being recognized, Luce. We are adding a real shark digitally."

They were adding a real shark digitally? What the hell was I doing in this suit?

"We need someone to stand in as the shark so the models know where to direct their fear . . ."

Okay, understandable. That made sense . . . But why the fucking suit?

"And Stefano thought it would be . . . inspiring, for you to, you know, wear the suit."

So basically, all I had to do was swim back and forth in the waves while the bikini-clad babes bolted from the sea. Seemed easy enough. I mean really, how bad could it be?

I pushed the mask tightly against my face and popped the snorkel into my mouth before hopping into the water. I pulled at the latex to let some of the cool ocean trickle in. I heard several voices go "Ohhhh man . . ." and just as I turned my whole body to look up—since I couldn't move my damn head—a giant wave surged over me and I spun and tumbled around and around until my enormous fin stopped me in the shallow sand. I coughed and spit the frothy salt out of my nose and mouth. A few lighting techs came over to help me to my feet . . . er, flippers.

"Take five!" Thank goodness Stefano needed a break

because I needed oxygen. I hobbled over to my messenger bag and flipped open my phone. Go figure, I had missed the one call that I was waiting for. I put the voice mail on speaker since my ears were inaccessible.

"This message is for Lucy Butler. I am calling from Eberly Properties to let you know that you have been approved for the studio apartment on Fountain Avenue. Congratulations! Please let us know when you can come in to sign the lease."

My own apartment! This was amazing news! "Wooooohoooo!" I screamed as I bounced up and down unapologetically, the shark nose bonking my head with each bounce. I had never lived alone before, but it seemed only natural that I would get my own place. I was, after all, Stefano Lepres' first assistant, progressively making my way into the studio and making a small but decent salary. I could barely afford the tiny first floor studio apartment but it would represent my becoming an independent young woman, aspiring photographer, assistant extraordinaire! Now was the obvious time to make this move since, beyond a doubt, my schedule would only get zanier as I gained responsibilities at work. I hadn't even told Sebastian or Julie that I had applied for the apartment because I wasn't sure if I would even qualify. Of course, their initial reaction was bound to be sour since we were now splitting the rent three ways, but it was never meant to be a permanent arrangement anyway. Besides, since I've been working so much, they've really bonded and probably won't even mind me moving out. Not that I was jealous or anything. Whatever, I was not going to let my worries about their reactions throw shade over this happy occasion. I tossed my phone back into my bag and happily belly flopped back into the sea.

"And . . . action!"

I threw my whole body up and down, side to side, getting from one side of the shot to the next. I could hear the models screaming as they pretended to be terrified of me. I began to recognize the difference of an authentic scream and a forced one—the real ones came right before a giant wave. When I heard those kind of yelps, I braced myself for the crushing waters that barrel-rolled me over and over and dumped me back to land. The last one was particularly harsh. I told the lighting techs to leave me for just a minute. I lay on my super-padded back, my eyes burning from salt, my face stinging from sand. Like a dark cloud, Stefano's shadow came over me.

"I want to have a party at Hidden tonight. Ten thirty."

I put all of my energy into rolling over and crawling back to my messenger bag. I managed to release an arm from the rubber death trap.

"Yes. I am calling on behalf of Stefano Lepres. He'd like to reserve the VIP room for a private party tonight at ten thirty . . . Sure, I can hold . . . Perfect." I paused a moment before I asked, "And could you also check availability for next Thursday?" Sebastian and Julie had been dying to get into Hidden for months. It was the hottest club in LA. I bit my salty lip, wondering if I could pull off getting my friends onto the most exclusive guest list in Tinseltown. Surely it would sweeten the news that I would soon be moving out. I had wanted to do something extraordinary for my friends because they were always seeing me reap various perks from my job, and this would be a great way to involve them in my new world. "Fabulous! If you could put the room under Julie Kaplan's name? It's her birthday, so we want to be sure it's extra special . . . Uh-huh. I can hold." I covered the mouthpiece, wickedly giggling. I wasn't totally lying. When I said "we," I meant Sebastian and I. The hostess was only assuming that I meant Stefano, I rationalized. "Wonderful. Thank you!" I couldn't wait to tell them! My friends were going to freak out!

Just as I hung up on the hostess, my phone began ringing. James Braves. He had been calling and calling and never at the right time. As if there ever was a right time for me. I decided to answer but keep it brief since any minute now they'd be calling me back to set.

"Hi, James!" Even though he couldn't see me, I was embarrassed to be dragging a tail fin from behind my ass.

"Hey, Luce! I'm so glad to have caught you!" Little did he know he'd just punned. "Did you get the apples?" Julie told me that a delivery of Washington apples had arrived without a card—we'd been snacking on them all week without knowing if they were poisoned or not.

"That was so thoughtful of you! Thank you! I'm sorry that I haven't called—things have been so busy. I'm actually at work right now."

"That's great! Are you kidding? Don't apologize! What are you working on?"

I swung my fin from side to side. "Oh . . . this beach shoot . . . hard to put into words."

"Nice! At least one of us is getting a tan . . . So, listen—I am thinking of coming down to LA next week and I wanted to see if you were going to be around?"

"Actually—I just booked my best friend's birthday party at Hidden for Thursday night. Will you be here?"

"I sure will! I am only there for the weekend, so make some time for me, okay?"

I jumped up and down, letting my tail thump against the sand. James Braves wanted to hang out with me! "Of course!"

We bid adieu and I unabashedly did a happy shark dance.

My excitement was halted when I heard Stefano calling out my name over the megaphone. I steadily leaned down to put the phone into my bag and slowly rose back up, pulled the mask off my forehead and pushed it over my eyes. I let out a little whine of frustration before popping the snorkel back into my mouth. "I will get to work on the set . . . I will get to *work* on the set . . . I will get to *work* on the set . . ." My voice sounded like Darth Vader as I repeated my mantras into the hollow tube.

chapter eight

The Extra with Extras

As I drove Stefano to the studio, I tried to imagine what type of duties I'd be assigned to perform on the shoot today. He was set to photograph Ky Zavala, teenage heartthrob superstar. Ky burst onto the scene about two years ago when he landed the starring role on a Disney show. Soon after came two platinum albums, a bestselling memoir, several blockbuster hits, a clothing line and hundreds of collectible items coveted by all of his cultlike fans. Stefano inserted his latest CD, *2Cool*, into the player and turned up the volume. Ky's unmistakable prepubescent voice crooned on about lost loves and late homework. It was adorable. Even Stef grinned when the kid sang out, "Girl, pass me back that note . . . Are you crushin' on me too? . . . Circle yes or noooo . . ."

I was about to pull into Stefano's reserved spot when a yellow Lamborghini cut me off and jerked back and forth before stalling out in the space. Stefano and I couldn't wait to see who the asshole was who had such audacity.

Out hops little Ky Zavala, who yells out to me in passing, "Sorry, babe! Just got my permit and not quite ready to handle the parallel parking, if you know what I mean!" He then twisted his yellow and purple Lakers hat to the side and flashed a peace sign.

"Kyle! Wait just . . . two seconds!" A slightly frantic woman exited the passenger side and dashed to my window. "I'm so sorry. His driving tutor has yet to explain the right of way, apparently!" She squinted her eyes and caught on that Stefano was in the car. "Oh—hi! Hello! I am Deena, Ky's manager. We are just so thrilled to be working with . . ."

"Mom! The door is locked! It's so freakin' hot out here!" Ky yanked off his Margiela motorcycle jacket and slammed it on the sidewalk.

She took a deep breath and gripped the diamond-encrusted cross that lay over her shirt. "Deena Zavala—manager *and* mother. Depends who you're asking, really." She said through a forced smile while bolting to her son's side.

Stefano exhaled. "Fucking mom-agers. Lucy, you have one job and one job only on this shoot: Keep that little shit away from me. Understood?" I nodded my head and drove forward into another spot. So much for getting to actually work on the set today.

The studio was busy prepping for the shot. The set was designed to look like a teenage girl's bedroom. The baby pink bedding, white eyelet dust ruffles and exaggerated curtains were accented with fluffy pom-poms, ceramic horses and snow globes. The art director decorated the room to look like a super-fan lived there by covering the walls with dozens of overlapping posters of Ky. She also accessorized the shelves with propped-up dolls and had decks of playing cards spilling out of the drawers of a vanity next to the bed. These and all other types of items were all emblazoned with Ky Zavala's likeness. It was overkill and it was on purpose, to showcase the mania caused by the little man.

"This is gay! This is so *gay*!" Ky shrieked when he saw the setup. Everyone on set heard him. I guessed that 70 percent of them were probably gay.

Roman responded, "Look, honey, it's not gay if it's you. Think about it . . ."

Ky jokingly punched him in the arm and playfully called him a homo.

"What did I say about those words, Kyle? I'm so sorry everyone. He had a late performance last night and we're all a bit tired. Ky, this shoot is for that contest where you show up to a fan's house—remember? And this is supposed to be her bedroom, yes?" Deena Zavala directed the question to Roman.

"Right . . . Her—or his bedroom," Roman said matter-of-factly.

"Eeeeewww, *gross*!" Ky fled to the dressing room. Roman grinned.

"I'm sorry—again. His assistant is being dropped off here any minute now and things will be a lot easier once he's here." Deena hurried back to the dressing room.

Stefano was in the farthest corner of the studio, discussing the shot with a lighting assistant. I contemplated tending to him, to see if he needed anything, versus checking on Liz in the office, to see if there was any assisting I could do for the production team.

"Girl, if you want to keep our Rottweiler calm, keep the yappy Yorkie in its kennel . . . I mean it," Roman warned. "We are ready to shoot in twenty minutes. Go . . ." He turned me by my shoulders to face the dressing room and pushed me forward.

I knocked on the dressing room door and was told to come in. Ky sat in the makeup chair, deeply involved with a portable game player while a groomer powdered his face. A stylist steamed a crisp, white Dior shirt before hanging it on a rolling rack, next to the other options. His mom-ager sat in the adjacent makeup chair. She had her cell phone nudged between her ear and shoulder while she clicked away on a laptop. She looked worn out.

"Can I get anything for anyone?" I asked quietly.

Deena held up a steaming mug and requested, "I am okay with this tea but I didn't see any sweetener out there . . ."

"Let me see what I can find!" I quickly left and returned with a brand-new box of Sweet'N Low found hidden in the office. "Stefano has a strong distaste for sweetener, and we don't usually have it out—so I'll leave it in here." I set the box down next to the multitasking mom. I felt awkward just standing there, so I left the room and guarded the door. I wasn't exactly sure who I was guarding, Stefano or Ky. I hoped that once Ky's assistant arrived I wouldn't have to babysit and instead I'd be able to do something—anything—photo related.

On the set, Stefano and his photo assistants were adjusting

the shot, and when they were ready, Roman gave me "the look." Again, I knocked on the door this time to let Ky and his mother know that they were ready for him. An art director instructed Ky to do various poses. For the first shot, he sat on the edge of the bed with his guitar, grinning into the camera. After a few shots, they removed the guitar and had him leaning forward, then reclining back. Once he got comfortable shooting he even jumped on the bed and high kicked midair. As much as I was annoyed with the kid, I had to admit, he was kind of cute.

"What's up, dick face?" Ky yelled out. He bounced off the bed and ran over to another teen boy leaning against a wall beyond the lights. The two of them took off for the dressing room. Stefano usually took at least fifty shots per look and Ky disappeared after somewhere around twenty.

"Kyle! Ryan! Get back here . . . please . . . ?" Deena chased after them. Stefano tightened his jaw and cracked his neck. I could tell that he was extremely irritated but holding back. I caught up to Deena and asked where this miracle assistant was. "He's here. That's Ry, Ky's assistant." I didn't know how to respond. The boy looked about fourteen years old. "And also his brother. His brother is his assistant."

"Oh . . . okay," I stuttered out. That kid is supposed to wrangle his not-much-bigger brother into submission? I didn't see it happening.

Roman was losing his patience as well. "Lucy, make sure that ADHD poster child is back here ASAP. We need to get through this shoot quickly—for everyone's sake." He motioned with his head toward Stefano, who was visibly trying to keep himself calm by closing his eyes and taking deep breaths. "Lushy is picking up coffee for the crew—you want anything?" Roman asked. I was touched that he asked me. It made me feel like I was becoming part of the crew.

"Thank you, but I'm okay." I dashed to the dressing room, which was pure chaos. The brothers were throwing cups and open bags of chips and anything else that they could get their hands on while Ky changed into his second outfit. I closed the door and snuck to the office to see if I could be of use to anyone else. Stefano was decompressing while the crew discussed Ky's antics.

I heard a lighting tech reason, "Yeah, man, he's just a kid in an adult world. He's got to get his fun in too."

Ky, Ry and Deena returned to the set and we all followed suit. Ky assumed his first position on the bed, now wearing a gold metallic DSquared jacket, his guitar in hand. Stefano walked around the giant lights and over to the camera. He pulled out his stool and plopped down into place.

"PHHHHAAAAAAAAARRRRRRPPPPPPPPPPPPPPP." A vibrating, echoing fart sound boomed from Stefano's seat. The entire crew looked at him while Ky and Ry fell over in hysterics. Stefano stood up and pulled out from under him a flattened whoopee cushion. It was nearly impossible not to laugh! I turned away from the group and pinched my arm hard to keep from laughing out loud. Tears were building up in Roman's eyes because he was holding back so much laughter. And he wasn't the only one. It felt as if the room was about to explode. Stefano, however, did not find it very funny. He quickly snapped approximately fifteen shots before storming off into the office and slamming the door. It was then that I realized that had I been watching Ky like I was supposed to, this would not have happened. I wondered if I would be to blame. Once the office door was closed, everyone instantaneously fell apart into laughter. Just as Ky and Ry were about to high-five, their mother/manager grabbed them by their wrists and dragged the boys into the dressing room, slamming the door once inside.

Liz's Aussie drawl echoed across the studio. "What's with all the ruckus?" She set two crates of coffees down on a table. "Is he in the office?" She picked up a venti cup marked "SL" and was immediately stopped by Roman.

"Give him a few minutes. It could be deadly in there!" He removed the cup from her hand and set it back down. They walked away from the crew and Liz started cackling while Roman described what had transpired. Members of the crew picked over the beverages and took what was theirs. I thought to write "Do Not Touch" on a Post-it and placed it on the lid of Stefano's coffee to avoid anyone mistaking it for their own. The office door swung open and Stefano's voice boomed, "Roman!" Roman scurried into the office. After less than a minute, my name was called as well. I swiftly made my way to the office. Stefano was pacing the room while running his hands through his hair. Once he noticed me, he stopped and dramatically held his shaking hands out like he was strangling a ghost or something. If I had been a few steps closer, he would have been choking me.

"Lucy . . . Our discussion earlier . . ." Terrified, I nervously nodded my head. "Your only fucking job today: Keep that kid away from me. I hate children. I hate teenagers. I hate little people. I hate Ky Zavala." His face was red and his hair was a mess. Veins protruded from his temples. Again, all that I could do was nod. Stefano sat down on a sofa and I took that as my cue to get the hell out of there.

Roman skipped after me. "Was that not Nick Nolte's mug shot come to life? Okay, you know what to do—make sure the kid stays out of trouble and I'll take care of the big guy. We have one shot—just one left! And actually, Stefano is doing pretty stellar, if you ask me . . ." I gave him a look that said, *Really?*

"Thing is, if he snaps on this tyke the tabloids will have a field day, and his reputation is already in need of rehab. So let's protect all our paychecks and get him through this last shot."

I entered the dressing room, this time without knocking. It was time to show some authority and let these kids know that they were messing with all of us and it was going to end now. Surprisingly, the boys were sitting in the makeup chairs, clicking away at their video games. Deena was on the floor, crouched over a script and her laptop while texting a message on her phone. The boys were being civil but it seemed too good to be true. "Everything okay?" I tested. Neither of them looked up at me but they started giggling in a guilty way. I looked around the room for any signs of disarray.

Ry broke the boys' silent treatment and responded, "Everything is . . . sweet." Both he and Ky nearly fell out of their chairs from laughing so hard. It was then that I noticed, in the corner of the room, the box of sweetener had been torn in half and at least twenty little packets had been ripped open.

"No!" I cried out as I bolted from the room and into the studio. Stefano's venti cup was gone! It was too late! I stood frozen between the dressing room and office on the vacant

set, unsure of what to do. Dare I enter the office and knock the cup from Stefano's hand before he has a chance to take a sip— or should I pray that somebody else claimed it as their own, despite my Post-it? One prayer was for certain: that this would not be blamed on me. How could it be? I was with Stefano when they did it! This whole day was pure ridiculousness, and what should have been a fun photo shoot was turning out to be the sequel to *Adventures in Babysitting: Hollywood Edition*. My mental rant ceased when Roman slipped out of the office and stiffly walked toward me. He was doused head to toe in what had to taste like liquid cake. I bit my lip and shook my head. What could I possibly say?

He used his damp silk pocket square to dab away a drip drizzling off his forehead. "This bitch wants to play Mafia wars? Oh, it's on. It is so fucking on. I'm about to get Antonia Montana out here to teach this little fucker what is what . . ." Roman had an evil glint in his eye as his fingers attacked the keyboard of his BlackBerry. Mafia what? None of what he was saying made sense to me. I didn't know if he was texting a hit man or what. Anything was possible at this point. He hooked his wet arm through mine and led me to the dressing room. "Hello . . . Ky, Ry . . ." The boys appeared shocked to see Roman's attire.

Ky was visibly contrite. He jumped up from his chair and tried to apologize. "We . . . I was only joking. Everyone knows that pranks are my thing and . . . Did he throw it at you?"

Roman put his hand up and made light of the situation. "Don't you worry about me, I'll be fine. Just stopping by to tell you that Stefano decided to bring in an extra, to make the set more realistic—more you."

"A cute girl?" Ky enthusiastically inquired.

"Only the best." Roman assured. "Now you boys stay put. We'll have lunch delivered to you in here. Besides, you should make a grand entrance—keep her waiting with anticipation." He winked and closed the door as the boys fist-pumped with joy.

"Roman, what is going on?" I wasn't buying any of it.

"Watch and learn, boo. Watch and learn."

Over the next forty-five minutes, the crew and I ate lunch next to the set while Ky and his small entourage were served in the dressing room. I kept a close eye on the door to be sure that the troublemakers didn't sneak out to cause more problems. Stefano, Liz and Roman dined in the office. At the end of the hour, as promised, a pretty girl was escorted to the set by Roman. She was about my age and dressed the part of smalltown teenybopper super fan in knee socks, a short plaid schoolgirl skirt and a tight turtleneck. We all crowded around to observe how things would play out.

The buxom blonde offered her hand. "Hi, I'm Antonia—a huge fan!"

Ky turned the charm way up and kissed her hand. "Thanks babe! Wow—and I'm a huge fan! Have you ever been in a music video?"

Stefano intervened. "Okay, kids. Let's start off with a serenade shot and take it from there . . ." I was surprised by how Stefano managed to pull it together. He was even in a good mood!

A series of staged scenes followed that included Antonia opening the bedroom door to find Ky there with flowers, them sitting on the floor, her awestruck as he sang and strummed guitar, them sitting side by side—taking turns kissing each other's cheek. It was a very sweet photo shoot and definitely a dream to many young girls. Thank goodness things turned out as they did, with the shoot appearing to be a total success.

After his standard fifty or so shots, Stefano announced that we were finished. Antonia stretched backward on the bed and exhaled a sigh of relief. Ky's eyes were glued to her rack.

Roman called out, "Tony! Thank you so much for coming out here on short notice to help us out!"

Ky flirted, "Yeah, that was pretty dope of you . . . to come out here lookin' so hot . . ."

Antonia sprung up and tugged at the neck on her top. "I'll tell you what's hot! These lights!" With that, she peeled off her blonde bombshell wig and started fanning herself. Ky jolted upright like a jack-in-the-box. Antonia continued in a deeper, less sultry voice. "Roman, are we going out after this? If so, I'm gonna wanna change, girl. If I don't un-tuck from this duct tape, my balls are never gonna be the same. . . ." Tony reached underneath the schoolgirl skirt to adjust his package.

Never in any scary movie have I ever heard a chilling little-girl-like scream such as the one that came from Ky Zavala. He flew out of that studio like a bat on fire.

chapter nine

Vogue, BC

The cover of Italian *Vogue* had once been a dream assignment to aspiring young photographer Steven Leper. But, after years of incredible success, Stefano Lepres had become blasé and jaded, treating plum assignments like this one as if he was shooting the Johnson family reunion at a state park. Obtaining a permit to shoot inside the Museum of Natural History was no easy feat, but Stefano couldn't bother with being on time or complying with the requirements of museum management. Liz had scored a major coup when she was able to negotiate clearance to shoot inside the cavemen exhibit. "The Cave" housed eight life-size replicas of cavemen in what would have been their natural habitat. Inside Stefano's trailer, out in the parking lot, Liz and Stefano discussed the shoot as the crew scrambled to prep the location. Stefano eye-rolled dismissively as Liz read him the conditions he was to follow in order to shoot on the premises.

I sat at the opposite end of the trailer, doing my best to be invisible, while I put together the shot list. A shot list is a checklist of images the client requires as an end product of the photo shoot. Today's shoot was a fashion spread, and the editor had sent various e-mails listing what needed to be featured. My plan was to go that extra mile and create one concise list. I'm sure Stefano would appreciate my efforts and see that I was capable of such tasks.

Liz's tone was serious and stern as she faced Stefano. "Stef, you have to at least pretend to hear me out. It says here we cannot touch or move anything at all, especially the replicas. That, they say, is bloody important."

"Not even just a little? Some of them are kind of cute, right?" he jokingly asked.

Liz glared at him. "Also, the obvious stuff . . . no small fires, candles, no smoking . . ." Stefano rolled his eyes as he poured himself a glass of scotch. Liz went on. "Don't worry, babe, I saved the best for last! It seems our mates here at the Museum did some research and got familiar with your work. It says here in no uncertain terms that "there is to be no reference of any kind to sexual activity while working in this family-oriented establishment . . ." The two exploded into laughter as Stefano threw his head back and gulped the remnants of his second drink of the day.

Slamming the empty glass down on the table, Stefano dug his hand into his pocket. "What about this? Did they mention any rules regarding our little friend here?" He tossed a film canister to Liz, who caught it and flipped it open.

"They most certainly did not!" She dumped the contents of the canister out on the counter and began sorting a giant pile of cocaine into thick, white lines. Peering in their direction, I attempted to discreetly confirm what I thought they were doing.

Roman entered the trailer as I watched Liz and Stefano nose-diving into the cocaine. Of course I had seen it done before at parties while in art school, but I hadn't expected to see it at work—at 10:00 a.m., nonetheless. Roman interrupted: "Alright kids, showtime. We need you to approve the shot." Stefano and Liz, laughing hysterically, hopped out of the trailer before skipping off to the set. Roman stepped up and carved himself a nice long line. He took a rolled-up bill and snorted the whole line in one long sniff. He squinted his eyes and rubbed his nostrils a few times before holding the bill out to me. I declined.

The Cave was amazing. The barrier that usually prevented the public from getting close to the exhibit had been removed. The crew had full access to the display. I touched the stone walls simply because I could. There were piles of flattened rocks and tufts of animal skins expertly put in their place. Toward the back, replicas of two burly cavemen carried long spears on their shoulders. Tied to the parallel spears was the dangling body of an extinct animal. A third caveman crouched over a pile of wood, rubbing two sticks together.

Three exotic-looking female models outfitted in Cavalli, YSL and Versace animal print couture gowns and vintage Van Cleef & Arpels diamond brooches as hairpieces were being readied with makeup and hair as they waited for instructions for the first shot. "I want that girl, the one in the pink glittery

Louboutins, yes her . . . Up on top, riding the woolly mammoth, but you know, looking sexy. Hit her with a fan! I want that bitch to fly!" Everyone on set began to chuckle as the model was lifted onto the behemoth creature. "And I want you—yes, you in the zebra print. Get beneath this Geico freak and wrap your legs around his neck. Yes! Very hot!" The model slowly crawled under a hairy prehistoric man hunched over and devouring an animal carcass. She moved slowly, careful not to damage anything with the heels. The crew continued to crack up but nobody howled louder than Stefano. He was beyond amused with his mockery. I admit, it was hilarious.

The European art director stepped forward, saying, "But Stefano, dees make ze girl look like she is being . . . how you say? . . . pleased by ze man, no?"

"Camille, trust me, dees is ze sexiest photo shoot I give to you . . ." The crew giggled as Camille backed down. "Okay . . . the last girl, yes, her . . . Switch her out with that fucked-up-looking fawn. What do you weigh, baby? Eighty pounds, give or take? She'll be fine." Obediently the crew disassembled the animal from the spears. I could not believe what was happening! Without a doubt, this exhibit cost a fortune. I looked around, wondering if any of the museum people were witnessing what was going down.

Liz stormed around the mammoth, stepping in front of Lepres. "Stefano . . . No! No! No! Listen to me! You know what you're doing. You're breaking every single rule they laid down . . ."

"Can I get a lit cigarette to the girl straddling our fire-starter? Have her arch backward and hold her smoke up to the sticks as if she's lighting it . . . Thanks, Paul. No, Lush. *Now* I have broken every rule." Liz disappeared, knowing there was no stopping him.

Passing an illuminated wall that showcased the stages of human evolution, I hurried toward my insane boss. He called out to me. "Laurie! Come here! Where have you been? I'm paying you, right? You should always be with me in case I want something."

"Um, it's Lucy, and here is a complete shot list that I put together. You'll notice *Vogue* mentioned featuring that the Rodarte piece. . . ." Stefano tossed it aside without so much as looking at it. My heart sank as I realized that my work would go unnoticed. There has to be a way to get ahead in this group, I thought. I pressed on. "Is there anything else I can get you?"

"It's your fucking job to *know* what I want. I shouldn't have to say it. I shouldn't have to even think it. That's *your job*," he snapped at me.

"Yes." I knew where this was going. I could hear it in my mind before he said it.

"So, Laurie, what do I want right now?" Looking down at me, he relished in the fact that he could intimidate me.

"Umm . . . I'm not sure . . . are you thir—"

"No . . . stop. Don't ask. Think. What . . . do . . . I . . . want?"

"An iced coffee?" I guessed.

"Hello! Is there anything inside that head of yours? We are in the middle of a prehistoric party! Do you see a fucking Starbucks anywhere? Maybe there's a caveman on a smoke break who can rub two fucking rocks together and whip up a mocha frappucino!" Holding up a megaphone, Stefano boomed, "Roman . . . I need a competent assistant over here stat, so skip your fairy derriere this way pronto . . ." The crew cackled at me as I was humiliated yet again.

Roman stepped in and transferred something from his hand to Stefano's. I didn't need visual confirmation this time to know that they were passing drugs around. It was with that observation that a lightbulb went off in my head. I glanced up at Liz, who was on the phone on a balcony overlooking us. She turned her back to the cave, lowered her head to a table before turning back around and winking at a set designer. He in turn gave her a head nod then, elbowing one of the grip guys, they went off to the bathroom together. How had I not picked up before that this was going on? Was I the only one who had been left in the dark?

I returned to the trailer to fetch Stefano a fresh pack of cigarettes. As I reached for the smokes, I took a closer look at the powder. I couldn't help but be curious. It seemed so white, so innocent, so inviting. I was curious to know what the big deal was. I put my pointer finger into the dust, stupidly taking a sniff but only to see what it smelled like. I could feel the dust sprinkle my face. I rubbed it away with my sleeve. What did this stuff do that made people want it, or in some cases need it so badly? My vision of a hard drug user had been from mug shots shown during the news, pictures of people in the ghetto with blotchy skin and rotting teeth. But my coworkers didn't look like that. In fact, they appeared and acted like the movie stars we photographed. Yet, they were all on drugs. I wondered, was it possible that I had been wrong about drugs all along? We are taught from a young age that drugs will derail your life, however it seemed to me like my peers were right on track. On my way back to the shoot, a lighting assistant pressed, "Stefano wants a Voss . . . what the hell is a Voss?"

"I've got it." I picked up a long glass tube of the designer water from the cooler, wiping it off with a towel. I handed Stefano his designer water and cigarettes.

Putting his hand on my shoulder, he said, "Thanks, baby! Now was that so hard?"

I let up a slight smile then turned around to see who was pulling at my T-shirt. Roman motioned for me to follow him into the Fossil Fascination room. We walked to Liz, who was on her headset deep in conversation. We all took turns looking intently at each other and listened to Liz as she wrapped her conversation. "No. I totally understand. We'll take care of it. It's done."

I then felt very paranoid. Did they know that I had touched the cocaine? Was it okay for everyone else to but not for me? How did they find out? Was there something on my face? I reached up and slyly wiped the bottom of my nose with the back of my wrist.

Liz took me by both hands. "Luce, I had to fire our production assistant, Marc. With him gone, I really need you to step it up and help me out by picking up his slack. This shoot needs to be edited and delivered to Camille Bestour's room at the Four Seasons by nine tomorrow morning. She's heading back to Milan at noon. The contact sheets should arrive at Stefano's house an hour after we wrap here. You've got to get on him and make sure he gets it done. This is very important and it's your responsibility. Do you think you can handle it?"

"You want me to make sure he finishes the edit and deliver

it to the Four Seasons by nine o'clock tomorrow morning?" An assignment that didn't include lattes or lighters! No problem! I would be assisting in the editing process . . . on a *Vogue* shoot! Hell yes! This was my chance to prove myself. Finally!

"Right. He can be a pain in the ass, as you know. Editing is not his favorite part of the process. But he's got to do it and you've got to see to it that he does."

Roman added, "There's a drawer in his office with red grease pencils and loupes. Just set up a table with everything he needs. Fix him one of his crazy miracle juices and wait. When he's done, it's all you. Got it?"

"Got it." I wondered if the edit would be done by ten o'clock, when Julie's highly anticipated birthday party at Hidden started. I had barely spoken to my friends since I made the reservations over a week ago. Lest I forget that James would be there! It was only six o'clock. We still had another two hours of shooting. It would take one hour to get to the house. He could start editing at nine. If things went smoothly, I could make it to Julie's party on time!

At eight forty-five, I realized I would never make the party on time. I snuck out of the cave and sent a text to Julie: Hey bday girl! Work ran late. Will b there 4 sure. 11? Call u! xo.

A round of cheers and clapping echoed from the nearly vacant museum as the shoot finally ended. A beaming Stefano swaggered outside, holding hands with the art director. They air-kissed three times as he turned to give the rest of the crew a peace sign. "Let's roll!" Stefano slid into a waiting limo as I followed him into the car.

"That was a great shoot! Didn't you think?" he gloated while adjusting his loose knit beanie.

"Yeah, it was! Those cavemen looked so real it was scary. And those models were gorgeous!"

"I know, right? Flawless." I was relieved to see my boss in such a chipper mood. I poured a glass of water from the limo bar and offered it to him, in an attempt to always anticipate his needs as requested earlier. "Did I say I was thirsty?" He looked at me like I had lost my mind.

"It's here if you, um, want it."

Stefano flipped over the clipboard that was on my lap. He took a film canister from his pocket, tapping out some powder. Maybe he was comfortable cutting up in front of me now that I had already seen him do it. "Cut this up for me, would you, babe?"

Not wanting to show my awkwardness, I took out my wallet and removed a movie rental card. I proceeded to create six white lines. Stefano took a bill, snorting three of the six lines. He then held the bill up to my face.

"Oh, no, thank you." He moved the bill closer to my face. "No, really, I'm good, thanks."

"We have an edit that's going to take all night. If you work for me, you need to keep up with me . . ." I looked at him with uncertainty. I felt pressured to participate but images of the "Just Say No" buttons the student council handed out in junior high flashed in my mind like sirens. He put his hand with the bill on my knee and gave me a tickle. "Come on, relax a little. Work should be fun!" I was happy that Stefano was being so friendly toward me, but I was not comfortable with his suggestion. He was my boss, after all. He turned away from me with a shrug, finished off the three lines himself, and ignored me for the remainder of the ride.

chapter ten

When at Home

Back at the house, Stefano quickly changed into a swim-
suit and cannonballed into the pool. I checked the time. Ten
o'clock. Not bad. If the proofs were there in fifteen minutes, I
would only be an hour late, two tops. I ventured into Stefano's
office, discovering the drawer Roman had told me about. I
took out two loupes and two grease pencils and laid them
neatly on the dining room table. Afterward, I poured Stefano
one of his detox juices. From the kitchen, I watched him dive
into the deep end of the pool.

My cell phone began to vibrate. Mom and Dad. Not until
then did I slow down to consider that I hadn't spoken to them
in over a week.

"Hey Luce! Are you still alive? We haven't spoken in so
long!" my mother began.

"I know. I've been working so much!" I sighed.

"Working? I'm so sure. Tell me, how many times did he send you to Starbucks today?" she mocked. How I wished that I hadn't told them in great detail about my job. I thought that they would be proud of my work ethic and willingness to start at the bottom. Instead, they were upset that I was "disrespecting" the degree that they afforded me by selling myself short. Either way, my mom loved to hear about the glittery things. "So, what movie stars have you met this week?"

My father immediately interjected, "Do you get health benefits?"

Without giving me a second to answer, my mother went on, "We've been telling everyone about your adventures in Hollywood with Stefano Lepres . . . Of course, we don't tell them that you are practically changing his diapers, but you know . . ."

My father continued, "Without health insurance, you're in trouble if you get sick or injured. You need to think about this, Luce . . ."

"I'm still technically working—and yes, Mom, working. In fact, I was . . . promoted to second photo assistant. I am no longer running errands and doing minion work. In fact, I am about to sit down to edit the selections for Italian *Vogue* right now." I didn't know why I was saying these things, but once I started I couldn't stop. "We shot Drew Barrymore for *W Magazine* on Tuesday, did a music video for Rihanna on Wednesday, shot the new Balenciaga ad campaign on Thursday, and *Vogue* wrapped about an hour ago . . ." I paused and grinned, registering what I had just said. I felt lucky to have been part of all that—regardless of my role. I chose to ignore my mother's snide remarks and reveled in knowing that she was eating her words. True, my big promotion was a big fat lie, but sooner or later it wouldn't be.

There was a knock at the front door. Balancing the phone between my neck and my shoulder, I signed for the box of prints before taking them into the house, all the while continuing the conversation with my parents. "We're not offered insurance on the job. I'll look into getting some on my own." I placed the prints on an entry table, separating them into piles. I set the date detox smoothie to the side on a gold coaster. "I promise I'll call you over the weekend, okay?"

As Stefano reentered the house through the French doors, he picked up his drink and headed up the stairs. "I edit in the living room, not the dining room. The dining room is for dining, not living."

I hoped the universe hadn't let my parents hear his nonsense. After a long silence, my mother spoke. "Alright, Lucy. Have fun!" I hated when my parents told me to have fun as if I were away at summer camp. I had a real job to do whether they recognized it or not. And, whether it was true or not. Dammit.

As I transferred the setup to the living room table, Stefano returned clad in a gray terrycloth robe carrying a platter adorned with a buffet of pills and powder. Sitting down next to me on the couch, he began to thumb through the contact sheets. "May I?" I asked, referring to the extra loupe.

"Be my guest." We sat beside each other, admiring the images. They were even more magnificent in print than I had even imagined. The giant mammoth looked as if he were racing through a jungle and the model was a sensual creature barely able to contain the beast. It was amazing!

"You may also imbibe," Stefano offered as he pointed to the array of drugs.

"I . . . I'm off to my best friend's birthday party after this, so I can't." I figured I might possibly evoke a sense of guilt in my boss knowing he was keeping me from my plans. I could not miss Julie's party!

"Really, Lucy?" He gave his signature eye roll to me and snorted a line. "You need to decide if you want to stay in this family. Don't be so judgmental—I mean, look at us, we are on top of the world! The best in our industry! You could truly be a part of it if you would stop acting like it's you against us." Stefano resumed indulging. "Even earlier today . . . we were having a ball on set while you were sniffling in the corner over a shot list."

After I got over the fact that he called me by my real name and acknowledged that I had created a shot list, his words began to sink in. He had a point. I was keeping myself away from the rest of the crew. How *bad* could coke really be? Liz successfully ran the studio and she was obviously doing well. Cocaine didn't appear to be hurting her, and she was becoming someone that I looked up to, professionally. On the flip side, how *good* could coke really be? I mean, I had been able to keep on the straight and narrow all my life thus far, even "just saying no" only a few hours ago . . . Why give in now? As if reading my thoughts, Stefano continued, "You remind me of Lushy when she started out. That girl had no clue!"

Was this my opportunity to finally fit in? Had I just gone for it in high school and drank the freaking beer instead of water, would things have gone better for me? I was tired of thinking, *What-if?* If there was ever a time to just go for it, this was it. I held out my hand. "When in Rome."

"When at home!" He warmly patted my back as I leaned down and sniffed my first line. A burning sensation spread across my face, numbing and tingling as it seeped through. When the burn subsided, I did another line and later on, another. My mouth got increasingly dry and no matter how much I drank, I couldn't quench my thirst. The surge of energy that I anticipated felt more like a restless, anxious type of feeling. It wasn't the best feeling in the world, yet for some reason my body just kept wanting more, more, more. I can't quite explain it.

We worked as a team as we went through the edit and shared the coke. Our dynamic changed that night. Don't get me wrong, I was still Stef's slave. But partaking in drugs did bring us closer. I knew I was compromising everything that I was all about, but if this is what it took to be part of the scene, I was going to do it. And really, it didn't seem that bad.

"Those models are so stunning," I said with obvious envy.

"I prefer Eastern Euro models. The ugly-pretties, I call them."

"Ugly-pretty?" I tittered, thinking he was being funny.

"Yeah, like you." His voice remained flat.

I lifted my head away from the loupe. "Like me?"

"Yeah. You're nothing special now but with the right hair and makeup, the proper lighting and some retouching, you'd be stunning too."

I was dismayed by his brutal criticism and used the restroom as an excuse to leave the room. Once inside, I checked myself out in the mirror. Did I have supermodel appeal? No. Was I completely misfortunate? I didn't think so. I made a mental note to start wearing more makeup. I glanced at the clock on my phone. Shit—eleven o'clock. Following a grunt of frustration, I sent Julie another text. *Still working! I AM SORRY. Promise I WILL be there.* After I'd sent it, I wondered how upset she was at this point. She hadn't replied to any of my texts. I felt like the worst friend ever, but what could I do?

With resignation, I returned to the editing process. Rounding the hallway, I stopped dead in my tracks, gasping in horror. *He was asleep!* I flung myself to Stefano, shaking his arm. "Stefano. Wake up, Stefano!" I hollered, to no avail. He did twitch. Well, at least he wasn't dead, right? Racing back to the kitchen, I called Roman.

"He's *what*? The man hasn't slept since the eighties! How did you let this happen?"

"I don't know what happened . . . He took some pills. . . ."

"What pills? Colors! I need to know colors!"

I raced back to the living room and eyed the remnants of the drugs. "There were more of these white ones before . . . It says 12.5mg AMB."

"Oh, *fuck*. Ambien CR, 12.5 milligrams. We are so fucked. No, YOU are so fucked. YOU let this happen! Fuck, Lucy!"

"Roman . . . don't freak out. He'll sleep it off. I'll have him edit when he wakes up. The edit will be at the Four Seasons by nine like I promised. You have my word!"

"Sleep it off? Listen, Seattle girl. Our boss man just took enough sleeping pills to put down one of those whales you

Northwestern folk like to sit around and watch from your igloos or whatever. He's down for the count and I have every right to freak out!" Roman hung up the phone.

I would wait it out. Several hours passed while I read every book on the coffee table. By then it was 1:00 a.m. I admitted to myself that Roman was right. Stefano was not going to wake up anytime soon. Sitting down next to Stefano's seemingly comatose body, I turned my attention to the contact sheets. I thought, you know—I could *do this*. Was I not his biggest fan? I knew Stefano's work like the back of my hand. Hadn't I been studying him for years? It was the obvious choice. I would edit the shoot myself. I picked up a loupe and went from frame to frame. Some frames were out of focus and others too dark. Swallowing hard, I picked up Stefano's limp arm and placed a red pencil between his fingers. Sliding the loupe around, I found a striking image, then dragged Stefano's hand around it. I aided him in drawing circles around my . . . well, his selections. At least this way he was sort of editing it. Albeit unconventional, I was finally assisting in the actual photo process! For *Vogue* nonetheless!

Every so often, yes, I would do another line of blow. That stuff kept me awake and I was convinced that it saved the edit and my job.

At 7:00 a.m, after working all night, I delivered the edit to the Four Seasons. Returning to my apartment, I parked in the lot but was too tired to negotiate the stairs to the lobby. I fell asleep in the car. It was the first time I had closed my eyes in over twenty-four hours.

Nearly three hours later, the buzzing of my cell phone jolted me awake. I answered with a hoarse voice. "Hi, Liz."

"Babe, you sound like a hot mess! Roman told me what happened last night. I don't know how you pulled it off, honey, but Camille is beside herself! She's rapt with the selections and is very happy! You should be proud of yourself, little Luce. We can't figure out how you woke him up and got him to edit! Bravo! Get some rest, darl. You deserve it!"

"Thanks, Lushy." I didn't even bother to reach for my phone when it fell under the seat.

With a slight smile of victory, I fell back asleep. My friends would understand.

chapter eleven

The Greatest Show on Earth

I sat on the cold cement floor of the studio with a laptop, flipping through pictures of Julie's birthday party that had been posted online. I wished that I could have been there. I knew that I should have been there. The silver lining was that, judging by the pictures, everyone looked like they had had a ball. At least I was able to secure the venue, if nothing else. Our shoot had wrapped about twenty minutes prior and I was waiting on James to pick me up for an early dinner before he'd have to catch a flight back to Seattle. As luck would have it, on James' last day in town, Stefano would be spending the later half of the day at the spa. I was caught up in the images and hardly paid attention to the buzz happening around me.

"Somebody needs to take her home," Liz stated, matter-of-factly. "Not it."

"Not it!" . . . "So not it!" . . . "Dude, not it," echoed the sounds of several coworkers.

I looked up to find everyone staring at me. "What?"

Liz raised a glittered nail and pointed behind me. "That."

I half turned my body around and couldn't believe my eyes. Adriana Darling, a twentysomething trust-fund titan turned model, known for her class and composure, was found flirting with a potted indoor tree. She stroked the trunk and tickled the leaves while swaying back and forth. We had just finished shooting her for a "Got Milk" campaign. She still wore the frothy mustache smeared across her upper lip. Her angel white hair was beginning to fall out of the updo she wore during the shoot.

Roman joined the group showcasing three empty bottles of booze. "This should explain the display of dendrophilia."

"Bloody hell! You put all that booze in her dressing room? She weighs less than my eight-year-old niece, Roman! Are you crazy?" Liz steamed.

"Am *I* crazy? Excuse moi, am I the one fondling a fucking fern? It was on her rider list—it's not like I had a choice . . ."

"You're right, you're right. Well, you're going to have to help Lucy take her home." Me? I couldn't possibly stand James up for the second time this weekend. I considered suggesting that we call her a car service. "It's strange that she showed up here alone because . . ." *Crash-thump-thud!* The sounds interrupted Liz and demanded everyone's attention from across the studio. We all dashed to the fallen tree.

Roman tossed the bottles into a wastebasket. "This place is a fucking *circus!*" he hollered on his way to help the others lift the tree upright. Adriana lay on the floor with a goofy grin, her milky mustache and ruby red lipstick smeared around her mouth in a clownlike fashion.

Liz seemed annoyed. She started clicking away on her BlackBerry, presumably to find directions to Ms. Darling's home. "Maybe we should sober her up?"

I asked, "How do we do that?"

"As if I would know . . . I've never actually tried to get *sober* before. Maybe a glass of milk to coat her stomach?"

We looked around at the seemingly endless supply of milk. She was, after all, the latest ambassador to the brand.

"Intolerant . . . am . . . I," the pretty girl piped in. We leaned in toward her.

"What was that, Bozo?" Roman teased. Liz elbowed his rib.

"I'm lactose intolerant," she lifted her head to say before letting it fall back down.

Of course.

I greeted James at the studio entrance and we shared a great big hug. We were the only people around in jeans and plain T-shirts and it felt like home being close to him.

"Show me around your digs!" James referred to the studio.

"Real quick, I'll give you a run-through, but we have to drive someone home in their car then swing back around with my coworker to get yours. Is that okay?" I didn't want to tell him that we didn't have a choice.

"Whatever you need to do . . . I'm in your world now."

He had no idea. I quickly walked him through the studio and introduced him to a few work friends. He was impressed.

"Wow, Lucy! You are really here! I am so proud of you . . . You really did it!" He put both hands on my shoulders and gave them a squeeze. "Is that Adriana Darling?" We turned our attention to the fern whisperer, who was now turning her charm to a suit of armor—a prop that had been used in a recent shoot.

"Yes, yes, it is. And we are taking her home. Welcome to my world, James."

Adriana was far too incoherent to direct us to her own home, so we decided to take her to her parents' place, a virtual Hollywood landmark that Roman could direct us to. He and James rode together, while I drove Adriana's Porsche with her passed out in the passenger seat. The Darling Estate was nestled in the prestigious Holmby Hills, not far from the Playboy Mansion. As we neared the residence, an increasing number of luxury cars lined the streets, making it difficult to get to the parking-lot-sized driveway. An attendant held up his hand and motioned for Roman to roll down the window of his Prius. They exchanged words before the attendant came up to the Porsche. I politely smiled as he peeked into the passenger seat and recognized Sleeping Boozy. Her right leg was up and out the window, the left falling to the opposing side. The attendant handed me a piece of paper that read VIP PARKING, which I placed over her lap.

I followed Roman up and around the dramatic driveway circling a fountain adorned with angels.

"Fucking fuck!" Adriana shrieked as she came to. She flipped over the vanity mirror and attempted to clean herself up. She dug into the middle console and pulled out a powder puff and compact. While dusting her forehead and hollow cheeks, she spoke to me for the first time. "My parents are having their annual . . . Save the . . . Something event . . . Fuck! I forgot! I can't walk in like this . . . I'm on the absolute cusp of being cut off as it is . . ." She covered her face with her hands and shook her head side to side. Her attire was less than appropriate. I could just imagine how her parents would react.

I looked in the rearview mirror at the guys and wondered what they could have possibly been talking about the entire ride here. I didn't know two more different men. Roman caught my eye and began tapping his wrist and raising his hands as if to say *What's the holdup?* I excused myself and told Adriana I'd be right back.

I leaned into Roman's car through his driver's-side window, peeking into the backseat. "Did you return those gowns from yesterday's shoot?"

"No. Yes. Maybe . . . Why?" Roman inquired. I eyed the vacant driveway, the unattended entrance to the massive cream tent encasing the backyard and Adriana still carrying on in the Porsche. Roman followed my gaze, catching on to what I was thinking.

"Are you high? You can't just walk into Bozo's Big Tent party uninvited, Valentino or not."

"We can't abandon her—especially in the condition she's in. She's already on thin ice with her parents . . ."

"And this is our problem because . . . ?" I looked up at the Porsche to see Adriana still falling apart in the passenger seat. I felt badly and related to her parental predicament.

Not too surprisingly, James was the voice of reason. "Lucy, that might not even be legal."

"Look at her, you guys . . ." Her head rested atop her arms, which were both dangling lifelessly out the window. "James, come on—I know that you of all people are always down to help someone in need. And Roman, I'm sure there have been at least a dozen times that you might have majorly disappointed your parents had a friend not covered for you."

"We're not her friends, Lucy," Roman corrected. Still, he released the trunk and stepped out of the car. "But lucky for her, I still have that Tom Ford suit Bradley Cooper wore last week and it might be my only chance to get into that man's pants." He turned to James. "As for you, my friend, you'll have to settle for Seth Howard's suit."

"Who?" James questioned.

"Exactly," Roman snipped.

Getting dressed behind a series of cone-shaped hedges was not my proudest moment. Shimmying an inebriated Adriana into a Herve Leger bandage dress wasn't Roman's either. I looked all of us over. Even in couture we looked like a motley bunch. The full-length L'Wren Scott gown I was wearing hardly covered up my Converse sneakers. I wasn't sure we could pull it off.

Roman and I each had one of Adriana's arms wrapped around our own as we supported and kept her stable, both literally and figuratively. James lifted an open slit on the side of the tent and we all inconspicuously slipped in.

Light pink silk tapestries elegantly draped from the center of the tent. A small orchestra sung out happy sounds from the adjacent lawn. Caterers sailed through the room showcasing hors d'oeuvres that looked too cute to consume.

"I can't believe we are doing this," James whispered in my ear. Did he think that I was certifiably crazy? I looked up and found a slight smile spread across his face and knew that he was having fun.

Adriana's head fell to my shoulder. Roman switched her right arm to his right hand and swiftly put his left arm around her shoulders to lift her head upright just in time.

"There you are, Adri. Mother has been looking for you. She's especially unglued today, which is beyond entertaining for me—not the best of news for you, however." Trey Darling Jr. sipped his scotch and gave me and Roman the split-second scan, to briefly check whether or not we were worth acknowledging (we were not). Trey was unfairly handsome. His perfectly parted blond hair and icy gray eyes completed his prep-school Ken-doll look.

Adriana's head flung forward as she attempted to utter a response and Roman instinctively grabbed her hair, jerking her head back into place.

"Oh my God, of course—you're drunk. This party is going to be far better than I anticipated." Trey chuckled as he arrogantly walked away.

"I'd like to water his elephant . . ." Roman quietly uttered.

"Let's find an empty seat for her. Maybe if she eats something it will sober her up a little . . ." James suggested. I was nervous and starting to think that this was not one of my best ideas. With slow, steady strides, Roman and I followed James toward the back of the tent where the less-desired tables stood.

"The bearded lady, three o'clock!" hissed Roman as we passed a rumored-to-be-closeted actor.

"Would you cut that out?!" I halfheartedly pleaded. Although it was entertaining, I desperately just wanted us to blend in. My plan was to help this girl keep it together long enough to fulfill her daughterly duties and then . . . Well, that was as far as I had planned for, actually.

We spilled Adriana into a chair and propped her up between a wall and the table. I poured a glass of water and placed it in her hand. "Adriana . . . Adriana . . ." It took a few times to get her to focus on me. "Drink this . . . We'll be right back with some food, okay?" She grinned and nodded while petting my face. I took both of her hands in mine and placed them around the glass of water.

"Roman, you stay here and keep an eye on her. James, follow me."

Had I paid any attention to the society page of *W Magazine*, I might have recognized those in attendance and played a game of "who's who?" in my head as I made my way to the buffet. Instead, I hovered over the fine cuisine, trying to figure out what Adriana might prefer to eat. Some bread? Definitely a good idea to soak up some of that liquor. Poached salmon, perhaps? Everyone loves fresh fruit. A small side of wild mushroom risotto? Why not?

"Welcome, friends." Jeanne Darling addressed the party using a microphone from atop a small podium. The crowd faced Adriana's mother and began golf-clapping.

"The Ringmaster . . ." Roman said over my shoulder.

"What are you doing here? You are supposed to be watching Adriana!" I seethed.

"Oh honey, that hot mess ain't going nowhere." He picked up a plate and began serving himself.

"I'll go," James offered. He took his plate and the one that I'd made for Adriana to the table.

"Girrrrrl . . . he loves you!" Roman hummed.

"No he does not. He was my guidance counselor and we're just friends," I corrected.

"Trust me, the only place he wants to guide you is horizontally and upside down." I swatted his arm. "If a man looked at me the way that he looks at you, it would be o-v-e-r . . ."

The well-to-do-lady next to us told us to *shhhh*.

Feeling sufficiently reprimanded, I quietly set my half-full plate and the silver tongs on the pink linen and did an about-face, giving the podium my full attention. Mrs. Darling was of average height and size, looking posh in a pink bouclé Chanel skirt suit. She had the same almost-white shade of hair as her son and daughter, although hers was pulled up into a hurricane-proof bouffant. She continued to speak purposefully about the importance of community, responsibility and awareness. It was clear from her remarks that she was an intelligent woman, not just another socialite making irrelevant noise. I couldn't help but nod along with the others as I listened to Mrs. Darling go on.

"Lucy. . . . Shit. Lucy!" Roman began frantically whispering and jabbing me in the arm.

"Roman, not the time!" I quietly sneered.

He began to panic and squirm like a toddler about to wet his pants.

"What is it? If it's another stupid circus pun, Roman, I swear I'll . . . Oh my God."

In a Godzilla-like manner, Adriana was making her way through the sea of somebodies. A mixture of *ouches* and *pardons* blended with the occasional breaking of a glass that followed her as she neared the podium.

James stood up from the table with his hand out. He must have felt like he had accidentally let go of a balloon, watching it erratically fly off in every which direction.

"Hold this," Adriana demanded as she pushed her glass of water into the hands of Melania, Donald Trump's wife. It splish-splashed across the model's chest and a collective gasp was heard from their table.

My jaw remained unhinged as I watched Adriana tornado her way toward who knows where. All we could do was watch her trip past her stunned mother and all her guests. An exclamation of concern echoed from the crowd. I balanced on the toes of my sneakers and craned my neck to catch a glimpse of Adriana plunging backward into the estate's stately fountain.

"The heiress wheel has fallen off its tracks," Roman concluded.

James joined us as Roman and I hurried out of the party through a slit in the tent.

chapter twelve

Isabella Blackstone

My palms were sweating as I gripped the steering wheel. Stefano and I were on our way to a shoot and running late as usual. As soon as I had arrived at Stefano's house, I knew the day would be rough. He was still awake from the night before, and clearly a mess. The good news was that he was still wearing his uniform of layers from the previous day, so I didn't have the absurd task of selecting his outfit. The bad news was that Stefano was acting bizarre, anxiously tapping his knees and maintaining an ominous silence. It made me very nervous.

James had called this morning to let me know that he enjoyed spending time with me even if it was "a little crazy." He also said that he thought it was admirable that I wanted to help a stranger and he hopes that I never lose my kindhearted qualities. His validation made me feel good.

But those good feelings had long since evaporated. Stefano and I drove in silence the entire way to a modern estate tucked away in the Hollywood Hills. I couldn't help but feel as if he might be a volcano on the verge of eruption. As we pulled up to the set, he became increasingly agitated. The second the car came to a halt, he dashed into the house, isolating himself from everyone. I immediately rushed to Roman, who was supervising the setup in the backyard, to warn him about Stefano's state of mind.

I stopped short to admire the expansive yard. An infinity pool looked like it was placed upon the edge of the world. Unobstructed views of Los Angeles could be seen from every angle, and the Hollywood sign commanded attention as well.

"Damn it." Roman grunted in frustration after I filled him in. "This will only get worse now that Ebony is gone!"

"His last personal assistant?"

"Yeah . . . Ebony used to . . . help Stefano with his antidepressants . . . by kind of, putting them in his shot of wheat grass every morning."

"And he won't take them if I give them to him?" It seemed any pill that you put in front of Stefano was gone before an official offer was made.

"Well . . . He didn't exactly know about it . . ."

"You guys drugged him?" Roman grabbed my wrist, dragging me to the other side of a near wall. He surveyed our surroundings to confirm nobody was close enough to hear our controversial conversation.

"Technically, yes . . . but not in a bad kind of way. I mean, look at the guy . . . He pops Klonopin like candy . . . it snows more frequently in his right nostril that it does during

Sundance . . . and really, it's in his best interest, our best interest. It keeps him healthy!"

"No. Balanced meals and the occasional nap would keep him healthy . . . I hope you don't expect me to do that." I sternly looked into Roman's eyes. "I won't do that."

Roman put his hands around my own and smiled. "Godspeed." We laughed at the craziness of the situation. It finally felt like we were on the same team.

"*Ugly!!!! Uglyyy!!!*" Stefano's raspy voice bellowed from inside the house.

Roman manned up. "I got this one. You find Liz and see what time Blackstone will be here."

"As in Isabella Blackstone?" I asked incredulously.

"The one and only!" Roman dramatically threw his arms up and snapped.

Isabella Blackstone was set to arrive any minute. Miss Blackstone is not only hands down the most famous woman on the planet, she is also the most beautiful. Men, women, straight, gay and everything in between have all fantasized about her. I learned the scheduled shoot that day was a Pepsi advertisement for which Blackstone had reportedly accepted over eight figures in return.

I found Liz in the kitchen, which had been turned into a makeshift production room. She too appeared to be in last night's attire and full makeup. "Hey kitten! What's shakin?" she called out. No matter how hungover—or let's be honest, still drunk—Liz was always kind. Although in retrospect, maybe it was because she was always drunk.

"Can I pick your brain for a minute?" I felt comfortable addressing her.

"What's left of it, absolutely."

"What do you think about me taking over Marc's job?" I bit my lower lip. I wanted this so badly and hoped she wouldn't laugh at the idea.

"It's certainly something to strive for! But darl, you're still very green." I had heard the term "green" before. The color meaning I wasn't ripe enough to join the other experienced fruits in their more respected departments. I knew it was the truth and part of me expected to hear it. I had no experience in production—why would they just let me sail on in? My knowing that I was destined to do more than adult babysitting wasn't reason enough. "That being said, you've been consistently showing us that you are capable of more. When you get a chance, word up Stefano and let him know you're interested. Then keep killing it like you have been!"

Roman slid the giant glass door open and stepped inside, his Prada sandals trailing in backyard dirt. "He wants you. What's with the nickname?"

"The nickname?" I didn't understand why Roman flipped his lip to express his sympathy. I was still confused until a crew member poked his head inside. He pointed a clipboard at me. "Are you . . . Ugly?"

I knew it would only be a matter of time before I had been blessed with a mean moniker. Something that "Lushy" Liz and "No-man" Roman seemed to embrace. "Yeah, I guess I am. What's up?"

"Stefano wants you. He's on set."

"This too shall pass, honey!" Liz advised as I made my way to the set.

The Pepsi set was designed to look like a pool party circa

the 1960s. The extras were in short shorts and dated swim suits. The area was littered with vintage bottles of soda and multicolored floating devices. Everything appeared authentic to the era. Not a detail was missing. Stefano sat with his legs in the pool, next to a handsome young male extra.

"There you are, Ugly! How great is this house?" Stefano stood up and rolled his pants back down. Together we walked back into the sleek estate.

"So, Stefano . . . about this 'Ugly' thing . . . It kind of makes me feel uncomfortable." I had to say something.

He stopped in his tracks and did an about-face. "Oh no, it isn't meant to! I'm really calling you pretty . . . like those ugly-pretty models. You're like them, remember? Special!" Although he seemed sincere, I knew him well enough to know that he was playing mind games with me.

"Okay, well, why don't you call me 'pretty' then?"

"Because pretty really isn't that pretty; pretty is ugly. You see? I'm *complimenting* you!" How could I even respond to this type of logic? This man had the maturity level of a five-year-old combined with the sense of a schizophrenic. I had no choice but to go along with it for the time being. He continued walking a few paces in front of me. "Come on, Ugly! Let's go meet Isabella Blackstone!"

We approached the luxury Star Waggon where Ms. Blackstone was preparing for the shoot. I couldn't even count the number of paparazzi who were being held off the property by barricades monitored by armed security guards. Stefano lowered his head and held his hand in front of his face as he passed them by, as if the photographers would be interested in getting his photo. Unbeknownst to him, they all imitated him doing this, which honestly made my day. I followed Stefano inside to find Isabella surrounded by admiring stylists. The makeup artist, wardrobe stylist, hair dresser and all of their assistants hung on to her every word and tended to her as if she were the most delicate of flowers. Her platinum hair was rolled up in glamorous pinup girl curls and her plumped lips were painted a dazzling plum shade. She looked like the ballerina in a jewelry box that I had as a young girl, also seemingly too beautiful to be real. Her perfect body was elegantly posed as she balanced over a platform while a girl airbrushed a bronze hue to her already tanned legs. Another girl pinned a tiny ruffled Rosa Cha bikini tight to her body. Suffice it to say, Isabella didn't look like a woman pushing forty.

"Stef! Oh my God! How exciting to finally work together! My favorite photographer of all time!" The voluptuous star bounced over to Stefano and gave him a half hug, careful not to let her freshly painted legs touch him.

"Bella, you look phenomenal! Really, you radiate! Look at you! Let my staff know if there is anything you need! My assistant Ugly would be happy to get you anything at all!" The stylists paused to glance at the girl named "Ugly." I quietly chuckled, pretending as if he were joking.

None of this fazed Isabella's sunny disposition.

"Okay, wonderful! See you both in a bit!"

While the extras waited in the unrelenting sun for Stefano and Bella to arrive on set, I decided to snap behind the scene shots with my "James" camera. Every time that I held it, it made me feel a little bit closer to home—even though I wasn't exactly homesick. My first shot was of a model from behind as she stood at the end of the edge-of-the-world pool and leaned backward. The Hollywood sign appeared to rest above her chest and fell perfectly into her curves. I took another picture of a male model's torso while the makeup artist airbrushed on a more defined six-pack, the dark paint slightly dripping in the creases.

Everyone including myself was thrilled when things finally wrapped ten hours later. It had been a long, hot and sticky day. I opened the driver's-side door to Stefano's stifling car when I heard Isabella's heels click-clicking across the pavement. "Stef! Wait! Come to Vegas with me! I have the most incredible penthouse to myself for the next two days! I'm leaving right now! I have a plane! Come with me!"

"Vegas? You're mad, woman!" he teased and rested his arm on the car door. "What the hell would we do in Vegas?"

"You didn't seriously just say that?!" she squealed in her signature voice.

Stefano buried his head in his hands, while mumbling, "Vegas . . . Vegas . . . Vegas."

"Say yes! It will be a whirlwind trip! Let's jump on my plane right now and just go!" Stefano scratched his head, looking at the megastar. Had anyone ever said no to this woman? I wondered.

Shutting the car door he said, "Fuck it. I'm in."

Isabella gleefully jumped up and down, skipping to her waiting limo. "Come on! Vegas, baby!"

"Lush!" Stefano ran to Liz and the two conversed. I blissfully thought of everything that I could do with four entire days of freedom. Even if he was only gone for two, I had requested the weekend off. There was laundry, sleep, finally unpacking the last of my moving boxes and most important, spending time with my friends who I had neglected to see for longer than I could calculate. Although Sebastian and Julie pretended like they didn't care when I told them I was moving, even going as far to say that they saw it coming, I could tell that they were miffed. What really pissed them off was my missing Julie's birthday party, and I didn't blame them. This weekend I would make it up to them both by having them over to my place for dinner! We could catch up on everything and really reconnect. These heavenly thoughts were interrupted as Stefano snatched the car keys from my hand and threw them to Liz. "I can't go without an assistant!"

I checked my reflection in the BMW's blackened window. Had I known there was the possibility of a trip to Vegas I would have packed things to wear besides the tank top, cutoff shorts and flip-flops that I had on.

"But I don't have anything, just what I'm wearing . . ."

"I told you, Ugly! Always be prepared for the unexpected!"

I shot Liz a quizzical look. *He did?*

"Honey, it's Vegas, not Siberia," she chuckled. "Besides, this might be your chance to mention what we were talking about! Take advantage of the opportunity!"

Roman walked between us and inconspicuously passed something from his hand to mine exactly like I'd seen him do to others before. I could feel right away that it was a container of pills about half full. He whispered, "For him—trust me."

I opted for the front of the limo, next to the driver, who put on his chauffeur's cap as the car sped away. The prescription label had been torn off the pills, so I couldn't tell what they were for exactly. I flipped the container over and over on my knee, watching the capsules spill back and forth.

I was overwhelmed with conflicting emotions. I'd never been to Vegas before, and to get to go—well, that on it's own is a thrill! But to go on a private plane! With Isabella Blackstone! I wished that I had a friend around; we'd throw our hands up and scream, "I can't believe this is happening!" But there wasn't anybody. What would I do for clothes? Toiletries? A phone charger? Where are we staying? For how long?

I took a deep breath and told myself to stop overthinking everything. It would all work out somehow. I figured, what's the worst that can happen? Besides, I had other things to worry about: My parents were visiting in three days.

chapter thirteen

What Happens in Vainness

"Miss?" A gorgeous flight attendant presented me with a tray of tightly rolled-up washcloths. She was not dressed in any typical airline attire. Instead she reminded me more of a member of Charlie's Angels in high-waisted slacks paired with a flowing silk blouse that tied into a giant bow at her neck. The tiny towel was ice cold and smelled like eucalyptus. It was so refreshing on just my hands that I wished I could take a few into the bathroom and wash the day off my entire body.

Although the plane could have sat eight, it was only the three of us flying. My seat was one of two in the front facing the cockpit, while Stefano and Isabella faced each other behind me where it looked like a small den with couches and a desk instead of an ordinary cabin. The cushy seats were a light beige leather and the details were all a dark, glossy walnut. The flight attendant handed us each a glass of champagne. Without further ado or any of those pesky in-case-of emergency demonstrations, we were off.

The instant the wheels of the Learjet touched down on the steaming Nevada tarmac, I exhaled. I released the pressure of my white knuckles gripping the armrest. I wasn't afraid of the flight. In fact, for some reason I felt safer on what I decided was a Mercedes with wings than I would on a commercial flight. I figured that Isabella only flew with the finest of pilots, but still, the prospect of crashing into eternity with Stefano was a terrifying fate. A pink stretch limo waited steps away from the jet. Magically, wherever Isabella went, there was always someone waiting to take care of her every need or want. On the flight neither the star nor the photographer had said a word to me, the invisible assistant. Welcoming the solitude, I was still a little uneasy in regard to what to expect on our arrival.

Arriving at the Bellagio Hotel with Isabella Blackstone was the equivalent of entering Buckingham Palace with the Queen. Crowds parted as staff hastily attended to Miss Blackstone's luggage. Security measures were implemented with the precision of a military exercise as Isabella, Stefano and I were quickly escorted to a private elevator. Stefano and I were shown to our shared suite just down the hall from Isabella's penthouse. Once inside, Stefano lit a cigarette and reclined on the luxurious bed.

"I'm going to have dinner downstairs with Bella. I need you to go buy me something to wear for when we go out later. If you order room service, be sure that it doesn't smell like fish . . . or meat . . . eeew . . . or cheese. Nothing worse than a stinky hotel room." Stefano rolled out of bed and stamped out his cigarette in the bathroom sink and swaggered across the room.

So far, not so bad, I thought to myself. In the living room, Stefano glamorously parted the delicate floor-to-ceiling curtains à la Joan Crawford before immediately slamming them shut. "Oh no . . . No! Not again!" He clutched his chest and stepped away from the wall of windows. I instinctively jumped up to investigate. Had there been a murder on the sill of our suite? Was there a mob boss's body in the final stages of rigor mortis dangling from the balcony? Not exactly. "Those damn fountains! I can't deal with those fucking fountains! Oh Lucy, you have to have them turned off immediately! They give me anxiety like you would not believe. I just can't deal!"

I peered down at the beautifully orchestrated water spectacle below. The stunning light show was world famous and attracted crowds of millions from all over the globe. Although I well remembered that Stefano was "always right," I decided to test him on this one. "What if we just switched to a suite on the other side of the hotel?"

"I'm not going to dignify that with an answer. Do your fucking job! Ebony was able to do it. I don't know why you have a problem with everything I say."

I wanted to yell back, "Because everything that you say is insane!" But I knew better. I sat on the half-moon couch on the opposite side of the suite, hoping to get far enough away so that Stefano wouldn't be able to hear me when I made a phone call.

"Bellagio VIP Services. This is Jennifer. How can I assist you today?" My inner voice pleaded, *Switch places with me?*

"I am wondering if I could speak to a supervisor regarding a . . . special request."

"Is there something I can help you with?" Gulp.

"Possibly." I struggled with the words. "We were wondering if there was any way that the fountains outside could be turned down . . . if anything, just a notch."

Stefano plopped down beside me and urged, "Tell her who it is for."

"Actually, I am calling on behalf of Stefano Lepres. He has a very important meeting tonight in your hotel with Isabella Blackstone . . ." He poked my elbow, giving a thumbs-up. "I know they would both appreciate anything you can do to accommodate them." I imagined the concierge waving down her coworkers as if to say, *You are never going to believe this one.* Me neither, girl. Me neither.

"Who?" she inquired.

"Stefano Lepres, the photographer and director, and Isa—"

"I am not familiar with Mr. Lepres. Besides, it's impossible. I'm sorry."

Stefano pulled on my sleeve and gave me hopeful eyes. Covering the mouthpiece, I lied. "She's a huge fan of your work."

"Is there anything else I can assist you with today?" I could hear her containing a snarky giggle.

"No. Thank you very much, Jennifer. I will let him know." I hung up the phone, turned to my deluded boss. "Done."

Satisfied he had successfully addressed the issue, Stefano grabbed his wallet and room key. "I'm off to dinner! See you in an hour!" I gave him a military salute that turned into slapping my forehead after he had left the room.

I raced to Barneys, where a stylist familiar with Lepres' style—thank God!—advised me to purchase an attractive Ann Demeulemeester ensemble. Luckily, the clerk thought nothing of letting me charge it to Stefano's credit card because in no way could I have covered the $3,600 (GASP!) total. It had occurred to me that I might be asked to tag along. Without hesitation I purchased a simple black DVF dress and charged it to my parents' "emergency only" Visa, rationalizing that technically I was avoiding a fashion emergency. With twenty minutes to spare, I laid out Stefano's new outfit and jumped into the shower. Room service arrived just in time. I couldn't shove the delicious turkey sandwich (sans the stinky cheese) into my mouth fast enough. It was the first time I had eaten all day. Realizing that Stefano could return at any minute, I took the sandwich into the bathroom, cramming large bites into my mouth as I blew my hair dry. Slipping into the new dress, I admired my last-minute attempt to look presentable. Not bad!

Soon after I prepared myself for a night on the town, Stefano entered the suite. Whistling at my transformation, he picked up the spotted sport jacket and skinny trousers that I had purchased on his behalf, nodded his head in approval, and said, "Fucking sick." After he swung the outfit over his arm, he searched through his leather backpack. "Where's my . . ."

"Your toiletries are in the bathroom. Ready to go!"

"Thanks, Ugly! You look nice. Pretty dress."

I wondered if he meant pretty as in ugly or pretty as in pretty. "Thanks. See, I'm getting better. Always be prepared!" I felt proud of myself for finally doing something right.

He shot me a puzzled look. "What are you prepared for?"

Stunned, I wasn't sure how to respond. Was he messing with me again?

"Oooh, you thought you were coming out with us to-night!" He covered his mouth and chuckled. "You're funny." Walking into the bathroom, he added, "No offense but . . . you're no Edie Sedgwick," before closing the door.

I quietly snapped, "You're no Andy Warhol either."

The door swung open. "What?"

"I said, I'd better get this food out of here." The door closed.

By 2:00 a.m. I was exhausted and back in my denim shorts, curled up dozing on the couch. I had long since returned my emergency purchase, knowing full well that my parents would not understand the urgency of fashion. Like a train off its tracks, a frantic Stefano burst through the door, flipping on all the lights. Forcefully shaking me awake, he shrieked, "My wallet! I lost it downstairs!! I was walking the casino with Bella and I know I had it . . . We were rushed by a crowd and . . . it's gone! You *have* to find it!!!" I sat up, confused after being roused from a deep slumber. I attempted to get the gist of what he was saying.

"Okay . . . I will find it. Give me a minute." I picked up the phone and dialed VIP services. "Hello, this is Mr. Lepres' assistant. He lost his wallet and . . . Oh, perfect. Thank you!" Hanging up the phone, I turned to Stefano, yawning out, "They have it downstairs. You left it at the craps table. They'll release it only to you—it's a security measure."

"*No.* I can't get it. *You* have to . . ."

"But . . ."

"*No!* Lucy, listen. I have a gram of coke in my wallet. They must have seen it when they pulled out my ID. The cops are probably down there now waiting for me and I can't . . . Oh my God! Fuck!" Stefano began pacing back and forth as he sweated profusely and wrung his hands. I got up from the couch, flinging off the blanket and tossing it aside.

He turned to me. "You have to say it's yours!"

"What? Are you . . . Why?"

"Because it's your job! Because I'm a public figure and I pay you to take care of things like this!" Grabbing my hands in desperation, he promised, "I'll bail you out, I swear." Realizing that my boss was paranoid due to his substance abuse and there was little likelihood the police were waiting downstairs to arrest him, I picked up the room key and rushed out of the suite. Thirty minutes later, I returned to find Stefano standing at the window, entranced by the fountains below. Without a word, I handed him his wallet. He took it into his arms, cradling it like a baby. Stefano roared with glee, believing he had foiled the police. It was the first time that I had grasped the degree of Stefano's pathetic state and how truly egocentric and clueless he really was. Without so much as a thank-you, Stefano exited the suite.

Two hours later, Stefano returned. "Lucy, Lucy! Wake up!" I opened my eyes and stared at my crazed boss. "You have to pack my stuff . . . I have to go to New York right away. Vegas is too much. I have to leave. Now." He walked into the bathroom and splashed his face with water. "And the fountains are back on! Turn off the fucking fountains! My God, they get bigger and louder by the minute! Fucking fountains!" Once again, he exited the suite. I got up and gathered Stefano's belongings. I was so exhausted that I could hardly stand up straight. Sitting on the bed, I thought, "I'll just rest for a few . . ."

• • •

Hours later, I woke up to a room drenched in sunshine. Startled, I realized I'd slept through the night and it was early morning! A chipper Stefano was eating breakfast in the living room.

"Morning, sleepyhead! There's toast and orange juice and muffins."

"I thought you wanted to leave? Was I dreaming?" I was so exhausted at this point that I felt delusional.

"Ha . . . you're so funny." He chewed a mouthful of pancakes and said, "I'm going to New York for a few days. Catch up with some friends. The car will be here in ten minutes. Get ready."

I secluded myself in the bathroom and washed my face with hotel soap. I then used my finger to brush my teeth. Leaning against the sink, I stared in the mirror at my puffy eyes. Studying my reflection, I shook my head. "What am I doing here?" I whispered to what used to resemble my likeness. The label-less pill container peeked out from the wastebasket. I picked it up to find it had been emptied. I couldn't help but look back at my poor eyes, which looked so haggard and sad. How much longer could I take this? He seems to be getting crazier by the minute, and the constant ups and downs were throwing me. I wasn't sure at this point whether I'd ever get to work on the set. I was starting to feel like a horse following the carrot. Yet, I kept on hoofing along.

"Ugly! Let's roll!" Stefano and I took the elevator down to the lobby and exited the air-conditioned hotel. The steamy Vegas air hit us like a sauna. Stefano climbed into the back of the limo and naturally I started to climb in behind him. "Whoa! Where do you think *you're* going?" He held up his arm like a barricade.

"What?"

"I'm getting sick of you always questioning me! Don't act like I'm fucking insane!" I stepped back as Stefano slammed the door shut. Rolling the car window down only a few inches, he said, "We can't just leave Isabella here alone. Help her. Assist her. I don't need you right now." I watched in disbelief as the limo rolled away.

Confused and dejected, I went back into the hotel and headed to the private elevator. I put my key card in the slot and pressed the button, but nothing happened. Great! Now the elevator is out of order? I waited in a long line at check-in only to be informed that my key no longer worked because we were checked out. The polished woman behind the counter smiled vapidly and said, "I'm sorry. It says on the system that Mr. Lepres closed out the account this morning, and the suite you were staying in has already been reserved by someone else."

I was too exhausted to be shocked. "I'll take any room. It doesn't have to be a suite or anything special. In fact, I would appreciate the least expensive room that you have." Would I even be able to expense this to the studio?

"I understand, but unfortunately the hotel is entirely booked for the weekend."

Completely bewildered, I walked like a zombie back to the VIP elevator. Luckily, the bellhop who checked us in remembered me and smiled. Desperate and unsure what else to do, I lied. "Excuse me. I forgot my key upstairs. My boss is upstairs in the suite. I just need to get to the floor." He used his pass to grant me access to the top level. The ride seemed to take forever. My eyes welled up with tears. The extreme fatigue combined with confusion and loneliness had taken its toll. Why had Stefano deserted me here? Why did he close out his room knowing that I would be staying? Did I have enough money to get back home? If I had to borrow money from my parents, how could I possibly explain this situation to them? My choices were limited. I stood in front of the penthouse suite and paused. I could just go home right now and quit my job. Julie could probably get me a hostess job at GiGi's. Where was this gig going anyway? I didn't see it going anywhere, anytime soon. But then again, nobody really thought I'd get the job in the first place. And I'd come this far; maybe I just needed to hang tight a little longer. I timidly knocked on the door. To my surprise, Isabella herself opened the door. She looked like a teen boy's dream, dressed in a sheer white Natori kimono robe. Underneath she wore the most minute white Malia Mills bikini. Nobody else in existence could have pulled off that outfit.

"Hi, Lucy! I thought you two were gone by now!"

I swallowed the knot in my throat, taking a second to contemplate how to put into words what I myself didn't quite understand. "Stefano thought you might need my help so he left me here . . . for you." I felt like a prostitute.

Isabella furrowed her thinly manicured eyebrows and put one of her dainty hands up to her chin. "Really?"

My mind raced. Would Isabella think she was stuck with me? Was Isabella a good person or was she another crazy? Her face lit up and she flashed a giant, blinding smile. Without hesitation, she reached out and pulled me into the suite. "Slumber party! This is great! You are officially on vacation with me!" Startled, but too in awe to react, I watched in shock as the star flew in and out of the bedroom waving a credit card and room key. She slid the cards under my bra strap. "Massages! Facials! Margaritas by the pool! This is going to be great! Take my card and treat yourself to anything you want because I know you don't want to be wearing *that* for the next three days!" She pointed her perfectly polished pointer finger up and down at me.

Isabella removed the Nikon strap from around my neck and looked into the viewfinder of my camera. "What's with this?"

"Oh, it's nothing." I didn't want her to think that I was like everyone else, wanting to take her picture and honestly, I wasn't.

"It doesn't look like nothing. Is it Stefano's?" I briefly wondered if she would have it confiscated. Maybe she assumed I'd take pictures without her knowledge and sell them to tabloids.

"No, it's mine." As if Stefano would put that dinosaur anywhere near his face. "I'm a photographer too. Well, not an actual professional photographer, but hopefully one day I will be."

Isabella lit up. "That's amazing! I'll take good care of it while you are on your shopping spree!"

"Isabella, thank you so much . . . but it isn't necessary to . . ." Before I could finish, she had rushed behind me and began to push me out the door.

"It's Bella . . . and when you come back, meet me at our

pool!" As I was being physically forced out of the penthouse suite, I glanced over my shoulder and took note of the private pool off Isabella's living room. Before I knew it, I was back in the elevator. I reached into my bra and examined the black American Express Centurion card that read "Isabella Black-stone, Inc." I have always dreamed of my parents giving me their credit card to spend on whatever I fancied—but now that I was met with the opportunity from a stranger, it just didn't feel right. I didn't feel comfortable spending someone else's money, let alone my boss's friend and client. I did how-ever need a few bare essentials to get me through the week-end, and since I'd likely be assisting Isabella, technically these purchases would be business related.

Upon returning to the suite an hour later, I found Isabella under the sunroof reading a fashion magazine. Naturally, she was on the cover. I reached into the Gap shopping bag, pulled out a basic blue bikini, and headed for the guest bathroom. I exited the bathroom with a plush cream hotel towel modestly draped around my equally as pale frame. Isabella stood over the shopping bag, her arms sternly folded across her gigantic breasts. "Are you out of your mind?" I was unsure of how to react, so I just stood there as Isabella investigated the contents of the shopping bag. Had I bought too much? Regardless of my frugal attempt, had I gone too far? "*One* pair of shorts, *two* T-shirts, what may be a dress but I'm not certain . . ." Isabella pulled out the dress, scrutinizing the price tag. Squinting her eyes, she called out, "What is that word, is this French?"

I stepped forward and read the red sticker aloud. "Clear-ance?"

Isabella swatted my arm with the dress. "I'm joking, Lucy!

I gave you a black Amex—you could have bought a jet and an island off Capri with that thing! I was kinda hoping you would! This is no time to be modest!"

Isabella clicked her kitten heels to the master suite as I added, "I got a toothbrush too!" She returned wearing a white crepe Halston jumpsuit. She flung an almost identical blue one at me. "Put this on." It was a Tibi! It probably cost at least five hundred dollars. I dropped the towel and did as I was told. It was without a doubt the most expensive piece of clothing I had ever worn. Isabella swung a monogram Fendi slouchy tote bag over her shoulder and pulled out two pairs of giant Chanel sunglasses, handing one to me. Was she kicking me out? I quickly stuffed my camera back into my messenger bag. Pushing me out the door for the second time, Isabella shoved the still full Gap shopping bag into the trash can outside the elevator. When we stepped outside the hotel, everyone turned to stare. Cameras and cell phones flashed as we made our way to yet another waiting limo.

Once inside, Bella instructed the driver, "Caesar's Palace Forum Shops, please."

"Right away, Miss Blackstone."

chapter fourteen

Right Away, Miss Blackstone

I had seen television shows about the indulgent spending habits of celebrities, but the spending sprees depicted on those shows paled in comparison to the shopping whirlwind that was Isabella Blackstone. Within no more than ten steps into the decadent clothing store, Alphabet, Isabella went into a purchasing frenzy. With wild abandon, she directed the store personnel to aid me in disrobing and trying on racks of clothing from the couture collections. Each outfit looked like something I had only seen in high-fashion magazines. This was like nothing I had encountered in Seattle or even in my wildest dreams! Bella was delighted to observe while reclining on a chaise lounge enjoying strawberries and champagne. She was like the crazy, rich stage mom that I never had or wanted. Not that I wasn't enjoying it!

"Why is this store called Alphabet?" I asked the Zac Posen look-alike employee positioning a Philip Treacy fascinator on my head at just the right angle.

"Because, darling, here you will find the ABC's of fashion," Posen explained. "Alexander McQueen, Balmain, Chanel . . ."

A Rachel Zoe wannabe removed a copper-feathered Helmut Lang vest from my shoulders and replaced it with a rose faux fur Fendi bolero while reciting, "Dior, Etro, Fendi . . ." Pushing my shoulder's back, she went on, "Gucci, Hermès, Isaac . . ." My knees went weak.

Bella ran up to us, champagne in hand, chiming, "I *love it*! Now *that's* a Hollywood Photographer!"

I defended what I'd always believed. "Nobody cares what the photographer looks like! We're behind the scenes . . ."

"Really? What is Annie Liebovitz's signature style?"

I knew this! She was one of my favorites. "Easy, black button-down shirts."

Bella shot me a knowing look and directed the attention to the stylists. "Ladies?"

They chimed, "Lanvin, runway."

I gasped. "No . . ." It was as if I'd been living a lie. Okay, that's dramatic. But come on! Next they'd try to convince me that Dian Fossey only wore Givenchy while working with the gorillas.

"Look, girlfriend, you're fresh on a scene that is solely based on smoke and mirrors! You've got to step it up."

"But it's not like I'm that . . . important. It's just me," I stated. I didn't want to sound lame, but why would anyone care what I wore? I am only an assistant, lady. Minimum wage. Nobody expects me to look like . . . well, you.

"Then you'll have to pretend that you are important if you really want people in our industry to take you seriously. You'll be surprised at how differently everyone treats you once they see you like this." She pointed behind me.

Faux Zoe rolled out a floor-length mirror. I was blown away by what I saw. I had never imagined that little old me could look so, so . . . haute couture! I twisted and twirled in the yellow Marc Jacobs layered organza dress as the fuzzy bolero tickled my chin.

"Wait!" Bella squealed. "You need a little something . . ." She wriggled two of the four gold bangles off her wrist and slid them onto mine.

"Ohhh, Cartier Love bracelets!" the stylists swooned. I twisted them around with my other hand and admired each tiny screw dotted along the way. I vowed never to take them off.

"Is that it?" Bella referred to the rack outside the dressing area, now loaded down with the dozens of luxurious labels that I had tried on. Everyone stopped twirling and fussing to do an about-face.

"Yes, Miss Blackstone," the man answered.

"Great! We'll take it all!" The sales duo and I froze in disbelief. Bella took me by the wrist and began pulling me toward the exit.

I must have turned beet red. "Bella, no. I can't! . . . I mean . . . that was . . . this is . . ."

"You're welcome! Let's go . . . Shoes are next! Lesson number two: if you're going to step on people to reach to the top, you might as well do it in stilettos!"

"But I don't think I have to step on anyone to . . ."

"So much to learn in so little time . . . I'm kidding! Come on. You haven't walked until you've Choo'd!"

As she yanked me out of Alphabet I felt beyond flustered.

Of course I wanted those things, but I didn't want her to buy them for me. I have a hard time letting someone buy me lunch unless I can reciprocate with dinner. Not in this lifetime could I ever reciprocate one third of what she had just bought me.

The Jimmy Choo boutique had hundreds of shoes displayed like individual pieces of priceless art. An enthused Bella plopped down on a lounge, kicking off her own Choos while telling an employee, "I'd like to see everything new in the last month that's over four inches. Size seven and a half. And, get whatever this beautiful girl wants . . . and two glasses of champagne, please." I strolled the perimeter of the store, reveling in the wonder of the amazing footwear. Flipping a black strappy sandal over, I could have fainted at seeing the $725 price tag.

I snuck away to call the one person who I knew would just die to be here . . .

"Julie! You're not gonna believe where I am . . ." I barely let her say hello upon taking the call. "Isabella Blackstone took me shopping and bought me all these clothes—Dolce & Gabbana! Chloé! And I'm even *wearing* your fave, Marc Jacobs! And now we are at Jimmy Choo and she just told the sales guy . . . Wait, Julie—are you there?"

"Lucy, I'm at work but haven't heard from you in so long. Not since my birthday party, to be exact . . ."

"Are you not hearing me?! I'm shopping with Isab—"

"I heard you! I just didn't think that you cared so much about that stuff. And I'm good, by the way, thanks for asking."

"Well, it's not that I care about that stuff . . . or I didn't . . . But I don't know, maybe I do?"

"I really do have to get back to work—we're in the middle

of a lunch rush. Have fun, Lucy." After cutting me off, she hung up all too quickly. I guess I hadn't considered that she might still be upset about the party. I had been so busy, we hadn't spoken about it—or anything, really—in a while. I would definitely make it up to her when I returned to LA.

I sat myself next to Bella, who was surrounded by boxes labeled with both of our sizes. I was still feeling increasingly uncomfortable accepting such lavish gifts from someone I had known for less than twenty-four hours. A small crowd was gathering outside, peering into the windows to catch a glimpse of the famous star. Several held their cell phone cameras up to take pictures. "What do you think of these?" Bella stuck out her legs, admiring the melon-colored, rhinestone-studded base of the five-inch heels she had on.

"They're gorgeous!" I smiled, thinking incredulously that Isabella Blackstone was asking *me* for fashion input. Up until fifteen minutes ago, the most expensive item in my closet was the prom dress I had bought from Macy's. Even during my high school years, the populars had never once asked me what I thought of an outfit.

"They come in five colors," said a well-informed and highly motivated salesman.

"Brilliant! I'll take them in every color . . . in both our sizes!" Before I could speak up to again explain how unnecessary the gifts were, Isabella was on to the next topic. "So tell me, what do you want to do with your photography?" The salesperson slid Bella's foot out of a turquoise satin strappy heel and replaced it with a chocolate brown zipped-up ankle bootie.

"I'd love to show at a gallery one day! That's pretty much my ultimate dream."

"That's easy! Some of my best friends own the most re-nowned galleries in the world. What would you show?" I couldn't tell whether she was simply pointing out that she knew "people" or if she was suggesting that she could help me get into a gallery one day.

"I'd definitely show portraits. I love to tell stories by cap-turing the unexpected sides of people."

"Stefano is the master of celebrity portraiture! Working for him will take you anywhere you want to go!"

"You think? I'd thought that too, before. But I'm starting to wonder if that's how it works." I wasn't sure how much I could confide in Bella. I chose my words carefully so I wasn't saying anything negative about my boss.

"Here's the thing. Stefano isn't going to help you. Holly-wood doesn't work that way. You have to help yourself." She gave the salesman a nod of approval and continued. "You need to start cultivating relationships within his network—become friends with everyone. Go to every party, every screen-ing, every anything, and then when you get there, network some more! Getting to the top is all about who you know—and who you blow, but that's a lesson we'll save for later!"

"Should I be taking notes?" I joked.

"Really, Lucy! You need to cut the wallflower act and be-come a force to be reckoned with! A force in Fendi!" She fluffed up the feathers on my bolero. "You're his assistant now because you act like one. Stop being part of the background. Do whatever it takes to stand out and get noticed, then you'll definitely get ahead!" She did make sense. I was not only dressing but was acting like an assistant.

"Okay, one more stop . . . my obsession!" Bella led me,

along with a curious crowd of tourists, to a store called Shady, which featured luxury sunglasses, also displayed like tiny Rodin sculptures. Bella headed straight for the back counter where the most expensive sunglasses were displayed. "May we see this tray?"

A stylish, pin-thin woman with a too-tight bun pushed up the bridge of her cat's-eye glasses. She then removed a large flat of shades from the glass case. Twenty oversized and over-priced pairs reflected Bella's face as I peered over them. Her hands flickered mid-air as she debated. Without further delib-eration, Bella plucked out a pair and put it aside. "I'll take these." The woman tugged on a white cloth glove, picked up the Marni glasses and carefully began ringing them up. "Oh, no. I mean these . . ." Bella pushed the entire tray forward, indicating that she wanted all but the singled-out pair.

Outside the shop, several clerks pushed the rack of clothes from Alphabet and the ten pair of Choos. Bella added a black shiny shopping bag full of sunglasses to the overwhelmed cart and marched on, with me following suit as we made our way out of the shopping center. The bellman cart barely con-tained all of the bags and boxes that looked about as stable as an elephant on a roller skate. I couldn't help but take advan-tage of the scene and memorialize it on film. In addition, it couldn't hurt to let Bella see me in action. I took out and tin-kered with the settings, adjusted the aperture and captured the shot, all while walking backward alongside Bella.

Just as we reached the exit, where two doormen leaped to attention, Bella selected two new pairs of glasses from the bag. Handing me a YSL pair, Bella instructed, "Put these on."

I giggled. "The sun's not even out."

She sang, "Don't say I didn't warn you . . ."

"Huh?" As the doors swung open toward the outside world, hundreds of flashes blinded us as we hustled to the waiting car. At least twenty paparazzi ran to the car, some jumping on its hood, and just as the shop attendants shut the goods into the trunk, the driver zoomed away.

"That wasn't as bad as last time," Bella noted as we leaned back into the leather seat.

"You know, Lucy, I hire photographers all of the time! I should hire you!" For a flash, I believed that the most miraculous opportunity had just been handed to me. Was this how it really happened? Were they lying to us in art school the entire time we were prepping our portfolios and learning about agencies and so on? Of course not. She hadn't even seen my work, how could she offer me a job? "No really! I bet you are super talented. I know an artist when I see one!" I thought back to the last twenty-four hours. Bella hadn't so much as seen me scribble my name let alone exhibit any type of artistic expression.

Regardless, I played along and said, "That would be incredible! I would love to!" But I mean, come on! There was no way one of the most famous faces in the world was going to trust some kid with a camera to shoot her next *W Magazine* cover. I officially felt like a charity case knowing that Bella felt so badly for me being ditched in the desert that she took me on a shopping spree and then offered me pity work to boot. It was very sweet of her and I appreciated the sentiment, yet I still felt like a total loser.

I gazed out the back window from behind her tinted YSLs.

chapter fifteen

Souvenirs

Everything seemed to be falling right into place. Bella and I were en route to LA just hours after my parents checked into their hotel. I called them earlier to explain that my job had taken me to Las Vegas and they offered to pick me up from the airport. Since Bella had been within earshot, I couldn't get into details. I wondered if they understood that they were picking me up from a small airport used only by private planes. They never would have assumed I was with one of the most famous women in the world either. They were soon to find out about both.

I grew anxious as we began our descent. There were so many thoughts firing off in my mind. I was supposed to have today and tomorrow off as requested, to spend time with my parents. Would those days still be granted since I wasn't with Stefano? Or due to the fact that he left me to "assist" his friend,

did today still count as a work day? I hadn't heard from Stefano since he deserted me in the desert—did I still even have
a job? Sailing from air to land at what felt like light speed inside a tin can that sat eight didn't help. I gripped the armrests
and held my breath as we landed on the short strip.

"Oh shit, shit, shit!" Bella shrieked clicking away at her
BlackBerry. "My driver had a flat on the freeway. He sent another car but the 405 is a parking lot. You said that you had a
ride?" *Oh no. Oh. No.* "Do you think that you could take me
home and my driver can come get the bags?" A ride? With my
parents? This was going to be mortifying. But what was I supposed to say? I couldn't exactly say, "Thanks for the ride back
via your private jet, but no, I'm sorry, we cannot drive you
home in our rental car."

"Of course. My parents are picking me up—if you don't
mind?" I had high hopes that she would mind, being that it
was beyond lame.

"That would be great! Thanks!" She returned to texting.

The plane circled the lot and I scanned the area for my
parents. When I was little, whenever we picked up a family
member from the airport we would bedazzle a giant welcome
sign. In my mind I pictured my parents holding up glittered
billboard-sized foam boards that read "Welcome Lucy Butler!"
while releasing bouquets of balloons and tossing streamers. I
would probably shrivel up and die on the spot. I was relieved
to see them leaning against their parked rental car, sans signs,
outside the gate. I unbuckled my seat belt and made sure that
I didn't leave anything behind. I wanted to get to them first, to
give them an update on what was happening, whom I was
with, and most important, beg them not to humiliate me.

"That Moschino is to die for!" Bella reminded me that I was dressed as the newer, improved version of myself. I put my hands in the pockets and looked down to admire the A-line dress that reminded me of something Audrey Hepburn might have worn. It was white and covered with little red hearts. I felt very feminine and extra-special in it.

"I love it! Thank you again, for . . . everything!" I wished that there were another word that held more weight than *thank-you* because I would have used it. She threw her hand out as if to say, *Please, it was nothing.* She began gathering her things and I prayed that she would need a few minutes to stay on the plane to collect herself.

We taxied right up to the gate, in front of my parents. The door to the plane was falling out at a snail's pace. As soon as the stairs landed safely on the ground, I promptly put both hands on the rails and quickly climbed down. How did Isabella make this look so glamorous in heels? I felt like I was about to eat pavement. I looked up to find my mom and dad completely awestruck. My father was taking pictures. Here we go.

I booked it to the car. Correction, I booked it to the teal Ford Focus hatchback that my parents rented. My parents sandwiched me in a smothering hug that nearly lifted me off the ground. I was excited to see them too—but I didn't have much time!

"Lucy! A private plane? Is that Mr. Lepres'? How exciting! Is he here too?" my mother gushed.

"You look great, kid!" My dad held my hands and pushed me out, giving me a twirl. Their enthusiasm made me even more excited to have them here because I couldn't wait to tell them the rest!

"Stefano isn't here—it's just me and my friend, actually. But I have to tell you about her and she needs a ride home and, okay, so this might blow your mind a little bit—especially you, Mom—so you have to try and contain yourself because it's important to me that you don't . . ."

"Of course we can give your friend a ride home and we won't embarrass you, Lucy, geez . . . What, are you still afraid of being seen with your mommy and daddy?" My dad poked me repeatedly in the sides, which I have always hated, but he did it anyway because it tickled and I always laughed uncontrollably. But really, it has always driven me nuts!

"Oh, Luce! Wait until you see our hotel room—you're going to want to stay with us tonight, and if you do, that's fine! We had them bring up a rollaway bed, just in case! It's close to Rodeo and around all these amazing shops. We can get up really early and go window shopping tomorrow . . ." She whispered into my ear, "Or really go shopping tomorrow . . ." She winked. I couldn't get a word in!

"And hopefully we can get a chance to see you in action at work! Or at least stop by the studio to see where you spend all of your time," my dad added.

"And I really want to see a celebrity! Where do you think we should go?! My friend said that there is this restaurant called the Ivy where . . ."

This is where I had to jump in. "Mom! This is what I need to talk to you about! My friend, Bella, is . . ."

"Here! I'm here! Sorry to keep you waiting! It's a pleasure

to meet you." Bella looked every bit the part of a star avoiding recognition in an enormous Eugenia Kim floppy hat and dark shades that could double as ski goggles. She extended her hand to my father first. "Please, call me Bella," she said, assuming that I had told them we would be escorting Isabella Blackstone home. He introduced himself warmly as Bill. She then air kissed my mother on each cheek, "So nice to meet you!" My mother introduced herself as Renee. We stood there for an awkward moment. I thought that they were letting it marinate, fully grasping the fact that they were in the presence of Miss Isabella Blackstone. I paused for reaction.

My father asked, "Where is the luggage?"

"The driver will pick up our luggage when he's able to get down here, which shouldn't be too long. Lucy, if you can text him your address, he'll drop yours off to you tonight." She handed me her phone.

My parents opened the car doors and flipped the front seats upright. We climbed into the back like little kids. Bella adjusted her skintight black tank dress so that nothing was exposed. Her hat was crushed in the confined corners of the backseat. I was pretty embarrassed that this was how we were rolling. Not that I was born into a Bentley, but come on—this turquoise roller skate was not a good look.

"Seat belts!" my dad reminded. We managed to click ourselves in despite being smooshed together like sardines.

My mom turned to us and gushed, "Private planes and drivers! You girls sure had the red carpet star treatment this weekend! I can't wait to hear all about it!" Bella and I looked at my mother and then each other.

They had no idea who she was.

"So where are we off to, dear?" my dad asked while wiping the face of his iPhone off with his button-down shirt.

"Malibu," Bella informed.

"Oh, very nice! I downloaded a GPS app on my phone that will show us how to get there by avoiding traffic . . ." My dad held his phone two feet away from his face and began sliding his finger across the screen. "If only I can just figure out how to open the damn thing . . ."

"You and your apps! I have something way more fun. The girls will get a kick out of this!" My mother dug around in her giant purse. Why were they suddenly acting like Jerry's parents from *Seinfeld*? Bella giggled. At least she was amused. "Look!" My mom held up a folded-up map that read *STAR MAP: Your Guide to the Homes of the Rich and Famous*. She spread the map across the dashboard. I wanted to die. "This guy was selling them at the freeway entrance and I couldn't resist!! . . . Here it is! Mal i buuu . . . You have some famous neighbors, Bella! But I'm sure you know that! Mel Gibson! Jennifer Aniston! Cher!" Ironically, all I could think was how much I wanted to turn back time. Now.

"Here we go . . . found the app. What's your address, Bella?" At least my dad was keeping it cool.

"17300 Pacific Coast Highway," she stated clearly.

"A perfect day for a drive along the coast." He placed his iPhone on his knee and took off. "So, Lucy—tell us about Las Vegas! Were you there for a photo shoot?" He glanced at me in the rearview mirror.

"No, Stefano decided to go last minute after our shoot in

LA the other day, so he took me with him." I chose my words carefully because I didn't want them to know it was part of my job to trail him like a loyal Labrador.

My mom was still scouring over the star map, but she added, "That was nice of him to take you on a trip. He must really like you!"

"Mmmhmm," I hummed.

"Stefano loves her. We all do!" Bella exaggerated. "Are you doing anything special with your parents this weekend?"

"I'll show them my new apartment today and then my mom wants to explore Beverly Hills. I think they'd love the view from Runyon Canyon, so maybe do that in the morning? Tomorrow we'll probably do something fun and touristy and at night we're having dinner at GiGi's—where my best friend, Julie, will be working."

"You also live right by Diana Ross! And Tom Hanks!" At this point I had just accepted that my mother was going to do this for the entire drive. She had her head in the map and followed her finger along the Pacific Coast Highway, calling out famous names. It was like she had some desperate form of celebrity Tourette's syndrome, dropping more names than Kathy Griffin.

My dad tuned it out. "It will be great to see Julie! It's too bad that she has to work the whole weekend." I didn't want to tell them that we'd had a falling-out, so I fibbed about her having to work.

"Isabella Blackstone!" My mom shouted. "You two are practically neighbors . . . I read last week in *Us Weekly* that she—"

I sprung forward and put my hands on my mom's shoulders. "Mom . . . Stop already!" Bella grabbed onto my dad's headrest and collapsed forward, laughing uncontrollably. I stopped taking everything so seriously and joined her in hysterics.

"What? What did I say?" My mother turned to us with an innocent dolphin smile.

Bella took off her scrunched hat and removed her sunglasses, then reached her hand out to my mom's arm and enthusiastically asked, "Tell me—what did they say about Isabella Blackstone? I have to know!"

I'm willing to bet that my mom peed in her pants a little, judging by the look on her face. She laughed nervously and folded up her star map. "Well, now I'm just embarrassed . . ." She covered her reddened face with the map and chuckled away.

My father obliviously asked, "What? What is it?"

Mom turned back around and asked, "So . . . do you know Cher?"

We pulled up to a hidden community, secured by a guarded gate, which granted us access when Bella waved from the backseat. The guard was probably wondering what the hell she was doing in that car. Her multilevel Mediterranean-style house was surrounded by drizzling fountains and covered in creeping ivy. I mentally checked myself and couldn't believe that my parents and I were dropping Isabella Blackstone off at her house.

She hugged me good-bye in the backseat and told me that she'd call me. I wondered if she meant it, or if during the ride she was reminded that I was in fact just an ordinary person. Why would she call me anyway? My father let her out of the backseat and she hugged him, thanking him for the ride home.

"Bella, would you mind if I used your restroom?" my mom asked from the passenger side. *Oh lord, Mom—please just let us get out of here without further awkwardness,* I wanted to say. They entered the house and I filled my dad in on who he had just driven home. He wasn't too impressed, but then again, he wasn't into such things. A few minutes later, my mother returned and got in the car. My dad backed us out of the driveway, and again we were off. My mom turned around and held up two small waxy starfish.

"What are those?" I didn't understand what she was showing me.

"Souvenirs!" she exclaimed as she folded the decorative soaps in the star map and tucked them away in her purse.

chapter sixteen

Killer (sons of) Bees

"Oh Lucy, do you have to go?" my mother pleaded. We were at Universal Studios, in line for the Jurassic Park ride. I felt horrible having to leave them like this, but if Stefano was calling me on my second day off ever, then it must have been extremely important.

"I'm sorry you guys! It's my job . . . I have to go—the taxi I called will be here any minute. I will meet back up with you in a few hours, promise!" They had to be proud of my work ethic at the very least.

My father tried to make sense of it all. "What could be so urgent in a photo studio?"

If only they knew the questions that were swimming through my mind. Had there been an overdose? Did Stefano finally kill one of my coworkers and need help hiding the body? Did he run out of decaf? Of course, I couldn't let my parents know what an emergency in my job capacity could mean, so I dug myself deeper into the delusion that I had invented. "I'm not sure . . . Sometimes Stefano needs me to switch out camera lenses for him when it's a hectic shoot. Or maybe the production team needs me to . . . produce something. It could be anything really! I'll find out when I get there and call you right away!" I couldn't believe that I was leaving my parents at a theme park—but what were my options? This could have been an opportunity to prove myself to Stefano! What if he was swamped with edits and needed me to make the selections for *Rolling Stone*? It could happen!

When we pulled up to Stefano's house, I paid the driver and sprinted from the taxi. I took a deep breath, braced myself for whatever was to come, and opened the front door using my own key. I scanned the room for any signs of chaos but everything was in its place. I heard a woman's laughter coming from the backyard. I stepped into the serene sanctuary to find Stefano and a lady friend lounging poolside with kiddie pool–sized margaritas.

He delightfully greeted me, which was slightly unsettling. Perhaps his good mood was an effect of the first day off from shooting that he'd had in months—or the margaritas. "There you are, honey! Are you having fun with your parents?"

"I am, thank you! Your text said something about an emergency? Is everything okay?" I was confused. Everything appeared to be just fine.

The petite woman spun her oiled legs around the lounge toward me and crossed them. She wore a gold foil Norma Kamali monokini—the kind that you see in magazines and wonder, *Who actually wears these, and to where?* because they couldn't possibly be meant for actual swimming, and the tan lines would make anyone look like the underbelly of a spider. She slid her dark Sama shades atop her head, over a silk turban. I immediately recognized Vanessa Benshaw. Vanessa is an actress whose career never completely took off until she married her husband, William, a star player on the Lakers. The public became obsessed with their private life once they decided to do a short-lived reality show, and ever since the tabloids were constantly featuring how-to guides on emulating her as a woman, wife and mother—and him as a husband, sex symbol and athlete.

She put her colossal concoction on the ground and reached up to shake my hand. "Lucy! I've heard so much about you! I'm so glad that you were able to come over and help me out." While Vanessa seemed nice enough, I was irritated that Stefano just loaned me out to his friends like Tupperware. "Come, sit . . ." She scooted over. Half of me couldn't believe that I was sitting with Vanessa Benshaw, and the other half was nervous about what they might have me do. Maybe they needed more margarita mix? Easy. I could run to the store in Stefano's car and have my parents pick me up in an hour, tops. This wouldn't be so bad.

Stefano dove into the pool from the opposite end and swam up to where we sat. "V is my best friend, Lucy. We have to take special care of her today!" He dunked back under the water and began breaststroking back and forth.

Vanessa put her hand on my arm and I readjusted myself to face her. "Lucy, we're having a . . . sensitive situation at my house. I came here to discuss this situation with Steffy and we decided it's best if I avoid being in the public eye today. Now, due to this . . . situation, I have had to let go of my staff and . . ."

Her eyes began to well with tears, and she slid the dark shades back down. "I am unable to pick up my children from school and my husband is unavailable. Stef says that he would trust you with his children, and I trust him, so . . . you wouldn't mind, would you?"

Ordinarily I would be offended by being called in on my day off to chauffeur the children of someone that I don't work for, let alone know, but in this case, I was touched that Stefano said those things about me, and I wanted to help Mrs. Benshaw. "Of course, I am happy to help." Besides, picking up groceries versus a few kids and bringing them back here—not a huge difference. I could still meet my parents afterward and manage to save the day for my boss's friend.

I left immediately in Vanessa's car because it had the booster seats for her two kids. She gave me directions and said that she'd call the school to let them know I would soon be arriving. If I was nervous to drive Stefano's cars, I was horrified driving the Benshaws' custom Bentley, which had to cost more than an average home in the valley. Small curtains were drawn on the backseat windows. I opened them to avoid any blind-spot issues. The steering wheel, headrests and rims all had a scripted *B* emblem prominently emblazoned on them. Everyone stared as I drove by in the gleaming white mansion on wheels. They were probably thinking, *Who is that?* The school was only about fifteen minutes away, and it took me an additional ten to find a parking spot that didn't intimidate me. I opted for a spot farthest from the school's entrance because there was nobody parked on either side and I didn't want to risk anyone opening their mediocre Mercedes car door into Vanessa's Bentley. The school looked like a small private college. The interior looked far too refined for an elementary school. The school's crest was centered between two large stairways that led to the second floor, presumably where the classrooms were. To the side was the main office.

I approached the desk manned by an older woman. "Excuse me," I said. "I am here to pick up two students." I leaned in and lowered my voice. "I believe that Mrs. Benshaw called ahead."

"Are you the nanny?" a well-to-do woman, sitting with who I assumed was her child, said from behind me. To avoid confusion or any chance of them not letting me take the kids from school, I fibbed. Well, actually, I didn't consider it fibbing because, at that point in time—for that hour—I *was* their nanny. Sort of.

"Yes, I am."

The woman raised her brows and folded her arms across her Birkin bag without taking her eyes off me. The receptionist requested my driver's license and left to make a photocopy. The mothers behind me were all whispering to one another behind my back. I didn't know what they were saying and I didn't care. I'm sure it had something to do with Vanessa Benshaw's nanny picking the kids up early from school, or something equally as stupid. The lady returned with my license and a sticker that read *The Academy: Visitor.* "Please wear this while you are on the campus, dear, and wait right here for the children." When I sat down in the only free chair, the group of mothers stood up and left the room with their offspring. Maybe they were too good to sit with the help.

Nearly twenty minutes later, William Jr. and Willa arrived. They were six and seven and absolutely adorable. Each had on a tiny backpack with the same scripted *B* that was all over the

Bentley. I knelt down to their level. I forgot how much I loved little kids! "Hi, guys! Your mom asked me to come get you from school today. My name is Lucy and we're going to meet up with her right now, sound good?" The little ones nodded their heads and each took my hands. We headed out into the parking lot, still holding hands. I wanted to engage them, make them feel comfortable. "Do you guys like music? We can listen to whatever you want in the car! Do you have a favorite song?"

Willa perked up. "I like Ky Zavala!" she beamed. Ugh, Ky Zavala.

William Jr. sassed, "That's not a song, dummy."

"Uh oh, that's not a nice . . ." Our brief bonding time came to a halt as strangers started charging us from every direction! Startled, I froze, and both kids tightened their grips on my hands as they buried their little faces into my sides. We were all scared. Who were they? They were all yelling and pushing and shoving each other, quickly surrounding us. What the hell was happening?

"Hey, nanny! How's the job going?" yelled one of the attackers. "Yeah, tell us what are the perks like." They all started laughing and heckling. I estimate that there were ten, maybe fifteen of them, and they all had huge cameras. Paparazzi, of course. I had to get the kids out of there. I secured them each in a booster seat, entered the driver's side, and locked all the doors before turning around in my seat.

"Are you okay?" I asked them while starting the engine. They looked like they were about to cry. I crawled into the back and closed the curtains on their windows, which made much more sense now. "It's okay, we're going to go see your mommy right away." A huge thud was heard from the trunk.

I peeked from the curtain and one of the paparazzi had shoved another into the car. Willa started crying for her momma. I crawled back into the front seat. Cameramen had their lenses nearly up against the windows, taking shots of the kids, of me. I knew that they were only cameras and not a true danger, but for some reason it felt like they were shooting us with weapons. These people, mostly men, were acting unruly and tyrannical—not caring at all that they were terrifying us. I put the car into reverse and slowly backed out of the spot. They continued to swarm us as I rolled out of the lot. I moved with trepidation because I was afraid of hitting somebody— not because I cared about those vermin, but because of the damage one might do to the car. What a relief to get on the open road! My phone began to ring and it was my parents. I would return their call once back at Stefano's. Then the car phone began to ring and the screen read "VB MOBILE" across the dash. "Um, how do I . . . answer this thing? Umm . . ." I fumbled while trying to drive and figure out the phone.

William piped, "The gween! Push the gween!"

"The what? I don't understand, buddy . . ." The car phone stopped ringing. My phone began ringing again and, without checking who it was, assuming it was Vanessa, I answered. "Hello?" I tried to sound calm.

"Lucy, it's Mom. Where are you?" Shit.

"Mom, I am still handling this work thing. I have to call you back, things are a little . . . crazy." In my rearview mirror, I saw two black SUVs peel out from a red light and another turn a corner—I knew it was the paparazzi from the parking lot and they were headed for us. I stepped on the gas.

My mother continued, "Are we still on for GiGi's? Because

your father is starving, so we'd like to go for a late lunch rather than an early dinner . . ." One of the cars pulled up along my side and a photographer leaned out of the passenger window, snapping shots of me. What did he want with *me*? I am nobody! I sped up once more and cut off their car. "Sure, Mom, just go now! I'll meet you there. Julie's working, she'll take care of you! I gotta go!" I threw the phone into the console and put both hands on the wheel.

The car started ringing again: VB MOBILE . . . "The *gween* one, *Woosy*!" William screamed.

Willa translated, "The green one, Lucy!" Oh!

I pressed the flashing green light on the touchscreen. "Vanessa?" I took a deep breath and tried to compose myself. I didn't want to freak her out too. The second SUV was on the other side of us now, snapping away—while the other two circled us. I slowed down and figured it wasn't worth getting into an accident. Heaven forbid! Sure it was scary and invasive and unnerving, but they were only cameras, not guns. The kids didn't have the same thought process. They screamed and cried for their mom. I'm not going to lie, I kind of wanted mine too.

"What's wrong? What's happening?" I could hear the worry in her voice.

"There were paparazzi at the school and they're following us in the car right now but we're on our way . . ."

I heard her repeat what I said to Stefano and I assume he took the phone from her because we were then talking. "Don't let them follow you here! Can you lose them—safely?"

"I . . . I don't think that I can." He didn't live in a gated community and at this point they were orbiting us like the sun.

There had to be somewhere we could go. Somewhere with a back door and security and other adults to help me protect these kids . . . My cell phone began ringing and I quickly glanced at it: Julie. "Stefano, I'm taking them to GiGi's."

"G-Spot, Lucy? I hardly think that's appropriate . . ." He thought I was nuts.

"My best friend works there, she can have security meet us in the back, escort us in . . . It's the only place I know!" I defended.

I heard him repeat my words to Vanessa, who I assume took the phone from him because she confirmed with me, "That's perfect. My husband and I will be there, but please don't tell anyone we are coming!" *Who would I tell?* I asked myself.

I called Julie back and she answered by saying, "Did you really ditch your parents with the dinosaurs?" Without time for explanation, I cut right to the chase. "Julie—I need you to help me and I can't explain everything right now . . ."

She sighed. "I know—your parents are almost here, get them a table and entertain them while you dodge flying objects thrown by your deluded boss . . ."

I was too focused on not killing everyone on 101 Freeway, including myself, to let her remark get to me. "No, actually—another favor. I need you to have security meet me at the back door in fifteen minutes, with someone from valet waiting in the back."

"Excuse me, has hanging with the Hiltons gone to your head? I don't think so, Lucy."

"It's not for me! Just trust me, please," I pleaded. "I'm in a white Bentley. Fifteen minutes!"

"Okay, okay—I got it . . ." I don't know who hung up on who, but I tossed my phone to the side and reverted my attention to the kids—and the road, and the killer-bee-like vehicles racing along within inches of our own.

I'd never felt so relieved to see that fucking restaurant. Julie was in the back and she pointed us out to the valet, who had thoughtfully shut the gate to the parking lot. They had opened it just for us and closed it off to the others. As this happened, cameramen jumped out of their cars to get one last shot. You would have thought Mariah Carey was with us. Naked.

As promised, there was a security guard waiting. I pulled up to the back door and handed the keys to the valet. Before I could address anyone else, I climbed into the backseat between the kids and faced them. I rubbed their little legs. "We're going to get something to eat and your mom and dad are going to meet us here okay?" They unbuckled their own harnessed seats.

Willa pouted. "No more papomoddees?"

I gently touched her reddened cheek. "No more paparazzi. They went away."

Julie held the door for us, pouncing on me the second we got inside. "Lucy, whose car is that and—whose kids are these? Your parents are here and they seem kinda pissed." I kept walking toward the dining room, not responding because my mind was still in overdrive. "Lucy!" She grabbed my shoulder.

"What?" I turned around. She gave me "the look."

"They're Vanessa and William Benshaw's kids. I had to pick them up from school and the paparazzi were chasing us off the road, so I had to come here. Vanessa is coming to get them soon." She gasped and looked down at the kids. "Thank you for helping me—I didn't know what else to do!"

"Is she coming with her husband?" Julie inquired.

"I don't know—I think so. Maybe." What did it matter, I wondered. When I saw my parents sitting there, I scrambled mentally, knowing that I hadn't thought this through completely. I'd have to wing it. The looks on their faces said it all. They love kids—but didn't expect them or understand why I had brought two to lunch. "Hey, um, Mom, Dad . . . These are my friends, William and Willa!" I told the kids, "This is my mommy and daddy." I assisted them in sliding into the vacant side of the booth and I sat down on the outside. Julie stood at the head of the table, hands on her hips, waiting to see how I would pull this one off.

My parents said hello to the children. In a falsely cheery voice, my mother said, "They're adorable. Who are they?"

I could do this. "Stefano's friend's kids . . ."

They leaned in, waiting for me to give them more information. I grabbed my mother's water and began chugging it instead.

"Is that what you were doing all afternoon? Babysitting?" my dad asked.

I shook my head no while continuing to drink the water. I felt safe with my face planted in the glass. It seemed like a reasonable excuse not to speak.

"Is her husband coming with her?" Julie asked again. I shrugged my shoulders, keeping my face in the nearly empty glass. What was with Julie? She isn't even into sports. Why wouldn't she let off about Mr. Benshaw?

Julie leaned in so the other patrons couldn't hear and

spelled out certain words so the kids couldn't understand. "Everyone is talking about how she caught him having an a-f-f-a-i-r with the n-a-n-n-y . . ." I spit out the last sip of water that was in my mouth. The kids thought it was hilarious.

"You didn't know? Don't you watch the news?"

"Not *E! News!*" Why would I?

"Maybe you should, since it's their world you're living in." She had a point.

I looked over at my parents. My dad tuned out, as he did with most girl talk. My mom, on the other hand, wanted in on the gossip. "Who are you talking about?"

Suddenly the rush of paparazzi made perfect sense. "Oh my God. Julie, I told a mom at their school that I was the nanny . . . *The nanny.* Oh my God. That's why . . . they . . . Oh no."

My dad checked back in. "I'm sorry. You're whose nanny—?"

My mother cut him off. "You're having an a-f-f-a-i-r? With their f-a-t-h-e-r?"

"No! Dad, I'm not a nanny. Mom, I'm not having . . . one of those. Their mother is friends with my boss and she couldn't pick them up from school, so I did. And I brought them here because it got . . . . complicated. So their parents are picking them up any minute. Okay?"

"Why you? You're his photo assistant—I don't understand how that's your responsibility?" Dad wasn't buying it.

"So they are *both* coming?" Julie was fascinated and wouldn't let up.

"*Who?*" Both parents burst out. They were fed up with this game.

The kids jumped up in their seats and hopped up and down with glee. "Mommy! Daddy! Mommy! Daddy!" they sang out. I stood up so they could get out and Vanessa, now wrapped in a vintage trench and still wearing the silk turban and shades, met me with a huge hug. William picked up both kids and kissed their bellies, which made them giggle and squirm.

Vanessa turned to my parents and introduced herself and her husband before unknowingly, completely selling me out. "Your daughter saved us today and we are so grateful. You should be very proud of her. Lucy, if Stefano ever loses you, you come find me because you are above and beyond the most wonderful personal assistant I've ever met!" Vanessa opened up her Prada hobo and stuffed a wad of cash in my hand. "Thank you, thank you, thank you! Stefano is so lucky to have you!" She kissed my cheek and said good-bye before leaving with her family.

I sat down and faced my stunned parents. Julie swiped the wad of cash and counted it out on the table.

My mother sternly said, "Personal assistant? You have so much explaining to do."

"Six . . . hundred . . . dollars? Six hundred dollars!" Julie squealed.

My father gulped down large sips of the scotch that he would ordinarily nurse.

"So I guess . . . dinner's on me?" I tried to be cute but my charm didn't faze them.

"Yeah, don't forget to tip your waitress," Julie said before walking away.

chapter seventeen

Oh My Gaultier!

After an exhilarating mini Vegas vaycay with Bella, followed by an exasperating weekend with my parents, culminating in being hunted down in a freeway car chase, I was very much looking forward to resuming work at the studio. I walked with a renewed spring in my step. I, Lucy Butler, felt a sense of confidence that I had never experienced before. I wasn't sure if it was the new wardrobe or the experiences I'd had, but I felt like a new girl. I mentally recited Bella's words of advice from our return flight. I had to stop being a part of the background and demand recognition. In addition to my hard work, I would dress and act the part of someone worthy of a real job in the studio. I had to act like I was part of the artsy family that I saw in *American Photo*. My own reflection in front of the studio's blacked-out window stopped me in my tracks. The frazzled art student geek had definitely died, and this new and improved version had been born. My curly hair was pinned up into a messy yet chic chignon that emphasized the asymmetric neckline on my Roland Mouret black sheath dress. "It's a cardinal sin to throw coffee on couture," Bella jokingly assured me when she insisted on buying me several "power dresses" for work. I smoothed out the structured fabric tugging at my hips and pointed my toe to admire the new Tory Burch ballet flats as well. I beamed and bounced into the studio.

"Oh my Gaultier! Is that a Vuitton? Good lord, child, let me touch." Roman held his arms out as if for an infant, slid the signature tote over his arm and sashayed to a mirror. The classic purse contrasted sharply with Roman's matched red and baby blue checkered shorts and cropped jacket. Striking several poses, he examined himself from behind while making kissy faces.

Liz spun me around. "You look beautiful, darl! How was your time off? By the looks of it, I suspect things went well!"

"It was fantastic! How was your weekend?" I couldn't help but gloat just a little bit. I was emitting joy.

"Girl, you are glowing! Are you . . . ya know . . . baking a pain au lait in that oven?" Liz squinted her eyes and leaned into me. An intoxicating mix of Elizabeth Taylor White Diamonds and vodka overwhelmed my senses.

"A who?" I leaned back, holding my breath.

"Roman! Look at this!" Liz cupped my face in her hands and spun me around.

Roman folded his arms, popping out a hip. "Tell me you didn't sign up for nine months of sobriety!" The two circled around me like juvenile hawks, poking at my belly, not allowing me to get a word in. Stefano stormed by.

"She's not knocked up, you dimwits . . . She was in Vegas with Bella Blackstone." I wanted to add that I had been with my parents, too—but that would have sounded less cool.

Roman and Liz stopped dancing around me and stepped back. "Oh child, then you *are* most likely preggers by osmosis." Roman held his hands up and made an *ick* face as I gave him the evil eye.

Liz added, "It's true, babe. That woman has had more 'seamen' than the SS *Saratoga*."

I put my hands on my hips and defended Bella. "I'll have you both know there wasn't a guy in sight the entire weekend, and not only is Isabella the nicest person I've met since—"

Liz put her arm around Roman and mock whispered, "I liked her better when she was pregnant."

Heading back toward the offices, Roman added, "No men? Sounds like a horrible weekend to me!" I dismissed my covetous coworkers and set off in search of Stefano.

Today was an exciting day on the set. Stefano had been hired to shoot the cover for the anniversary issue of *Vanity Fair*. The issue was a celebration of "Young Hollywood" and would feature interviews with several intriguing and influential stars under thirty.

First to arrive was Paige Sheedy, an eighteen-year-old who had already scored her first Oscar. Her glossy dark hair and cocoa eyes enhanced her feline appearance. Paige was low-key. She did not make a scene or command attention. Instead, she quietly followed Liz and her assistants to the largest makeup room. Brett Berkeley's camp arrived next, and he was escorted to the room adjacent to Paige's. At twenty-two, Brett was the most pursued male model in the world. Brett had multimillion-dollar contracts with Burberry and Tommy Hilfiger, with H&M showcasing his new namesake clothing line. A rising country singer, Brooke Sands made an entrance with a ten-person entourage that included her mother. Lisa was only twenty years older than her daughter and, with the assistance of multiple plastic surgeries, looked anything but maternal. They were known as "The Sands Sisters" and often were photographed on the party scene, sharing good times and bad men. Brooke's breakout album had gone triple platinum and had transformed her from a self-described "country bumpkin" to a bona fide diva overnight. The shoot would have been incomplete without a rock-and-roll lothario, and they had snagged the crème de la crème—Jax Phoenix. For the past year, he and his British rock band, Phoenix Rising, had dominated the airwaves and Billboard charts. His shaggy dark hair, chiseled features and liquid eyes mesmerized females of every age.

I rushed about the studio, trying to make myself useful while remaining unobtrusive, hoping to avoid Stefano, who was agitated and anxious about the shoot and most definitely would take it out on whoever was in his path. I replaced dirty towels, picked up trash from the floor and handed out ashtrays. After tossing a pile of dirty towels into the laundry room, I checked my dress for smudges and lint as I walked through the narrow hallway. While concentrating on the status of my clothes and not watching where I was going, I slammed right into a shirtless Jax Phoenix. "I . . . I am so sorry . . . I'm really . . . just very . . ." Embarrassed and overcome, I got locked into his bedroom eyes.

"Sorry! I think I'm lost," he joked in a British accent through his boyish smile.

"Yeah, me too." I fell back against the wall, which seemed to knock a little sense back into me. "Wait. You're lost? Where are you lost . . . to?" I could hear the gibberish that was spewing from my mouth and I wanted to die.

Jax opened his arms, and in one hand he held up a hanger with a royal blue D&G dress shirt, and in the other he held a matching satin tie. "I just need to wash up before I change into this. Is that the washroom?" His immaculate physique was distracting and turned me into a babbling idiot. Nodding yes, I watched him walk into a room and immediately walk out. "Should I put myself on the permanent press or the delicate spin cycle?" I had sent him to the laundry room! Idiot!

"Oh! No! The restroom is the door straight across," I corrected, pointing to another door.

As he walked toward the restroom, he paused to face me and held out his hand, simply stating the obvious, "Jax."

I put my hand in his. "Lucy."

He lifted my hand to his lips and kissed it gently. "Thanks, Lucy." My entire body went numb and I had to consciously keep my jaw from staying ajar. Jax turned to continue his quest to get dressed.

From the slightly open door closest to me, Roman's hand reached out and forced me sideways into the dressing room. Liz and Roman had been watching the scene unfold and we all quietly gushed, "Ohhhh my God!" Like a symphonic trio we engaged in a contained chorus of *oohs* and *aahs* before collecting ourselves and proceeding to the set to continue our duties on the shoot.

An incredible carousel had been delivered the week before. The art directors had painted the entire thing a glossy black. Lit exquisitely from behind, the carousel was dazzling. Each of the stars was dressed and specifically placed to complement the dramatic scene. Paige was posed front and center in a dazzling purple Elie Saab halter gown, resting her head against the lead horse. She evoked a classic Elizabeth Taylor *Black Beauty* aura. Brett was shirtless, dressed only in Rag & Bone jeans, seated backward on the same horse and tipping an orange Stetson. Brooke stood on top of the horse behind them and to the left, draping down the pole, sizzling in a sequined yellow Armani tube dress. And finally Jax, in his dress shirt and tie, leaned against a palomino, his chin on his forearms, gazing seductively into the camera and simply oozing sex appeal.

After nearly a thousand flashes, Stefano stood and yelled, "Stick a fork in it, y'all! We are done!" The stars climbed off the set and huddled around Stefano. Brooke's ever-present mother, Lisa, joined the group. "We need to celebrate. Come on, everybody!" Throwing her arms around Stefano and pressing her breasts into his arm, she batted her eyes. "What do you say, Steffie?" Liz shot me a raised eyebrow and a look that read, *What the hell?* Was Lisa Sands hitting on Stefano? What was wrong with her? Was her gaydar out of batteries?

Stefano appeared oddly flattered. "That's a great idea! Roman, get us a table somewhere fabulous. Lushy, we need a limo—maybe two."

"We have a limo!" Brooke shouted as she headed out of the room with her entourage.

"Alright then!" Stefano stood up, raising his arms to stretch as he headed into the office. "So, what do we have tomorrow, guys?"

Roman's assistant handed Stefano a printed e-mail. "The shoot has been scrapped, something about a direction change for the album. We'll know more tomorrow."

I removed the Vuitton from under Roman's desk—nice try buddy—and placed it in the crook of my forearm. "Since you're going out, I guess I'll just see you in the morning. Bright and early, right?"

.   "Actually, we could use an extra hand in the production office tonight, if you're interested in learning the ropes?" Roman offered. I'd been waiting for those exact words for so long!

"Lucy! Absolutely not! You have to go with them. Jax Phoenix is hot for you!" Liz insisted. She clutched her throat. "Oh my God . . . I'm living vicariously through . . . her?" Poor Liz was far too sober to accept this devastating epiphany. I looked up at Stefano and shrugged. The studio wasn't going anywhere—but the lure of a glamorous outing with the celebrities seemed few and far between. Shit . . . I wanted to prove myself in the studio and earn my keep, but I also wanted to establish that I was no longer a stupid wallflower . . . And, obviously, Jax-freaking-Phoenix! Need I say more?

Never one to mince words or miss an opportunity to belittle, Stefano looked me up and down with distaste and replied, "I'd say come along but you are hardly dressed for the nightlife." I smiled. This was another encounter I had hoped for. I dropped the bag and pulled out a pair of neon pink patent Brian Atwood pumps. I tucked away the flats and stepped into the heels. Roman approved. "You go girl!" I shook my hair out of the chignon, fluffed it out Bardot-esque and stepped forward. I couldn't help but think Bella would be so proud! Wallflower no more!

"Jesus Christ. Have we met?" Stefano stammered. I put my arm through Stefano's and escorted him to the waiting limo.

"Always be prepared, right?" I confirmed. Most people have out-of-body experiences when they are about to possibly die. This was mine. I saw myself walking in an incredible dress and towering stilettos, with my va-va-voom hair. I knew that I was moving my body as if on the prowl, like I had seen girls do on a runway—on TV, of course. It was like a dream. I made my way into the white lights—the limo's headlights, that is. A bewildered Stefano looked behind him at his equally amazed crew as we joined the others. The geek in me wanted to completely freak out and break into the running man, however I remained cool, collected.

The limo raced through the city in search of a location worthy of the group's patronage, finally pulling up in front of a setting all too familiar to me. As we entered the G-Spot, my mind was flooded with not-so-distant memories of joining the staff for free family meals in the kitchen and getting grilled by my own family in the dining room. Why couldn't I get away from this place? Was Julie working? Would she even recognize me in this getup? I was not sure how to be both versions of myself in the event that she did.

Jax seemed to sense my awkwardness, and he took my arm to make sure I didn't get left behind with the salivating paparazzi. While once I had been too timid to approach my idol in this very place, now I was arriving as his guest and on the arm of the hottest rock star in the world. The seasoned young celebrities were unfazed by the throngs of photographers, even lingering awhile so that their images could be frozen as they saw fit to grace the pages of the tabloids. A hostess that I did not know led us toward a large round table in the back. I took note of the stares of other patrons. Among the gawkers was Julie, completely awestruck in her all-black servers uniform. I released my arm from Jax's and made a beeline to her.

"Oh, my God. You're working! I didn't even know we were coming here until we pulled up! We just wrapped a shoot so we came out to celebrate and . . ." Julie had not taken her eyes off the party who proceeded to take their seats. She could hardly contain herself and exploded with shock.

"You were holding hands with *Jax Phoenix! The* Jax Phoenix! He's my screensaver! Is that Paige Sheedy? What are you doing with them?" She grabbed my forearms, hoping to engage in a gabfest. I looked back at the table where Stefano was motioning, demanding my return.

I slipped my arms from her grasp and held her anxious hands. She was smiling and staring at me intently, waiting for me to fill her in as she always had done with me. She squeezed my hands and pushed, "Well?" Where to start? There was just so much to tell. Again, I glanced back at the table where Stefano was still glaring at me. Jax had kept the seat next to him open and had his arm draped over the top of the chair. I visualized myself sitting there, his arm being around me. I released one of my hands from Julie's and nervously ran it through my hair. The pressure from both sides was off the charts and I didn't know what to do! Although I just saw her yesterday, our time was limited and I wanted more than anything to catch up with Julie one on one to make sure that our friendship was still intact. But I also really wanted to be at that table to continue living out my fantasy evening. When would another night like this ever happen to me again? Julie had been my best friend for years and she wasn't going anywhere . . .

"I, umm . . ." I took a few steps backward toward the table, letting my other hand go from hers. "I want to tell you, but I can't right now. But I heard someone mention going to Hidden after dinner! You and Sebastian should meet us there! I'll call you on our way, I'll take care of you—I promise!" Julie looked on as I quickly made my way across the room and took the last open seat, apologizing for my tardiness.

I sat down and looked back at Julie, who was visibly flustered. I'm sure she too couldn't help but be thrown by the turning of the tables. In what world was I being summoned by the cool crowd while gorgeous Julie paid her dues? I hoped it wasn't too big of a blow to her ego. Although, mine soared excitedly for the first time. So this was how it felt to be "cool."

Tapas-style plates were passed over conversations about first on-screen kisses, and rumors of on-set behaviors swirled. I tried to appear engaged and not as if the words "Oh my God, Oh my God, Oh my God" were consuming all of my thoughts. When we did make our way to the exit like a school of fish, I was able to catch Julie's eye and gestured to her as if we were talking on the phone while mouthing the words, "I'll call you."

Upon arrival at Hidden, I had put together that Brooke and Paige were both under twenty-one and, had they not been rich and famous, they certainly would have been carded and denied entrance. Once again, a sea of photographers was drawn to the limousine like moths to a flame. The group was imme-diately hustled past the red velvet ropes and into the tiny venue. The bass from the music was so intense I could feel my blood vibrating to the sounds. Gesturing to a side door, Jax motioned if I cared for a smoke. Now, I do not smoke and I despise the smell of cigarettes. However, the notion of some time alone with Jax seemed worth the health risk. Jax led me through the door, through the kitchen and out the back door. He seemed to know his way around. The night was balmy and it felt good to get away from the dark intensity that per-meated the club. Jax lit two cigarettes, handing me one, and smiled wickedly. "What?" I asked.

He shook his head. "I don't know," he said, leaning his hand on the wall just above my shoulder. I squeezed Bella's Cartier bracelets behind my back, hoping they'd magically in-still some confidence or luck or miracle or whatever magic they might possess. I guess it worked, because I don't know what came over me as I cocked my head and arched toward him in a teasing manner, out of nowhere finding confidence I never knew that I had.

"Oh really?" I purred.

"Really." He leaned in closer. He exhaled a stream of smoke and I tried not to gag.

Our solitude was interrupted as the door was flung open and a dapper man stepped out. "Hey, kids, you'd better get back to class before I start handing out detention slips." Jax looked delighted as he faux-punched the man in the stomach. He responded by picking up Jax and then putting him down. Jax introduced us.

"Lucy, meet Quinn. He owns all the best bars in LA, including Hidden."

"Establishment, my friends. Bars are for savages. Lovely to meet you, Lucy," Quinn said as he gallantly held out his hand. Quinn's appearance was the epitome of Hollywood. He had slicked-back hair, wore a shiny suit and topped it off with Ray-Ban sunglasses even though it was nearly pitch black inside. I was transfixed on the cocktail straw he gnawed on as he passed it from side to side with his tongue.

"Likewise." I accepted Quinn's hand as I air-kissed both his cheeks. Repeat: I air-kissed both his cheeks! Why the hell did I do that? I have never air-kissed in my life! Did he think I was European? Did I think I was European?

"Ready to get completely knackered, Miss Lucy?" Quinn asked in a mischievous tone. Jax offered his elbow as we followed Quinn back into the club, er, establishment. I ditched my cigarette outside while Jax, above the no-smoking-inside law, kept on smoking. Quinn led the way up a stairway to a private room with a balcony that overlooked the dance floor. Settled in already were Stefano, Lisa, Brooke, Paige and Brett. They had been joined by Presley Dalton and her friends. In the darkness, I could make out a private bar and plush leather couches surrounding a large mirrored table. Quinn turned to lock the door. He pulled a large manila envelope from his suit jacket. "Who's ready to fucking party?" Presley threw her arms up in the air and let out a wild "Woohooo!" With that, Quinn ripped open the envelope and dumped copious amounts of cocaine onto the table. I gasped out loud, and if it weren't for the deafening music below, everyone definitely would have heard it. Reaching behind the bar, he tossed a handful of straws into the air. Everyone cheered as they were showered in straws. Those seated around the table scooted in closer to it.

Presley was yelling, "Lindsey! Lindsey!" I glanced up and realized that Presley Dalton was calling out to me.

"Friend of yours?" Jax teased. I gave him a playful shove and crouched down beside Presley.

"Hey Presley! It's *Lucy*, remember?" I shouted.

"Of course I remember! How can I forget the girl that saved my shoot? Hope you didn't bring any cops with you tonight! Ha! Here, sit with us!" She scooted to the side, making some room for me. "These are my friends, Deb and Amalia. Girls, this is Lucy! She's a way important person in photography." The girls nodded with enthusiasm as they sipped their cocktails. Presley continued, "Deb's dad like owns Mega Records and Amalia is a huge pop star in Armenia that Deb's dad just signed. How hot is that? Here, let's do a line together!" Presley snorted a line off the table and handed the dollar bill to me. All three girls were looking at me with their enormous approving pupils; the debate of should I or shouldn't I wasn't really an issue. I leaned in for the kill.

"*No!*" Stefano swiped the bill from my hand. "Don't you know what kind of diseases are carried on dollar bills? That's disgusting, Presley. Think about who might have touched that dollar!"

"You're so right! Gross people rarely touch hundreds, and I think I have one . . . Oh yes, here you go!" She rolled up the hundred-dollar bill found in her clutch and handed it to me. I snorted the line. Followed by another and another. Close to two in the morning, the group decided the current hot spot was getting cold.

While waiting for the car, Jax opened his arms and warmed me with his hands. As I nuzzled my head on his chest, I looked at the line of hopefuls waiting to get into the club. I remembered my not-so-distant days of waiting in line, hoping that I was "cool enough" to make it past the velvet rope. I looked over those in line, one after the other, in their desperate-for-attention slinky dresses and bedazzled shirts, wondering who would actually make the cut. Quinn and an equally as slick promoter stepped in and out, judging and ve-toing people as if they were Heidi Klum and Michael Kors on the season finale of *Project Go-away*. *Auf Wiedersehen*, losers! And then, I saw them. Sebastian and Julie stood staring at me with their mouths wide open. With horror, it dawned on me that I had failed to make my promised call. I hadn't even checked my phone, which I just knew had dozens of their missed calls and unanswered texts! As they stared at me with anger and hostility, I didn't even have enough time to ac-knowledge them. The limo pulled up and Jax pulled me in. I felt helpless and completely out of control. I fell back into the car just as it quickly sped away.

chapter eighteen

All in a Day's Work

The next morning, I woke up in bed. But it wasn't my bed. I shut my blurry eyes and tried to recollect what had happened the previous night. I remembered arriving at Presley's house, declining the Ecstasy Lisa had offered, and watching an impromptu inebriated performance by Amalia. Maybe these memories need not be recollected, I joked to myself. I slowly stretched as I unfolded a heavy comforter away from my body, looking up to find a massive portrait of Presley seducing me from above the bed. Location verified. I had fallen asleep wearing my dress. My pink heels were next to the bed on an end table. Propped against them, was a note: *"A diamond amongst the stars. JP"* I pressed the note to my heart before putting it in my bag. Was I really in the midst of a reciprocated crush with Jax-freaking-Phoenix? Why yes, I was!

I freshened up in the bathroom before heading downstairs. The entire house was decked out in glamour shots of Presley and mirrors—lots of mirrors. Her style was flashy and feminine, and very over the top. In the kitchen, I discovered Presley having her hair and makeup done. Through the bay windows, a photo crew was setting up by the pool.

"Hey doll! How wasted were we last night?" Presley inquired, expertly not moving her lips as the makeup artist applied rouge lipstick with a tiny brush.

"What happened? I don't even remember going to bed." A housekeeper handed me a mug of coffee. "Thank you."

Presley explained, "Jax put you and me to bed before he left. He tucked us in and everything. How cute is he? I can't believe we've never hooked up!"

I mentally sighed in relief. "Where is everyone?"

"Well . . . I know Phoenix Rising starts their European tour tomorrow, so Prince Charming is probably halfway over the Pacific by now."

"Atlantic," I corrected before taking a second nip of coffee.

"No, I think they're with Jive. But anyways, the girls left to go shopping and my assistant drove Stefano home about an hour ago . . . Do you need a ride?"

"Actually, I think that I'm going to walk." Stefano did only live just down the road and I felt weird being an assistant, having another assistant assist . . . me.

"Babe, nobody walks in LA!" Presley teased.

"I know, but I have a few phone calls to make and the fresh air is just what this hangover needs." I put the warm mug to the side of my head.

Presley took the phone from my hand and entered her number, saving it as "P.D." "Call me, bitch!"

We air-kissed as I exited Presleyland and made my way to the gates surrounding her estate.

I called Julie immediately. No answer. I called Sebastian. No answer. I called Julie again. Straight to voice mail. I knew I had really messed up.

After a few minutes my cell phone started singing the song "Girls Just Want To Have Fun"—Julie's ringtone! I opened my phone. "Hi!"

"I don't even know why I'm calling you back."

"You have every right to be mad at me. What I did, forgetting to call, is inexcusable. But in my defense I was still technically working . . ." I knew it was a stretch, and even as I said it, I regretted it.

"What does that have to do with treating your friends like shit? Let's not forget that you missed my birthday party for the first time . . . ever. Do you have any idea how many times I've tried to connect with you in the last three weeks?"

"No. I . . ."

"I've called you six, maybe seven times, and you haven't so much as texted me back to let me know you still exist—or that I still exist to you."

"But you . . ."

"I suspect you're too busy with your fancy new friends to bother with your old ones. We're not cool enough for you anymore, is that it?"

"No! That's not it at all . . ." Okay, so I knew that those people weren't my friends. I met most of them only twenty-four hours ago. It's just that I didn't understand why she couldn't let me have these experiences and be happy for me. "Look, I am allowed to have other friends . . . You don't have to be jealous."

After a long silence, Julie's voice grew angry. "Jealous? Take a good look around and ask yourself what is real. People out here have a shelf life shorter than milk and you're no different! When they get tired of you, you'll be dead to them. Then what will you have?"

I didn't have an answer. I regretted the jealous remark as soon as I said it and was disappointed in myself for being such an outright bitch. All that I could say was, "I didn't mean that. I'm really sorry."

"Your apology will be accepted when you get off your high horse and meet me halfway."

"Fair enough. I will fix this, Julie. Promise."

"Don't forget what you came here to do: photography. The rest is all hype." With those words I winced, noticing that I didn't have my camera on me. I stopped walking and felt around my neck even though I knew it wouldn't be there. Where had I left it? How could I leave it wherever I had? Oh, that's right, it's at the studio in my messenger bag. Phew! "Have fun at work, Lucy. Sebastian is waiting for me in the car and we're heading to the beach."

Fun at work? How badly I wished that I too was in that car. "Thanks. Tell Sebastian that I'm sorry."

By the time that we hung up I was at Stefano's front door. I wanted to cry and felt very much on the verge of a breakdown. It wasn't like me to let down my friends. Things needed to change. I went inside and straight to the kitchen. I poured myself a glass of water and leaned my back against the sink. I just needed a minute to myself.

"That fucking guava tree spits out sap like a goddamn viper, I swear . . ." Roman walked in through the back door and tossed a paper bag full of guavas on the counter. He dismissed the fact that I was wearing yesterday's clothes, likely because that was par for the course when working for Lepres. Except when it came to Roman. I had yet to see him wear the same thing twice. "What's wrong with you? You look like you're about to . . ."

Before he could finish his sentence I started wailing. I don't know if it was the guilt of what I had done to Sebastian and Julie, the disappointment I caused my parents, the lack of sleep or the overwhelming sensation of everything happening so quickly and at once. Whatever it was, it all came out right then and there.

Roman dumped out the guavas from the paper bag, pressing the bag to my mouth as he pushed me against the kitchen counter. "Just breathe!" he told me with authority.

"But I don't need . . ." I wanted to tell him the bag really wasn't necessary.

"Shhh . . ." He looked behind him over each shoulder to ensure the coast was clear. "Look, he's an asshole, I know. I've been there." The bag inflated and deflated with every breath. I stopped crying because I was in shock. Roman had never expressed any animosity toward Stefano. He whispered emphatically, "You are under great pressure and I feel for you. But, you'd better get it together, sister"—he put his forefinger and thumb an inch apart—"'cause you are this close to being promoted into the studio."

My eyes widened and I made some happy sound through the bag. Roman shook his head and said, "You heard me . . ." Oh my God! It was all happening! Yes!

Stefano bounded into the room and spotted me breaking down into the bag. "That's an interesting look . . ." Holding up his house phone, he announced, "Bella Blackstone. She wants to know if she can steal you for the day. Poor thing is having a hard time finding a decent assistant." He rolled his eyes while handing me the phone. "Which I can fully relate to."

I pulled my face away from the bag and took the phone, covering the mouthpiece with my palm.

Irritated, Stefano demanded, "Roman, are you ready? What is taking you so long? Are you taking me to brunch or should I call a cab?"

"555-1212," Roman snapped.

"What? What is that?"

"The number for Yellow Cab."

"Well, aren't you clever?"

"Not as clever as that knockoff Rolex." Stefano quickly covered his wrist with his other hand, scooting Roman from the kitchen to the front door.

"In the car . . . Now . . ."

Once they left I answered the phone. "Bella, your timing is impeccable!"

"Will he cut you loose for a few hours?" Her upbeat demeanor was like a breath of fresh air.

"Are you joking? Who's going to say no to you?!"

"Great! Meet me at the Bungalow Hotel in Malibu. I signed in as Minnie Mouse."

"I'll see you there!" I didn't waste another second in Chateau Crazy. I quickly ran home to change and found a substantial, expensive-looking floral arrangement at my door.

Who would send me flowers? Sure enough, the envelope had my name on it. The card was typed out and read: *XO, J*. Jax Phoenix had sent me the flowers! Was this for real? How did he find my address? I suppose that he could have had his agent or someone like that contact the studio or something. The details didn't really concern me because I was so excited that I could jump out of my skin! This was really happening!

I changed into a Bella-bought Rebecca Taylor sundress, put the card in my purse and headed to the hotel. I wondered what Bella could possibly need from me.

The Bungalow Hotel is a posh haven overlooking the sea. It is known for its private pools and lush gardens. It is a frequent retreat for celebrities who need a refuge from the prying public eye. As I went through the simple modern entry, a kind looking man approached me. "Welcome to the Bungalow, miss. How can I assist you?"

"Actually . . ." I smiled and felt a little ridiculous stating, "I'm looking for my friend . . . Minnie Mouse."

The man laughed, motioning to the large French doors leading out to the garden. "Miss Mouse is lying by the pool. Follow me." He led me through a maze of small trees, aromatic blossoms and fountains, passing several private pools. At the last pool, he gestured toward the cabana. There I found Isabella topless, face down and glowing in coconut-scented oil. Her luscious blonde hair draped over the side of the padded lounge. A tray of strawberries and a bottle of iced champagne were by her side.

"Lucy! Come sit!" I sat on an adjacent chair.

"This place is *amaaazing*!" I exclaimed with enthusiasm.

"It's my home away from home. I couldn't live without it."

"So, are you working from here today?"

"Yeah . . . working on my tan!"

"Oh. It's just that Stefano mentioned you needed my help with something."

"I do need your help. I need you to help me lie by the pool. Always have a swimming buddy—pools can be dangerous!" We broke into laughter. I was so happy to get away from Stefano that I could cry again, this time happy tears. Bella handed me her room key.

"Go on up to the room. I have everything up there . . . bathing suits, sunscreen, whatever."

I took the key and bounced out of the chair. "Bella! I would hug you . . . but you're topless and all greasy."

"If I had a nickel for every time someone said that . . . !" she quipped.

I skipped to the elevator.

The scorching Southern California sun gleamed down on the Bungalow pool. We sailed next to each other on floating lounges. Blended strawberry margaritas filled both lounge cupholders. "How is work going?" Bella asked me. "Has Stef eased up on you at all?"

"Not really, although he didn't call me 'Ugly' once yesterday! I'm guessing because I was wearing those beautiful clothes." I smiled.

"That's a good start. I totally understand what it's like to be degraded by men. Every guy I've ever married did that to me. Next time, things will be different." Bella, a true romantic at heart, had a habit of falling in love quickly with the wrong men. Her last three marriages were highly publicized disasters. Her relationships had created so much fodder for the tabloids that VH1 had created a show titled *Bella's Blokes.* The program might just as well have been called *Bella's Blunders.* Bella's lovers had been chronicled and analyzed by gossipmongers and sex therapists as everyone offered their opinion of "what went wrong."

"I don't know why guys get off on putting us down. I guess, in a way, I get off on them putting me down. Otherwise, I wouldn't keep going back to the same type, right? That's what Dr. Dumb Bitch said on that bullshit *Bloke* show, anyways. What about you? Any boyfriends?"

"No, not me. Guys don't see me like they see my girlfriends. I've always been one of the guys, everyone's geeky little sister."

"You don't look like one of the guys!"

"Well, I've never been the hot girl, the one that guys fall head over heels for. That would be my best friend, Julie. I've always been the pretty girl's friend that guys like to pal around with. It's hard to explain, especially to you!" I sipped my margarita.

"In a weird way, I think you're totally lucky. I've never had any guy want to be my pal. I've never been friends with a guy, ever. No man ever wants to talk to me. They only want to sleep with me." She took a sip of her margarita.

"So we're both screwed," I conceived.

"Actually, it sounds like I'm the only one getting screwed here!" We laughed as I splashed Bella with my foot.

I asked, "Don't you have two daughters?" Anyone not living in a cave for the last decade knew about the celebuspawn children of Bella and her second husband, the infamous Noah Sierra. Noah is the Food Network's bad-boy chef, who keeps their censors working overtime with his rock-and-roll style cooking segments. Mr. and Mrs. Sierra's marriage owed its demise to Noah's never-ending addiction to drugs, alcohol and other women.

"The twins are great. They'll be six years old next month. It's unreal. I can't believe I'm a mother of two at thirty-two!" Thirty-eight, I mentally ticked. Bella went on, "So, explain to me how you are becoming a master photographer by slaving for Stef."

"Well, I thought that being his assistant meant that I would be assisting with actual photo shoots. I didn't realize that you had to start off where I am, fetching coffee and pretending to turn down fountains . . ."

"As odd as the job is, you do have it easy as far as Hollywood goes. Think about all of the models and actresses who have to sleep their way to be where you are . . . With scruffy directors and sleazy agents . . . On top of their ugly, itchy casting couches in the valley . . ." Bella drifted off and began unconsciously scratching her upper arm.

"Well, how did you get started?" I naively questioned.

"Certainly not by running into Spielberg while serving him cocktails, I'll tell you that much!" Bella laughed at her own joke. "Cheers to that!"

We clinked the empty glasses together and signaled an attendant for refills.

"Excuse me, Miss Blackstone, your five-o'clock massage is ready in the spa." A pretty blonde hotel clerk placed a plush white robe inside the cabana.

Bella slipped over the side of the lounge and sauntered out of the pool. "I almost forgot I booked one! I'm going in—feel free to stay here, keep drinking, whatever!" I sat up in the float and found I had more than just a minor buzz going on. "Yeah, I'll lay out for a while. Thanks for everything. Today has been so great."

"I know! I'm so glad we're friends. We're going to have to make a weekly habit of you assisting me!" Bella wrapped herself in the robe, refilled her margarita and headed into the hotel. I climbed out of the pool to refill my glass before retiring to the shaded lounge inside the cabana. In my inebriated haze, I decided to enjoy the rest of my afternoon lying down . . . watching the palm trees sway . . . closing my eyes . . . falling into a deep . . . deep . . . sleep.

chapter nineteen

Crash. Boom. Bang.

I opened my eyes to find myself alone in the cabana. I waited for my eyes to adjust to the light then discovered they were already adjusted and it was evening. I picked up my cell phone and, glancing at the time, was surprised to see it was eight thirty. I had six missed calls from Stefano. Quickly, I gathered my belongings. I attempted to return his calls but his cell phone had been turned off.

Pulling into Stefano's driveway, I was relieved to see Roman's car. A soft light coming from the house exuded a serene vibe. The sound of crickets chirping and a calm and peaceful breeze filled the air. I wondered if Roman got Stefano to sit down and complete an edit. I made my way up the steps toward the front door. As I fit my key into the lock, the door swung inward.

Roman was on his way out and he looked miserable. His

bow tie was undone, his face was flushed and his red eyes were tearing up. "I can't do this anymore. He's all yours. I mean, really. It's a fucking phone charger."

I was afraid to ask. "What do you mean, it's a phone charger?"

"He can't find his cell phone charger. Do you know where it is?"

I shook my head slowly from side to side. Roman held the door open for me and, after I entered, he slammed it shut behind him. I stood there frozen, looking at the living and dining areas. Cushions, pillows and books were strewn about. Chairs were turned over on their sides and a destroyed and expensive-looking sculpture was in pieces on the floor. "Hurricane Stefano," I whispered to myself. From where I was standing, I could see a sizable amount of cocaine cut into lines and spilled across the dining room table. I had become so used to such chaos that all it meant to me was that I'd have a hard time putting Stefano to sleep. *Crash, boom, bang!* Noise erupted from upstairs. "*Fuck!*" Stefano's voice echoed down. I carefully snuck up the stairs on the balls of my feet, one foot slowly following another, balancing on the edge of each step. *Bang crash, thump thump!* I froze midstep at the turn of the stairwell. I rested my hand on the wall as I strained my upper body around to get a glance of the upstairs hallway. *Creeeeeek—* the stairs loyally alerted the man of the house. "Lucy? *Lucy!*" Should I turn around and make a run for it? The hairs on my arm went straight and I became frightened. "I know you're there. I saw you pull up! Get your *ass up here!*" I took a deep breath and decided to just find the stupid phone charger and get the hell out of there. Stefano was pacing in figure eights around the sparse master bedroom, throwing and kicking everything in his path. I hesitantly entered the room. He glared at me as if I had done something unimaginable. "Where is my fucking phone charger, *Lucy*?" He said my name as if it were the most repulsive word he'd ever uttered.

I swallowed. "I . . . I don't know. The last time I saw it . . . I put it in your backpack." The satchel had been dumped out next to the bed and its contents scattered on the floor. I fell to my knees and checked the pockets with my trembling hands.

"My iPhone is dead and I want to call my mother. You'd better find it." This was the first that I had ever heard of Stefano's mother. Without looking up at him, I timidly suggested, "Why don't you use the house phone while I look for the charger?"

"Fine," he sulked. I briskly exited the room and went downstairs. I stopped in the bathroom to splash water on my face. My hands were now noticeably shaking and I attempted to shake them steady while trying to calm my nerves. I squeezed my gold Love bracelets tightly, as ridiculous as it sounds, and wished that I wasn't alone with Stefano in that house. I gave myself a good look in the mirror, staring into my sorrowful eyes. I glanced at the reflection of the mountain of cocaine on the dining room table. My eyes indecisively glanced back and forth from my own reflection to that of the drug. Biting my lower lip, I stopped to contemplate the demons. Proceeding into the dining room, I carved two large white lines, quickly vanishing them into my nose through a straw. I thought that it would help numb the intense emotions I was experiencing. I retrieved the portable phone for my manic boss.

He was sitting on the edge of the bed when he snatched

the phone from my hands. "You can't do anything right! How the fuck did you get here? You're pathetic and completely worthless! You think you're going somewhere . . . like all the other losers who try to use me as a stepping-stone . . . but I'll have you know that you are nothing and you will always be nothing." Right then and there, my heart broke. I could actually feel it shatter. I froze and looked down at the floor, unsure how to respond and unable to physically move. He continued rousing me. "Because you're fucking stupid and ugly and you do not belong here!" I looked into his hateful eyes and felt my own well with tears. Why was he being so extremely cruel? What did this have to do with his phone not being charged? Did he really think that I couldn't do anything right? Did he really think that I was stupid . . . and ugly? My dream had become a nightmare. This was not what I had wished and prayed for all those years worshipping the great Stefano Lepres. I had placed him on a pedestal and thought of him as this great symbol of awesomeness and inspiration, and here he was making me feel that I was better off dead. My pride, at least what was left of it, wouldn't allow him to see me fall apart, and I could feel that I was on the verge of a meltdown. Turning my back to him, I took a few quiet steps toward the door . . . when *BAM!* I pressed both hands tightly against the back of my head. Horrified, I half turned and saw the portable phone broken into pieces and spinning on the hardwood floor. He had hurled the phone at my head! He turned ballistic. "You fucking bitch! You broke my phone! Get out of my face you stupid . . . ugly . . . bitch!"

I stood horrified, in shock as the words cut through me like a dozen flying daggers. How could Stefano Lepres hate me so much when all I did was love and admire him? It was worse than any heartache caused by a boyfriend or fight with my parents or any other type of pain I had ever experienced before. He lunged forward and I bolted from the bedroom. I sprinted as fast as I could away from the house, dropping his keys on the driveway before fishing my own out of my purse. Running on fear-driven adrenaline, I got to my beat-up Jeep, which was parked up the street. Since I'd started working for Stefano, I hadn't even touched my own car. Without allowing even one second for the engine to warm, I peeled out of the spot and sped away from the house.

My entire body continued to quiver as I broke into a cold sweat. I dialed Julie's number. I couldn't be alone like this. She didn't answer. Next, I tried Sebastian, but he didn't answer either. Liz answered the phone but she was at a club and couldn't hear me. My parents certainly wouldn't understand and I was far too embarrassed to confide in James. I had nobody to call.

I sharply turned onto Highland Boulevard. I was alone and I deserved it. *Stefano is right,* I thought. *I am stupid.* Stupid enough to shut out my friends, stupid enough to think that I belonged in that world and stupid enough to have run out on Stefano-goddamn-Lepres. Did I do the right thing leaving like that? Did he just need a few minutes to cool down as Liz had rightfully suggested the times before? I had just thrown it all away and I knew it. Would he blacklist me from the industry? Could he do that? I began to really panic. Was this the end of my career? I eyed the dark highway, observing the oncoming cars speeding closer. My hands were shaking and so numb that I could barely steer the wheel. What did I have to look forward to? Nothing. Like he said, I was nothing. I had nothing. I'd always be nothing. Pulling over to the left, I shifted gears. My heart pounded like it might punch through my chest. What if I could just end it, right here—right now? Would Stefano then feel badly because he finally sent someone completely over the edge? Just do it, I thought. Nobody would care if I did. Or would they only care about me after I did? I wondered if I felt this intense because of those few lines I had just done at the house. Regardless, I didn't care. On impulse, I closed my eyes and careened the car into the oncoming traffic. The Jeep barely missed the first car, tipped up on the two left wheels as it weaved between the second and third cars. I came to a screeching halt at the opposite side of the road. My head slammed into the steering wheel. I burst into sobs.

Who and what had I become? Where did things take such a wrong turn? It was then that I decided that my time working for and worrying about Stefano Lepres was over. I was willing to sacrifice much of my self-esteem by letting him belittle me with his mind games. I even accepted the fact that I compromised many of my standards to be part of his cult-like studio. But was I willing to hit the ultimate low and tolerate being abused physically? No.

I stretched to the side, reaching for my purse, which had spilled out in front of the passenger seat during my near crash. Beneath it was the bikini I had borrowed from Bella, still damp and smelling of chlorine. I smoothed it out over the passenger seat and thought; if everything happens for a reason, which I do believe, maybe working for Stefano was meant to lead me to Bella, who in turn would be the one to get me where I really wanted to go. Was it possible? There was only one way to find out. I picked up my cell phone.

Isabella sang out, "Lucy-goosey! How was the rest of your day?!"

"Bella . . . it . . . it wasn't good." I decided not to tell her everything. "I'm calling to let you know that I am leaving Stefano." I never in a million years thought I'd say those words. They returned me to reality. I had to cover the mouthpiece so she couldn't hear me whimper as tears streamed down my cheeks.

"Well, I can't say that I'm shocked. You are a great photographer and you will never make it this way." Her insisting that I was this great photographer intensified my insecurities and emotions because she had never seen my work! But still, I knew that I was good. Perhaps if she gave me a job, even out of pity, she'd be blown away and would help me launch my career.

I took a deep breath and faked my disposition. "Thanks! So I am wondering . . . Does your offer still stand to hire me as a photographer?" I crossed my fingers on both hands and closed my eyes.

"Of course it does! Let's put together a show at a fabulous gallery! I'll invite everyone we know!"

Only momentarily did I consider that "we" didn't have mutual friends and I knew nobody. Still, it was everything that I needed to hear. I opened my eyes and grinned ear to ear. "Really?"

"Yes! Oh my God, you can shoot a whole series of . . . *me*! It will be like a documentary on my life! At the beach, with my kids, behind the scenes of other shoots—it will be fabulous! Once all my famous friends and editors see how talented you are, they'll all hire you for sure. How does that sound?"

Again I suffocated any voice of reason reminding me of the fact that Bella had never even seen my work. "It . . . it sounds too good to be true . . ." I chuckled.

"Well, it isn't! I will help you become the most celebrated photographer in Hollywood! We will bump Stefano What's-His-Face right off the radar! Okay?"

I laughed out loud. "Let's not push it!" I pulled myself together and started my car. "Okay, Bella. Thanks again . . . for everything. You don't know what this means to me!"

"Great! We'll meet next week and begin making plans for all of your dreams to come true! Good night!"

I clutched my chest, inhaled and exhaled deeply. Everything was going to be okay. I think.

"Good night, Bella!"

chapter twenty

WWJD?

Goodnight was the understatement of the year. On the fifth evening of isolation, I remained buried in bed with my eyes glued to the television. I wasn't ready to face the world otherwise known as my friends and parents. How would I even begin to explain what had transpired? I flipped through the channels in search of something light to escape to, some comedy maybe, anything to take me away to another place—at least for an hour or four. Nothing in the world could have prepared me for what I saw on *E! News*. The split screen behind Ryan Seacrest and Giuliana Rancic showed two stock images of Jax Phoenix and Jessica Amore with the words "Breaking News" splashed across. Jessica Amore is a bubbly, blonde songstress with girl-next-door appeal. She is effortlessly adorable, admired globally and the last person on the planet anyone would want anywhere near their boyfriend . . .

or could-be boyfriend, in my circumstance. I hurled myself to
the edge of the bed and turned up the volume.

Ryan amped up his legendary charm, "Reports are flood-
ing in from France that two of our hottest songbirds are making a lot more than beautiful music. Giuliana, what do you
think of the story? Another rumor or a match made in har-
mony heaven?"

"Well, Ryan, my sources aren't just telling, they're showing. Take a look."

Various images rolled across the screen of the enraptured
couple strolling in Paris. Jax looked fantastic in a loose knitted
beanie and Jessica looked like she always did, happy and perfect. Ryan continued, "It looks like this duet might actually
be duet'ing it, if you know what I'm saying . . ." A final picture
flashed of the two from behind, walking down a cobblestone
street with their hands in each others back pockets.

I was sick to my stomach. I turned off the television and
disappeared into my comforter.

Forcing myself up, I decided it was time to come back to
the land of the living. I took a quick shower and looked at my
phone. "Twenty-one new messages?" I stared at my blinking
answering machine in disbelief. It had been almost one week
since I had turned my ringer off and there were messages that
had gone unheard for weeks before then. The machine ran as
I rolled my wet hair into a towel turban. I tightened the belt of
my silk kimono and shuffled across the cluttered floor, sifting
through boxes labeled "kitchen." (Considering that I'd technically lived in this apartment for eight months, I'd barely spent
any time here at all.)

"Hi Luce, it's Julie. I'd leave you a message on your cell

phone but it says your voice mail is full. Anyways, my parents are flying in tomorrow and they'd love to see you. Call me." I bit my lip. That message was clearly more than just a few weeks old. I put a cup of water in the microwave to make some tea.

"Lucy . . . it's Mom. I'm sure you're busy at work. We need to talk about what happened in LA as well as discuss your Thanksgiving plans. I love you, here's Dad."

My father continued when my mother left off. "Hi, Luce. I mailed you some insurance forms. Please take care of that. You can't go another day without health insurance. Okay? Call us back." I glanced at a large envelope stacked in the midst of the other unopened mail.

"Hey, it's Julie . . . again. Sebastian and I are going to an outdoor movie at the Hollywood Cemetery—you had said you always wanted to go, so we thought you might be interested. My parents missed you but send their best. Don't be a stranger." Carefully balancing a full mug, I climbed my way to the window and opened the curtains to let in the morning light.

"Ugly . . . where are you? You know I can't get out of bed without a smoothie. I mean, if you can't do these things I ask of you, maybe you should just . . ." I could hear my own voice faintly in the background. Stefano clearly was unaware I was already at his house. I heard my own voice again, "Good morning, Stefano!" Stefano's voice continued on the message machine. "Umm, thanks, Lushy. See you at the studio." I nearly choked on the tea as I laughed for the first time in a while at Stefano's attempt to hide his idiocy.

"Hey, Butler, it's Braves." I was surprised to hear his voice. "I ran into your parents at Pike Place Market of all places. I was surprised your father remembered me from orientation. They sounded ... concerned. We need to talk." I curled up on my chair. "Anyhow, I'm going to be back in LA for my cousin's wedding the sixteenth through the nineteenth, and I thought we could get together. I'd love to see you again. Call me, e-mail, send smoke signals, whatever ..." I jumped to check a calendar for the date. It was Sunday the nineteenth. Maybe I could still reach him!

Immediately I dialed James's cell phone number. I paced the room while biting my thumbnail.

"About time!" A friendly and familiar voice, at last!

"James, I am so sorry! Everything has been ... I don't even know what to say! Are you still in LA?"

"I am ... my flight isn't until ten tonight. What are you doing? Can you meet up?"

"Yes! Let's do lunch?"

"*Do* lunch? Oh, Butler ... that is *so* LA ..."

"Oh shush! Where do you want to meet?"

"How about Cafe Med? It's close to my hotel ... and I'm pretty sure we don't have to sneak in through a tent," he joked.

"Sounds great—I'll pick you up!"

"It's just down the street—I'll walk."

"Oh, James, nobody walks in LA."

"See you at the restaurant, Lucy," he said through a chuckle. I wasn't sure if he thought I was kidding or not, but I was elated either way.

I tossed the remnants of my tea into the sink and bolted to my closet. I wanted to show James how grown up and sophisticated I had become in the short but life-changing month that had passed. I *had* to look amazing! Sliding the hangers from side to side, I pulled out several pieces of clothing and tossed them onto the bed, grabbing the latest issue of *Harper's Bazaar* and flipping through it for inspiration. There was a stunning picture of Presley Dalton at a Hamptons party and I wanted to emulate her look. As if . . . But maybe with couture courtesy of Isabella Blackstone I could get close enough. I pulled a taupe box labeled *Camilla Skovgaard* from under my bed and reverently unwrapped a pair of the designer's draped leather sandals. The coveted shoes were a borrowed gift from a stylist that had to be returned "within the week" from the photo shoot they were used for. I mentally calculated that it had been two weeks since I swore to return them. I made a promise to myself that I'd return them the next day. A striped 10 Crosby Derek Lam dress had the same effortlessly chic vibe as the one in the photo of Presley. I eyed myself in the mirror. Something was missing. Presley's stylist had accessorized the dress with a gold chain belt, but I didn't own a belt like that. Knowing I would have to compromise, I dumped out my jewelry box. Taking apart all my gold necklaces, then reattaching them together, I created my own chain belt. Removing a Hermès lock from one of my purses, I slid the lock onto the ends of the necklaces, attaching them to the other side once wrapped around my hips. I clapped in glee, smiling to myself, proud of my resourcefulness. I smoothed my hands down the sides of my torso. I had never been so slender in my entire life. Being stressed and never having time to eat was really starting to have its benefits! I turned to look at myself from behind and lifted the stripy skirt. My legs were teeny tiny! After twisting my hair into a tight knot, I grabbed a oversized Chanel croc tote and matching shades. With one more glance of approval in the mirror, I said out loud, "Thank you, Bella!"

As I sped up La Cienega wearing borrowed accessories and Isabella's clothes, my anxiety grew with each passing minute. Just before reaching the hotel, I pulled off to the side of the road, checking the mirror one last time. It was too much. On impulse, I pulled out the bun and shook loose my long red hair. I removed the makeshift belt from my waist and wrapped it around my wrist. Rolling into a parking spot adjacent to Cafe Med, I immediately spotted James waiting outside with his back to the elevated patio, handsome as ever in a vintage Doors T-shirt and dark jeans.

James's jaw dropped as he watched me shimmy my way through the slower moving pedestrians. When I got close enough, I pounced on him and threw both of my arms around his neck.

He took a step backward. "You look . . . Wow! Holy . . . Lucy! You are Lucy, right?"

"Ha, ha. Very funny."

"You look fantastic!"

"Thanks." I smiled and blushed.

"Hey—by the way, these are for you." James turned around, taking his time picking something up from behind him. My mind raced . . . what could it be? Perhaps an article in the school paper about successful alumni? Some hokey Seattle souvenir?

James did an about-face, however I couldn't see his face because it was obstructed by a massive bouquet of purple hydrangeas and white roses.

"Those . . . are for me?" I was thrown off, suffice it to say. Now I was really blushing.

"I thought the hydrangea would remind you of home . . . and the roses were my own special touch. Do you like them?"

"They are absolutely beautiful . . . I love them." I pressed my face toward the center of the blooms and took in a deep breath, not because I was particularly interested to see what the arrangement smelled like but because I felt like it was what you were supposed to do upon receiving flowers.

"You didn't say anything about the last flowers I sent, so I wasn't sure if you got them or if it just wasn't your thing . . . But I thought, what girl doesn't love flowers, right? I'm sure you've just been busy. . . ." I hid my blushed face in the bouquet, silently mouthing, *Oh my God!* That arrangement was not from Jax. *J* stood for James. I felt so stupid. I should have known.

"They smell like heaven. Of course I love flowers! Thank you, times two!" I smiled nervously. "Ready to have lunch?"

"What? You don't want to *do* lunch anymore?" James snarked. While following my lead into the restaurant, he briefly put his hand at the small of my back, which made me nervously shudder and widen my eyes.

We both giggled, albeit for different reasons, as we hovered over the hostess podium. I grabbed James's arm and gestured with my head. He looked over to see what I was gesturing to and recognized a glammed-up Joan Rivers dining with an equally enhanced friend. Both women were dressed and bejeweled to the nines and had identical permanent expressions of surprise on their plastic-surgeoned faces. Naturally, James and I slowed down to eavesdrop.

The comedienne was first to speak. "Priscilla, you look absolutely marvelous. That suit is to die for. Is it de la Renta? It's simply fabulous."

"Thank you, darling . . . Actually, it's Ferragamo."

"Oh, my, looks like it's time for me to get my de la *retinas* tested!" Both women rocked back in laughter, their frozen faces still possessing the same expressions of surprise.

"It's always an event doing lunch with you. Truth be told, I just stare at my wardrobe and think, *WWJD?*"

"Priscilla, I didn't realize you were so religious . . ."

"Oh, no . . . No . . . Jesus trims my hedges! What Would *Joan* Do, dahling!" The women erupted into another bout of laughter. Still no change in facial expressions.

Turning to me and shaking his head, James said, "I still can't believe you live here."

An attractive hostess showed us to a table and a few heartbeats of silence passed as we perused the menu. I decided on the appetizer-size tuna tartar while James selected the BBQ-chicken pizza.

"That's all you're ordering?" asked James.

"I had a late breakfast," I lied.

"You aren't dieting, are you? You've lost a lot of weight and you don't need to lose any more."

I perked up. "Hey, thanks!"

"That wasn't a compliment. It was an observation. So . . . how is your dream job going? Tell me more about it . . . What is he like?"

Not wanting to spoil the mood with my sob story, I blurted out, "It is . . . well, it was really great. Inspiring. But not right for me. Not what I thought, so I . . . left. How are your students this semester?"

"Cut the shit!" He dismissed my response and thought that I was kidding.

I took several large gulps of ice water and averted my eyes toward the ceiling and then glued them to the napkin on my lap. I was so focused on the wardrobe that I failed to consider the most relevant topic that would come up in conversation. I looked up to find James looking at me intently with a puzzled expression.

"Lucy . . . You were barely there one year—what happened?"

Should I tell him the truth? And how much of the truth? Or should I make something up? I used to tell James every thing that was on my mind regarding my dreams and aspirations, however something felt different now. After a short, heated debate inside my head, I looked up with sad eyes and elaborated. "It wasn't right for me. Stefano was kind of a mon ster and I was starting to get caught up in . . . I just . . . I was wrong—I don't belong there after all." I felt like a balloon with a small but rapid leak.

"Why didn't you call me?" he sympathized.

I shrugged. "I don't know. I didn't want to let you down."

"You could never let me down." He reached across the table and put his warm hand over mine. "I knew that you were too sweet for this place. Remember our chat about the sharks?"

I let up a slight smile. "Yeah."

"By the look in your eyes, it seems like you came face-to-face with a great white." I agreed to his cheesy reference with a nod. "Which is why I want to talk to you about coming back with me—to swim happily with the friendly salmon . . . where you belong," he said playfully.

"Move home?" I exploded into laughter and slipped my hand out from under James's to cover my mouth and muffle the loud expletives. "Holy shit, James—you're fucking hilarious!"

James was stunned. I had never sworn like that in front of him. He watched as I squirmed in my seat, unable to calm myself down.

His bright smile fell. "I . . . I'm serious."

My outburst came to an immediate halt. "What are you talking about? Why would I do that? What would I even do there? I have built a life here and I'm not going to run away just because of . . . him."

"Yes, I agree. You shouldn't leave because of him, but per-haps for someone else." He was brightly blushing and I didn't understand why. "Okay, so here it goes. Come back for me, Lucy—or for us, rather. I have feelings for you—I always have, but it just hasn't been the right timing and . . . Not that this is the best timing, but I figure, if not now, when? Right? I can't go a day without thinking about you and . . . I can only hope that you feel the same way about me. I am hoping that you might want to consider coming back and seeing what could be?"

Flabbergasted, I sat there with an astonished look on my face. I anxiously choked the napkin on my lap.

He continued. "Was it not obvious enough?"

"Was what not obvious enough?" What was he talking about?

"The special attention . . . The advance notice of opportunities . . . Calling you into my office for any reason that I could come up with . . . Do you think that I care to that extent for all of the students? Or chase them down in LA? You make me feel . . . I don't know what. I just know that I miss you and think about you everyday . . . I've never met anyone like you, Lucy, and I know that we would be great together. I just want you to come back and try this with me." I could tell that he felt he might have said too much. After his rant, he sat back and gave me some time to take it in.

I stared out onto the boulevard, feeling overwhelmed and in disbelief. James was everything that any girl would want. At one point, he was everything that *I* wanted. My parents would indubitably approve. How stupid would I be to decline him? Our eyes met and we both smiled. All through school I had imagined what being romantically involved with James would be like. I revisited the fantasy. We could live in an artsy cottage-style house in downtown Seattle. I would shoot family portraits or maybe even weddings too. And then we would even end up getting married, having children . . . He would be an amazing father. The picture-perfect future would be serene and drama free. Ideal, really.

His voice cracked as he broke the silence. "Excuse me, we didn't order champagne." The waitress paid James no attention and popped the bottle of bubbly, poured it into two flutes and returned it to a silver standing bucket. She then motioned to a table in the back and informed us, "Compliments of Miss Dalton." James arched his back as Presley Dalton blew me a kiss. She and a Johnny Depp wannabe were dining in a corner, both on their cell phones. I mouthed my thanks to Presley and she responded with a wink.

"You know that talentless twit?" he griped.

"Sort of." I took a big gulp of the bubbly. Then it dawned on me. In what world does Presley Dalton send me champagne? The first name on my resume was Stefano Lepres! Although brief, I did sort of date Jax Phoenix, and he might one day come back around . . . I was about to go into business with Isabella Blackstone, for crying out loud! My life was just beginning to blossom, really. Who knew what other excitement was ahead! Not to mention the fact that I wasn't about to go back to being the nerdy wallflower art student geek that I was back home. I finally felt actual confidence and excitement for my life! I had fancy things and fabulous friends—why would I go back to the old me? I couldn't disclose all of these reasons to James because he likely wouldn't understand, since I assumed he had always been a golden child with a charmed life. Instead, I gave him one reason only, the one that I believed he would support and relate to.

"James, I already have a new job with Bella Blackstone . . . I am not moving back. This is where my life is."

"Isa-bella Blackstone? What on earth would you do for her?" I observed that every time I referred to her as "Bella" others responded with "Isa-bella?" as if they were making sure their ears were not deceiving them.

"Photography, of course. She has commissioned me to shoot a series of portraits for a gallery show we are putting together. The concept is sort of up in the air—but it's all happening, it's going to be a major deal." I heard myself come off like one of those Hollywood types and I mentally gave myself a slap.

James noticed too. "You have changed," he concluded.

"Yeah, I have." I lowered my voice and leaned in to the table. "But what about you? You show up here with flowers, James . . . Roses . . . And you are telling me to abandon everything to be with you because all of this time . . . you had these feelings . . . and I am supposed to give up all of this . . ." I gestured to the boulevard and Presley.

James lowered his voice to my almost-whisper level and leaned in to the table. "All of what? You came out here to work for that freak and it didn't work out . . . But you are staying to hobnob with halfwits like Presley Dalton and has-beens like Isabella Blackstone?"

The waitress returned with the beautifully presented meals. James took a deep breath and attempted to turn things around. "Sorry, Lucy. I just don't want to lose you to this place. You're the last person that I want to see 'go Hollywood.' I just figured that you would come here, hate it and come right back."

"James . . ." I downed my champagne before I continued. "I've been out here for over a year. You have no idea what I have been through. You guided me and helped me get to this place—and now you want me to just leave it all and give up just like that . . ."

"Lucy, I was your guidance counselor while you were in school—it was my *job* to *guide* you in the direction that you *chose* to go! But my job ended when you graduated and left . . . and I thought that we had something, this connection—I thought that there was more to us than just that. I never thought of you as *just another student.*"

I fought tears as I verbally vomited a response. "And I always thought of you as *just my guidance counselor.*" It was a flat-out lie.

James removed the napkin from his lap and placed it on the table. He appeared absolutely crushed. "I can't do this. I am so sorry but I am . . . humiliated . . . and I really need to go." James stood up and fished a wallet out of his back pocket.

I too stood up and grabbed James's arm. "James—please don't go . . . Please, let's just start all over again. I will even leave and come back and we can act like none of this conversation just happened. . . ." I gave him my best puppy dog eyes as they welled up with tears. I desperately clung to his wrist with both hands. What had I done?

"This conversation did just happen . . . not everything is a staged set, Lucy. No re-shoots." Dropping two twenty-dollar bills onto the table, James stepped around the table. "I'm sorry." He kissed me on the cheek.

I watched James disappear out the door. I sat back down and began to grasp the reality that I had officially alienated myself from every person that I could always count on. I took his camera out of my bag and held it on my lap. I had planned to show him some of my recent prints and the new lens I had saved for. I looked up at Presley and Faux Johnny Depp, looking ridiculous at their romantic bistro table, both on their phones. I couldn't help but take a telling picture.

chapter twenty-one

I See London, I See France

"Pack your bags! We are going to London . . . tomorrow!"

I lifted the satin sleeping mask away from my eyes and sat up. "What?" It was 10 p.m. on a Saturday night and I was still in hiding. Although perhaps hiding wasn't the correct word, being that nobody was exactly seeking. In fact, this was the first and only phone call I'd received in the three days since the James incident.

Bella continued, "A car will pick you up at seven in the morning! Private plane! Parties! Are you in?"

"Ummm I . . . don't know." I couldn't imagine going to a party. I couldn't even imagine taking a shower.

"You don't know? Of course you know! The only acceptable answer is yes!"

I stood up on the bed and paced from one end to the other.

"Lucy, are you there? What do you say?"

"Can I think about it?" What did I need to think about? Who says no to a free trip to Europe with Isabella Blackstone? It was a sudden invitation and I was in such a haze that I couldn't think straight. Bella might have been used to these impromptu trips to and fro, but I wasn't accustomed to that type of spontaneity.

"Of course! Text me when you decide . . . but Lucy, you're totally coming!"

"Thanks, Bella. I'll text you in a few." I tossed the phone into the comforter and it bounced off my bed, then knocked into the nightstand, tipping over the vase of flowers James had given me days before. It was a reality check by roses. As I collected the bouquet from the floor, I considered the rough ride I'd recently had. Maybe getting away with Bella would be good for me?

Giving up my "dream job" was devastating. I had yet to tell my parents, which scared me more than Stefano. Sebastian and Julie had seemingly given up on me. I couldn't have been more insensitive toward James. I felt like a major failure all around. As I continued to pick up the flowers, my mind went to battle with my heart. Am I making the right choices? Stefano really broke my spirit. What could I have done differently? Liz and Roman are able to hang on, why couldn't I? Was this my fault? And what about James? Did I have to be so harsh? Could we have tried to do a long-distance thing? I couldn't believe that I let him walk out like that. Julie would have known what to do in that situation, and I wished that we were on better terms so I could have turned to her. I tossed the floral arrangement into the trash and flipped on the lights.

I plucked my dirty clothes off the floor and tossed them

into a wicker hamper. A quarter fell out from a pair of J Brand
jeans. I retrieved them from the hamper and shook out the
pockets. A few more coins fell out before a tissue and a tiny
plastic bag. I'd forgotten about that bag of blow. Stefano had
me hold it for him weeks ago. I hugged the jeans close to my
chest and stared at the small bag on the floor. I briefly considered flushing it down the toilet. Then I rationalized, it was
Saturday night and everyone else was out having fun, doing
it in clubs right now . . . Why couldn't I? It would no doubt
motivate me to pack for the trip, should I decide to go. I sprinkled a few lines onto my nightstand and snorted them with
a Post-it.

A few lines later, I took an inventory of my surroundings.
The roses upside down in the trash. A sink full of three days'
deliveries of half-eaten chinese take-out. Cocaine on my
nightstand. Was this really a snapshot of my life?

I picked up my phone and sent a text to Bella that read
YES!!!! She responded almost immediately with the word
Duh. It made me smile and feel grateful for something to look
forward to. Correction, something insanely out of this world
amazing to look forward to!

I pulled my only suitcase from under the bed and swung
it open. Piece by piece, I folded the best of my gifted wardrobe
and organized it into piles. Reaching farther under the bed, I
pulled out three boxes of glamorous shoes. Removing each
pair in its velvet encasing, I neatly added them in the suitcase.
The Rolling Stones were pumping from my iPod, which I
turned up louder when my favorite song "Get Off of My
Cloud" came on. As Mick Jagger belted out the chorus I felt
like he had written the lyrics just for me, intended for every-

one creating thunder over my cumulus cloud. Rocking out in my boy-shorts and a tank top, I bounced around my apartment and collected toiletries plus other small items and zipped them into a lavender travel bag that had my initials scripted in white. I sprinkled out a few more lines and continued to pack and snort.

Knock! Knock! Knock! I looked up in disbelief at the door. In my speedy haze, I was unable to decipher whether or not I actually heard the noise. Did I imagine it? *Knock! Knock! Knock!* Voices could be heard mumbling in the hallway. I slipped on a pair of jeans before unbolting and swinging open the door. Sebastian and Julie were standing there, yelling, "Surprise!"

"Um . . . surprise?" They were the last people that I expected to see. I thought it might possibly be Roman and Liz, stopping by to check on me. I hadn't heard from them since quitting.

Julie held up a pink box and Sebastian untied a bow made from a (likely) counterfeit Coach scarf. He dramatically undressed the box then folded back the lid à la Vanna White. A giant strawberry cheesecake, my favorite dessert, glistened under the hallways overhead lights. They stood there, eagerly waiting for me to invite them in. But, I did not. I could not! There were drugs on my nightstand, and God forbid they knew what I was up to! Leaning against the door frame, I put my hand to my stomach explaining, "I wish I could invite you in but I'm actually not feeling so good. I was about to go to sleep . . ."

"Are you running away?" Julie strained to see behind me. "What's with the suitcase?"

"I am leaving tomorrow for work . . . I was going to call you in a few to tell you about it."

Sebastian raised his eyebrow and quipped, "After you went to sleep?"

"Where's the job?" Julie eyed the spiffy spread across the bed.

"Bella invited me to go to London with her to work on some stuff."

"Isa-bella . . . Blackstone?" an astonished Julie asked. I nodded.

Julie continued the interrogation. "What are you doing for her?"

"It's complicated." I didn't want to get into it.

Julie shut the cake box and passed it to Sebastian. "So, you gave up on your friends and now you gave up on photography too? Is that right?"

"No, not at all! It's nothing like that . . ."

She firmly placed her hands on her hips and continued. "You haven't so much as returned my calls, but when Isabella Blackstone invites you out—you pack a fucking suitcase?"

Sebastian tried to calm Julie down by putting his hand on her arm. "Julie, come on . . . Let's just . . ."

"No!" Julie snapped her arm away. "You can't spend an hour catching up with your friends who've been there for you all along. But, when Miss Movie Star calls, you can't toss all of your fancy freebies together quickly enough! You are becoming everything you hate, Lucy! I don't even know you anymore! I don't even recognize you!"

I shifted my hands from my back to my front pockets several times. In my mind, I imagined the words I wanted to say, yet I was unable to vocalize them. My eyes darted around the hallway as I clenched my jaw tightly. I was unable to look my friends in their eyes. I was spinning.

"You . . . are so high," Sebastian insisted. Julie stopped quietly hissing something to herself as she was about to walk away and re-faced me. Horrified, I widened my dilated eyes as I glared at Sebastian. He continued his accusation. "Well . . . are you not?"

I stepped away from the frame and put my hand on the door. Without further response, I shut the door in their faces and secured the dead bolt. Click.

The enormous jet to London was like nothing I had ever seen. The white leather love seats and lounge chairs were detailed with a cherry wood grain. I couldn't believe that I was once again on a flying Mercedes-Benz, let alone going all the way to Europe. I accepted a glass of champagne from the friendly flight attendant who would accompany us. I hoped it would quiet the guilty knot in my stomach from all that had transpired the night before. I couldn't wait to get out of LA for a while. I was upset about my friends accusing me of . . . well, I guess catching me doing . . . that stuff. But still, I shouldn't have closed the door in their faces. They deserve better.

I decided to leave the drama in LA and focus solely on my photography in London. As we took off, I was not only literally but also metaphorically putting LA behind me for the time being.

"Cheers!" Bella accepted a flute of champagne from the attendant and touched it to mine.

"Cheers! So . . . why exactly are we going to London?" I still hadn't been informed.

"A whole lot of press. The itinerary is a little crazy. Some television and radio publicity . . . and of course there will be some fabulous parties!"

I patted the padded camera case beside me. "I brought enough film for a lifetime!"

She kicked her heels up on the adjacent seat. "Film? As long as you use Mariah's retouching team, it's all the same to me." She smiled and pointed to the barely there wrinkles in the corner of her mouth. "Alright girly, Ambien was invented for long plane rides, and I could really use a good nap." Taking two capsules from her pocket, she popped one into her mouth, chasing it with the champagne. "Want one?" I had never taken a sleeping aid before, but the idea of dozing off until we reached our destination sounded like a dream come true. I accepted the pill and washed it down with my drink too. We reclined and settled in for the long haul. I quickly blacked out and slept through the entire flight.

The plane taxied to a small hangar away from the main area of Heathrow Airport. The captain and co-captain emerged to thank us for flying with them. Bella slid into a long J Mendel sable coat, fluffed out her blonde tresses and pushed a pair of dark sunglasses over her dewy face before stepping out into the crisp air. I zipped into a pair of fur-lined Michael Kors boots, snapped my pea coat together and also donned a pair of shades—even though the gloomy sky didn't require shielding. I felt so chic living Bella's opulent lifestyle, even if it was only temporary.

"There she is! Isabella!" Piercing screams and loud roars echoed across the runway as at least fifty fans pressed against the gates. "Miss Blackstone! Over here!" They jumped and crammed against each other, hoping to get a glimpse. Bella quickly moved down the steps and into a warm Bentley limousine. Attendants carefully handled an assortment of Prada and Vuitton trunks, along with my generic black one. As the limo slowly rolled past the gates, the crowd erupted in chaos. Airport security opened the fence and the fans clamored to the car windows. Pounding their fists against the glass, they tried to open the locked doors. Bella politely smiled but I was somewhat petrified. What if a door was left unlocked? Would the fans pile in and pull at her coat and hair? It seemed likely. The car gradually gained momentum and, within a minute, we were sailing toward the city.

The Sanderson Hotel was magnificent. Several paparazzi politely snapped photos as we entered the double doors, which were held open by two handsomely uniformed doormen. The Baroque-meets-modern interior sparkled with fantasy. We were escorted past a velvety red couch shaped like a pair of lips. I was in awe.

"Isn't it beautiful? It's my favorite hotel!" Bella beamed.

A warm gentleman welcomed us. "Ladies, I'll be showing you to the penthouse. Right this way . . ."

We moved to the top floor in the elevator, not needing to wait or even check in. The man unlocked the door to the enormous suite and held it open.

If I was any more awestruck, I would have started spinning in circles while singing "I Think I'm Gonna Like It Here" from the musical *Annie.*

Each room was more impressive than the one before. The rich white curtains showcased an unbelievable view of the city and the famous London Eye. The ultra contemporary bathroom featured a stand-alone stainless steel tub, like the kind you see in the movies. Accommodations fit for a modern-day queen. I returned to the living room and found Bella popping open a bottle of complimentary Cristal in the dining room. She filled two flutes. Handing one to me, she said, "Cheers to a great trip!" It was my second glass of champagne for the day on a completely empty stomach.

Outside the large bay windows, the gray blue London sky was somber. Bella plopped down on the sofa, kicking her heels up over the side.

"So, what do you want to do? I don't have to do my thing until tomorrow."

I stretched out on the faux fur rug. "What thing?"

"My perfume is debuting. I just have to go in for a few hours, take pictures with fans, sign autographs . . . Easy." She sipped her champagne. "Mmm . . . and the ribbon-cutting thing."

"Ribbon cutting?"

"At Harrods. They're making this stupid perfume thing a big deal."

"Sounds like a big deal to me!"

"Don't be ridiculous! What time is it at home?" She glanced at her rose gold Jacob & Co watch. "We should go do a late lunch." She grabbed the bottle of Cristal and walked out of the den.

It was the best thing I'd heard all day! I was imagining biting into something warm, juicy and delicious. We went to our separate bedrooms to change and freshen up. Bella kept her black Citizens of Humanity skinny jeans on and paired them with a backless eggplant Loro Piana cashmere top. I stayed in my black leggings and added a slouchy Missoni sweater. We complimented each other and strutted to the elevator.

The appropriately named Purple Bar is a purple-hued lounge that is as dramatic as it is decadent. We settled into a pair of lavender-colored seats at a discreet table. A smartly dressed young woman in a violet dress placed two delicate menus on the table. Bella read it through, scanning the words. Even though the menu was in English, I felt as though I were reading a foreign language. The delicacies included foie gras crostini, mini haddock cakes, and blood pudding. I was open to trying new things but didn't quite know what any of that meant. Nor did I think I was ready to consume anything containing the word "blood."

"Do you like oysters?" Bella asked.

Flipping over the finely printed menu, I said, "I don't see them on the menu."

"Everyone has oysters." Bella motioned for the maître d'.

"Yes, Miss Blackstone?"

"We'd like an order of oysters and a champagne menu please."

"Right away, Miss Blackstone." He politely nodded and disappeared. I wondered if we were going to just have oysters for dinner. Since working for Stefano and spending time with Bella, I had become accustomed to barely grazing, but it didn't mean that I didn't like to eat when time allowed. I wasn't comfortable ordering more for just myself, given that I likely couldn't afford it and I didn't want to be too much of an expense for Bella, even though she definitely could afford it.

With that thought in mind, I was ready to get down to business. "So, where do you think there will be room in your schedule for us to shoot? I'm thinking that I'll scout locations for inspiration while you're at Harrods tomorrow?"

"Oh no! You have to come! You'll meet my publicists and manager and agent and everyone you just have to know!" It made sense that I would have to meet those people if I was going to work with their star client, and perhaps one of them could help me work with her schedule.

The maître d' returned with a bottle of Krug Clos du Mesnil wrapped in a dark, velvety cloth. "From a friend, madame."

Bella turned in her seat and eyed the sparse crowd. "A friend? I don't know anyone in here . . ." I also turned around even though I knew there was no way that I had any friends there. Bella quietly squealed, "Lucy, this is easily at least a thousand-dollar bottle of vintage!"

"One . . . thousand . . . dollars?!" The bottle was expertly opened and its contents poured into elegant crystal glasses. I calculated how many glasses added up to my rent. Bella closed her eyes, moaning in satisfaction. I'll admit that it tasted good . . . I mean, it must have been impressive to a refined palate. But I'm not going to pretend to know what set it apart from others. I didn't want to appear unimpressed, so I too let out a sigh of satisfaction. A waiter brought a lovely silver double-tiered tray laden with an assortment of oysters to the table. They were displayed all curved in the same direction, creating a giant swirl. I shook my head, reminding my-self to take a mental picture. I had flown to London via private plane with the most famous woman in the world. I was stay-ing in a penthouse that looked like a Salvador Dalì painting come to life, sipping thousand-dollar champagne and slurp-ing oysters that weren't even on the menu. Unreal.

A man's thick Italian accent bellowed from above. "Bayla, my beautiful friend. So good to see you! But in another de-signer's clothes, is not so nice . . ." Bella shifted around to see whose hands were resting on her shoulders. "Roberto!" She darted up and they air-kissed three times. "Please, join us!"

"No, dahling . . . I'm afraid I've had too much. Please, enjoy . . ."

"Roberto, meet my very good friend Lucy Butler. She's a fabulous photographer."

"It's an honor to meet you!" I stood up, offering my hand for a handshake. Roberto gently held my hand and kissed each of my cheeks three times. I blushed and smiled. He had tight tanned skin and a charming smile. His fashionable char-coal suit highlighted his long, manicured gray hair. Taking both of our hands, he said, "You must come with me to Paris tonight. I'm having a party and it wouldn't be right without you!" We giggled while Bella took his hand into both of hers. She knew how to amp up the charm as well and I was taking notes.

"I can't go to Paris tonight! I have to be here in the morning."

"I will have you returned in time for your work. There isn't a reason to say no!"

Bella and I looked at each other and grinned. She bit her lip and gave me a look that said, *Why not?*

Roberto raised his arms and stepped back. "Ahh! Bellissimo! I insist you wear my new line and nothing else! You both are ready for dressing at eight o'clock, yes?"

Bella clasped her hands together, exclaiming, "Yes!"

Roberto kissed both his hands and threw them out, calling as he left, "Ciao, Bayla! Ciao, Lucy!" I considered myself to be the luckiest girl in the world. I tried not to let the fact that I couldn't tell Julie what had just happened dim my excitement.

chapter twenty-two

One of Us

Immediately upon returning to the suite we prepared for our impromptu trip to Paris. I poured a miniature bottle of Molton Brown bath gel into the filled bathtub and sank in. I wondered what my parents were doing back in Seattle. We had played phone tag for long enough and it was time to come clean.

"Hello?" my father answered the phone.

"Hi, Dad!"

"Hey, Luce! Here, wait a sec . . . Renee! Lucy's on the phone!"

My mother picked up the phone. "Hello?"

"Hey guys! Sorry that I haven't called you lately but I've been dealing with a lot. I have a few things to tell you. Do you want the good news or the bad news first?" I was treading softly.

"How about the truth?" my mom rightfully requested.

I took a deep breath and exhaled. "I no longer work for Stefano." I heard her softly gasp. "I wasn't fired—I quit. As you know, it wasn't the job that I had hoped for. There's more to it but I don't want to dwell on the negative, so I'll leave it at that." Neither of them said anything. I thought maybe we were disconnected. "Hello?"

My dad moved the conversation along. "And the good news?"

"I am calling you from London! Bella hired me! I'm going to get to travel with her everywhere and we have this really awesome idea we're working on for a project . . ." I couldn't wait to tell them!

"Excuse me?" My mother sounded livid. I thought for sure she would agree it was pretty amazing and glamorous. "What about finding work since quitting your supposed dream job?" Did she not hear me? London! With Isabella! "We supported you through school so that you could become a photographer—or at least work for another photographer . . . How could you think this is an acceptable alternative?"

"Mom, you don't understand! I am going to continue my photography! We are here putting together this project . . ."

She kept going. "You're just going to give up everything that we've all worked for to babysit some train-wreck slut in Europe—that's great, Lucy." She must have been referring to a recent article about Bella in *Star* magazine. It labeled her an alcoholic and accused her of sleeping with anyone and everyone, which obviously wasn't true.

"No, Mom. You don't understand . . . Dad, help me out here? I'm here to work as a photographer, for Bella!"

My dad didn't say anything.

"So now you don't want to work in photography?" my mom questioned. She wasn't even listening!

"No, listen to me. I—" I was about to explain everything. That I was going to be finally taking the pictures and on the right path—a far better path.

"Lucy, I have to go to work," my dad cut me off. I remembered that it was early in the morning there.

"Some of us actually *work*," my mom verbally stabbed me.

"Fine." I catapulted my cell phone across the floor. Bella stopped the phone with her pointed toe. I was very embarrassed that she had witnessed my childlike meltdown.

Bella sauntered into the bathroom wearing a blue lace bra and matching panties. "Parents?"

"Yeah . . ." I stared into the bubbles.

"Mine never approved, either." Bella stood tall, scrutinizing herself in the mirror, pinching at skin on her waist and inner thighs. She sat on the edge of the tub and put her legs into the water. "But, look how things turned out for me! They'll come around. And if they don't, screw 'em!" She blew a handful of bubbles into my face, attempting to lighten my mood. The doorbell chimed. "Yes!" Bella cried out, springing into the foyer.

I patted myself dry with a towel and wrapped a snug white robe around my pink cotton bra and panty set. Bella, comfortable in just her underwear, answered the door and found Roberto and two of his assistants. Unfazed at her scanty attire, she invited them in. They trailed in, wheeling a rack of dazzling dresses behind them. Isabella flung off her bra, holding both breasts in one arm while sliding the hangers with the other arm to examine the dresses. "Oh . . . Roberto . . . They are all so beautiful!"

"Yes. This one is the one for you, Bayla," he said, pulling out a glittering fuchsia satin dress. Bella gasped, reaching out to touch the buttery fabric. The assistants rushed over to zip Bella into the gorgeous gown. It was held up by a gold snake chain that wrapped around Bella's neck. The dress hugged every luscious curve and enhanced her breasts to perfection. She rushed to the mirror, gushing, "This is brilliant! I *love* it!" before running back to Roberto, kissing him on the cheek. I timidly watched from the hall. Roberto held his hand out to me. "Come! Your turn now!" I clutched my robe as I entered the living room. Bella pointed out, "She has amazing legs! Show him, Luce!" I reluctantly untied my robe, modestly opening it just enough so they could get an idea of my figure. I was shocked when one of the assistants snatched the robe from behind me and tossed it aside. I was nearly naked! I bit my lip, silently praying they would all look away. I fully covered my chest with both arms. Roberto pulled out a ruffled, off-the-shoulder spotted frock. I turned my back to everyone, raising my arms so the assistants could professionally pull it over my head. I glanced at my reflection in the mirror and loved what I saw.

"Thank you so much!" I kissed the icon just like Bella had. Patting one of the assistants on his back, Roberto headed for the door. "I'll see you downstairs in thirty minutes, yes?" Both Bella and I responded gleefully, "Yes!"

We finished getting ready in Bella's bathroom. She removed luscious blonde locks from a velvet case. One by one, she clipped the pre-curled pieces in with her own hair. "Voila!" So that's how she does it, I observed. I loosely braided my own and twisted it up into an invented updo. It was the best I could do with what I had. As we applied our makeup, I watched Bella carefully for tips to use on myself.

Bella expertly lined her pout with a pencil as she spoke. "You're bringing the camera tonight, right?" Obviously!

Bella cloaked herself in a white mink coat, loaning her black one to me. As promised, Roberto was in the lobby. He was impeccably dressed in a black suit and vibrant fuchsia satin tie. He and Bella looked like the prom king and queen. We stepped into his chauffeured Rolls-Royce and were promptly driven to a nearby airport.

A small black single-engine prop glistened under the moon. Bella and I staged a shot before taking off. She wanted a glamorous image of her stepping into the small plane. She slid the mink coat off her shoulder and posed in the door, kicking one leg out. To me, it mimicked a cliché Guess ad from the Anna Nicole Smith days. It looked very staged. I knew that she wanted it to look like she was getting into her plane, appearing so rich and decadent. I understood what she was going for, but it wasn't really my favored style. I hoped that she'd allow for some candid, more journalistic shots along the way too.

We were in Paris less than two hours later. We arrived at Le Blanc, a trendy Parisian hot spot Roberto had rented for about a hundred of his closest friends. As we entered the club, I spotted Madonna, Mick Jagger, Paul McCartney, among others. Ashley Olsen, Presley Dalton, and Jessica Amore lounged on a sofa. Steven Tyler and his daughter, Liv, were also at a nearby booth. When Roberto and Isabella walked in, the entire room rose and cheered. I followed behind the duo and quickly got lost in the chaotic scene. I immediately thought of Julie and how starstruck she would be if she was here. I missed her. Presley spotted me and called out my name.

"Hey, Presley! I'm so glad to see you!" I leaned down and air-kissed twice.

"Are you here with Stefano?" Presley asked.

"No . . . why, is he here?" My pulse must have stopped for those few seconds.

"Not that I know of . . . I was just saying, since you're always with him."

"Actually, Bella Blackstone hired me to shoot some stuff for her . . . so I don't work for him anymore," I proudly namedropped. Jessica Amore and Ashley Olsen listened to the exchange while they sipped their cocktails.

Presley enthused, "That's so sexy! Stefano is a fucking bitch and you deserve better. Come, sit." The girls slid over to make room for me. I was shocked by Presley's statement. She and Stefano had been friends for years and it didn't seem right that she would say those things about him behind his back.

I settled in between Jessica and Presley, extending my hand to Jessica. "Hi, I'm Lucy."

"Nice to meet you! I love your dress, it's beautiful."

"Thanks! It's one of Roberto's."

The girls snickered as Ashley explained, "Everyone is wearing Roberto's designs. It's his party!" I blushed, feeling foolish. "I'm Ashley. It's nice to meet you. Are you from LA or New York?"

"I'm not from LA, but I live there. We're only in Paris for the party. Bella has to be back in London by tomorrow morning."

"I'm going to London in the morning too!" said Jessica while applying a sparkling Dior lip gloss to her voluptuous lips. "I have to cruise the West End with Jax before their sound check."

My heart sank when it was confirmed that Jessica was still dating my crush. Jessica pursed her lips together, offering Ashley the gloss.

Ashley accepted and applied the gloss, asking, "So, Jess . . . are you seriously dating Jax Phoenix?"

Jessica replied, "Oh gosh, no. We have the same manager and his band needs the extra publicity to push ticket sales . . . so I'm helping them out."

Ashley handed back the lip gloss. "That's cool of you."

"Well, the guys are so nice. They've become like brothers to me." Standing up, she straightened her cobalt blue corseted creation. "I'm going to say hi to Roberto. I doubt he'll be able to make the rounds in this mob!" Ashley also stood up, sending dozens of charm bracelets crashing down her arms. "Me too. See you girls around."

Presley pounced on me, taking her black cat suit all too literally. "Did you hear that?"

"Hear what?"

"Shut up! You and Jax are both in London. And both single!"

"So? Like he would even remember me. Plus, I don't have his number."

"So? You go to his concert! He will totally remember you!"

I cocked my head, shooting Presley a look that said, *You're not serious.* She enthusiastically continued, "I saw the way you guys were at my house . . . worst case scenario, you check out a great concert!"

Bella joined us, champagne in hand. "Isn't this a great party?"

"Hey Bell! Your girl has something to tell you about to-morrow night!" Presley schemed. I glared at her.

"What? What is it?" Bella leaned in, waiting to be let in on the plan.

I took a deep breath and smiled as I told Bella, "We have to go to the Phoenix Rising concert."

"Wooohoo!" Presley threw her arms up and picked up two glasses of champagne, handing one to me and keeping the other for herself. She raised her glass and further explained, "Let's just say our girl here is about to make Phoenix rise!" Bella and Presley clinked their Clicquot to each others then both to mine. My cheeks blushed redder than the rosé we were toasting with.

chapter twenty-three

Phoenix Rises

As promised, just before sunrise a plane returned me and
Bella to London. Flying alongside the sun rising was a magi-
cal way to begin the day. Bella promoted the perfume at Harrods for the obligatory three hours while her publicist and I
secured VIP arrangements for the concert. The perfume debut
was madness and there was no time to discuss our photo
plans with her management team. This was fine with me
since I was still adjusting to the time change and lack of shut-
eye. The day was over in a flash and, before we knew it, it was
show time. Dressed to the nines, Bella and I hunted backstage
like a couple of groupies. A security guard led us to the green
room where we made our own cocktails before being escorted
to the side of the stage. I hardly watched where I was going as
I scanned the area for Jax. The arena was buzzing with a de-
voted crowd that quickly filled the floor and cascading bal-

cony tiers. On our way to our seats, Bella took my hand and pulled me into an empty dressing room, locking the door behind us.

"What are we doing?" I asked, anxious to find Jax. Bella unhooked her Alexander McQueen knuckle-box clutch and clicked open a small mirror, placing it on the vanity table. She unscrewed a vial and tapped out a sizeable amount of powder.

"Relax! You can't go to a concert sober, first rule of rock and roll." Dipping her long acrylic pinky nail into the pile, she sniffed the powder into her left nostril. She then refilled her nail and held it under my nose. "You could use some snow support! This is going to be major!"

I sniffed the coke from Bella's nail. We each took another bump and then checked ourselves out in the mirror. Bella's backless black Alaia halter dress revealed more than just the sides of her ribs, leaving little to even the most devious of imaginations. Her signature blonde hair loosely flowed down her bare back. She dabbed at her nose with a tissue and tucked it away in the top of her over-the-knee boots. I pulled my extra-long red curls over my shoulders, careful not to get them caught in the chain detail of the Sheri Bodell sheath dress Bella let me borrow. Earlier I had purchased a set of my very own ginger clip-in extensions. Balancing on the tips of my borrowed pumps, I leaned in for a closer look at my smoky eye makeup. I stepped back, taking a final gander. "I hardly recognize myself!"

Bella smacked my bottom and added, "You look freaking *hot*. Lover boy is going to freak out!"

"Yeah . . . if he even remembers me!" I truly didn't see this going as planned.

Bella cupped my breasts and pushed them all the way up. "Make him remember!"

I laughed, swatting Bella's hands away.

We returned to the security guard patiently waiting outside the door. He mumbled into his headset and escorted us to the side of the stage, where a small area had been roped off just for us. The auditorium went pitch black and the crowd began to roar with excitement. Wide beams of light swirled around the audience and a machine wafted fog from the stage. Drums began to pulsate, commanding attention to the stage. A large circular platform lined with vanity bulbs was lowered from the ceiling, hovering above the stage floor like a UFO. Still dark, the only thing visible were the flashing bulbs around the perimeter of the raised podium. The drums continued playing wildly for a minute or so until, quieting down to a less frenetic pace, Jax Phoenix's raspy voice echoed as he slowly sang the first line from his latest song. "Watch out . . ." The crowd went mad. "She's having deep thoughts . . ." The bright lights blasted the stage into life just as Jax grabbed the mike from the stand, jumping forward to belt out, "Agaaain!" The band wailed to the popular hit as Bella and I danced and drank, rocking out with the band. I was entranced by Jax. He was incredibly talented and impossibly good looking. His aura was mysterious and seductive yet safe and approachable. I enjoyed the fact that I could stare at him intensely and he couldn't see me standing there beyond the lights. The concert was the best I'd ever been to and this was by far the best concert seat I'd ever had. They closed the show by covering The Doors' "People Are Strange," which made me think of James. The last time that we spoke he was wearing a Doors

T-shirt, and boy did he wear it well. Why was I still thinking of James? I wondered. Just let it go. You're here now, I told myself.

Once the band finished their two-hour set and the pyrotechnics closed the encore, the massive crowd quickly filtered out through the exits. Bella and I were led back up the side of the stage. A few people waited there, hopeful for a photo with the group. Security guards pushed the fans aside and assisted us up the stairs. As we made our way back to the dressing room, my heart beat like a bongo in anticipation. I smoothed out my hair and moistened my lips just in case I saw him. Security swung open a door marked *Private* and we stepped inside. The band was pounding beer and kicking back. The musicians welcomed us inside. Paul Pardee, Mot Callahan and Jacob Story were jovial, still coming off their stage high. Like proper English gentlemen, they offered us their seats and each a beer. Several magazines, including *Rolling Stone*, *Billboard* and *Spin*, were laid out on the table. The band was featured on the cover of every one displayed. Mot sat down next to Bella, his giant boots kicked up and planted atop the magazines. Mot, the drummer, was the least proper member of the group. He was more famous for his rowdy bar antics than for his musical talents. Naturally, Bella and Mot immediately engaged in conversation.

"Where did Phoenix head off to?" Jacob, the bass guitarist, shouted out from the bar area.

"He went looking for that bloody ring . . . lost it during the second set." The lead guitarist, Paul Pardee, downed his beer. "That damn thing falls off every time. I don't see why he wears it when we perform."

Since Bella was busy, I left to explore the hallways, hoping to find Jax and catch his eye. I carefully stepped through a maze of ropes, tape and wire behind the stage.

A large security guard flashed his small flashlight, making his way over. "Hey, you can't be back here. I'm going to need to see some credentials."

"Oh, sorry. I'm lost. I'm with Isabella Blackstone. We're in the band's room. Just looking for the restroom."

"Like I haven't heard that story twenty different ways tonight."

"No, honestly. We were just back there . . . down the hall by the . . ."

"By the restrooms."

"Um . . . well, okay. Yeah, but I was just . . ."

"Lucy? Lucy from LA?" Jax effortlessly walked through the wires and put his hand on the bouncer's back. "She's cool, Dane." The beefy man left us alone. Jax teased, "Let me guess . . . you are lost?"

"Yes . . . I mean no, but . . ." I stammered for the words, attempting to conceal my blatant nervousness. "That was an amazing show, the best I've ever seen!"

"Thank you! You look . . . stunning. I love this." He touched the chains that decorated my dress. I tried to remain cool as I melted inside. The collared shirt he had on earlier was now completely unbuttoned and his skinny black tie lay casually over his neck. I mentally warned myself not to stare at his muscled chest. It had turned me into a jibberish-speaking fool last time. "Thanks."

We both leaned on the ropes and smiled into each other's

eyes like love-struck teenagers. I wondered if he was flirting with me or simply reacting to my flirting with him.

"I wondered when I was going to see you again," he said, touching my chin with the back of his hand. This was not happening! My body temperature rose as I fantasized about tearing his shirt off and kissing him passionately right there. Jax shifted gears. "I've lost my ring. It's my lucky ring and I know it's somewhere on the stage. Do you mind?" He held out his hand.

"Not at all!" I took Jax's hand and we made our way past the thick dark velvet curtains.

I stepped on stage and was swept away. "This is . . . unreal." The seats were dimly lit and seemed to go on forever. Less than an hour ago, a massive gathering was there. Now each step I took echoed in the vast, empty arena.

"Mad, isn't it?" Jax said as he scoured the floor for his ring.

"Yeah, it is." I began searching the stage, hunched over and kicking aside several water bottles in hopes of being the one to find the ring and save the day. A few guitar riffs ricochet off the concave walls. Jax walked toward me, his guitar strapped across his chest. I nervously tucked a lock of hair behind my ear and smiled. Jax stood in front of me, improvising a melody. Feeling slightly awkward, I turned my back to him, continuing to search for his ring. Unexpectedly, Jax lifted the guitar over me and put it across my torso. I was strapped between the electric Gibson and Jax as he continued to play. I instinctively put my hands on his forearms as his hands continued to create entrancing sounds. He nuzzled his face into my neck. I boldly turned my body toward him, wrapping my arms around his neck. He lowered the guitar and drew me even closer. Looking into each other's eyes, our lips barely grazed. I could feel Jax breathing. He smelled so masculine. He put his hands in my hair. Suddenly, crashing noises banged from the audience as the janitors dragged large trash bins across the pit below. Jax removed the guitar and set it on the ground. He took my hand and led me off the stage. I leaned back against an amplifier as he wrapped the velvet curtain around us and lifted me onto the amp. I sat up straight on the giant box, bringing us to the same eye level. Jax wrapped my knees around his waist. Pressing one hand on the small of my back and the other on the side of my neck, he grasped my hair in a tight grip. I ran my hands through his thick hair. He pressed his lips to mine forcefully and then kissed my chin and neck. I feverishly ran my hands under his shirt, stroking his chest and back, and pulling him closer. I lifted my legs around Jax's waist, gripping him with my knees. As we continued, I felt a sharp object jabbing my left knee. Turning my head to the side, my hand reached into his back left pocket. As Jax kissed my décolletage, I laughed out loud.

"What's so funny?" I held up an engraved platinum band with an emerald stone. We both cracked up as I slid the ring onto his finger. "What are you, a magician of some sort?"

"I prefer the term *illusionist.*" I smoothed out the front of his shirt with my hands. Jax stepped back, placing his hands on each side of me. With his help, I hopped off the amplifier. We made our way through the ropes and wires returning to the dressing room. Jax opened the door and we found Bella straddling Mot on the couch in what was basically a simulation of sex. Jax cleared his throat and I covered my mouth with my hand. Bella and Mot didn't pay us any mind.

"Dinner?" Jax suggested.

"Drinks!" Mot and Bella shouted in unison. Jax and I looked at each other and shrugged. Bella stumbled away from the couch and hooked her arm with mine. "Powder room."

Mot took a drag from his cigarette, and in his husky Irish accent, shouted, "Don't forget the powder . . ." He tossed Bella her compact of coke.

"Right! Thanks!"

What could she possibly see in that guy? I wondered. She could have any man in the world and . . . him? He was so sweaty and burly and kind of gross.

In the restroom, Bella crafted her pinky nail special. "So, tell me everything!" She sniffed, digging into the pile for another round before putting her nail in my face.

I sniffed. "Well, I really like him! We made out and it was *amazing*!"

"Nice! Are you going to fuck him? We should all go back to our suite and party. You should definitely fuck him." I looked at Bella, shocked by her crudeness.

"I was kind of hoping we could take things slower . . . like, not hook up right away. This is the second time we've met!" Bella rubbed her upper gums with her pinky then rested her hand on my shoulder.

"Take things slow? Does this look like a high school locker room to you? Lucy, he's a freaking *rock star*. Dating doesn't exist in his world. Hell, it barely exists in ours."

I wasn't entirely sure what "our" world was. I thought that I was along for the ride in her world if only for a few days. "I think he's different. Besides, I don't want to sleep with him because he's famous. I *really* like him!"

"Of course you want to sleep with him because he's famous. Get real. It's okay to screw people for sport! Who am I to judge?" I eyed my friend skeptically as she went on. "Don't get your hopes up, is all. I've been in this business a long time and I have yet to meet one man any different from another. They're all the same."

"Okay. Thanks for the heads up." I forgot to consider how jaded Bella must be when it came to men.

Taking the lead, Bella darted back down the corridor. "I'm going to fuck Mot."

I sighed. "I know."

chapter twenty-four

A New Method

"What happened last night?" Bella groaned. Both my and Bella's lifeless bodies lay sprawled out beside each other in the aisle of the private plane.

"We went back to the hotel and partied all night," I reminded her.

"I remember that, silly. I'm talking about you and Jax!"

"Oh! We totally connected. He is something else . . ." I basked in the glow of my crush. "He was so sweet, didn't even try anything cheeky. I mean, we made out, of course. But that was it."

Bella snorted. "He probably can't get it up on blow!"

"No, I'm telling you. He is different. What about Mot? How did that go?"

"How do you think it went? I could barely hike the stairs of the plane."

I covered my face with my hands. "Why did I even ask?"

"He did leave me a parting gift." Bella pulled a tiny bag full of small crystals from her bra.

"Blow?" I could hardly look at the bag without getting queasy. I had had enough.

"No . . . glass!" Bella tossed the baggie into her purse.

I sat up, my head pounding. "Glass? You mean crystal meth? Bella, you've got to get rid of that. Do you have any idea what that is?"

"I know it's way more fun than coke!"

"They make that in meth labs, aka trailer parks in towns we've never heard of. I watched this documentary once. They take household cleaners and bleach and rat poison and dump it into a bathtub or trashcan. Then, when it evaporates, they scrape the residue into tiny baggies." Bella hardly reacted. "It rots your teeth and makes your hair fall out. Promise me you won't get in to that! Is that what Mot is in to?" I was very upset and not prepared to be introduced to any more drugs. Bella pulled my arm out from under me, forcing me to lie back down.

"Relax, Mother Teresa. I'm not an idiot."

We slept the whole way home. I returned to my apartment happy to fall asleep in my own bed. The next day, I called Presley to fill her in on the rest of my trip. She didn't answer her phone but text messaged an hour later: Hey, sexy. See you at Sasha's house tonight—5647 Doheny.

At only nineteen years old, for the past year, Sasha Hart had been the guilty pleasure of pop culture. Preteens idolized her and parents gladly added to the billions spent on her bubblegum movies and endorsed products. Sasha's home was located in Beverly Hills. More than a dozen luxury cars were crammed into the driveway and along the street. I contemplated whether I should knock or just enter, when out came half of this morning's *Page Six* mentions. The door was held open for me and I thanked them. The interior of the house did not reflect the lifestyle of a young Hollywood starlet. Plastic plants and ceramic ducks decorated the dimly lit living room. Two young dudes on a plaid couch were smoking from a bong. "Is Presley here?" I asked, assuming they knew that I was speaking of the one-and-only Presley Dalton. They pointed down the hall. I warily put my ear to a closed door, where I heard several voices. I knocked delicately.

"Who is it?" I recognized Sasha's raspy voice. She herself opened the door slightly.

"Hi. I'm meeting Presley here."

"She's my girl! Let her in!" Presley shouted from behind the door. Sasha opened the door to let me into her bedroom. It looked like mine did . . . when I was eleven. Presley was reclined on a floral Laura Ashley bedspread, sitting alongside pop singer Marisa Daniels, also a teen idol. *All of the Disney Channel is here*, I thought. Sasha hopped up on the bed. I sat myself on a corner. The bed was covered with tabloids, good, bad and ugly. "Where's Bella?" Presley asked.

"I'm not sure . . . Home, I think. Should I text her?"

"Yeah!" they all replied as if it was the obvious thing to do. I hadn't thought to call Bella given that Presley and her friends were about twenty years her junior. It was borderline inappropriate for *me* to be hanging out with teenagers.

Presley held out an assortment of lollipops. I popped a purple one into my mouth. My text message to Bella read: Come to Sasha Hart's house! 5647 Doheny. I assumed she would decline, thinking she'd be spending time with the twins after being away. Almost immediately, Bella responded: Be over ASAP! XOX BB

"Bella's on her way," I alerted the girls.

"Sweet. Love her," Marisa piped in. I wondered what Bella could possibly have in common with these teens other than fame.

The scene took me back to a high school memory: Just hanging with the girls at one of their parents' houses, gossiping about boys and procrastinating on homework. Although instead of textbooks, these girls were studying the tabloids intently. Marisa held up an *Us Weekly* to Sasha. "Loving this Temperley top you wore to Urth Caffe."

Sasha flipped through *In Touch Weekly*. "I'll trade you for the Ted Rossi clutch you wore to the VMAs!"

"Eeew . . ." Presley put down *OK! Magazine*. "I was so not seen canoodling with that douche! Ick!" She flipped to the next page, taking the sucker out of her mouth. "Oh my God, Lucy! It's *you!*" The girls leaned in. A photo of me with Bella, Jax and Mot exiting the hotel covered an entire page. Mot and I had been cropped in half, making it look like Jax and Bella were together. The headline read, "Isabella and Jax: Their Steamy Night at the Sanderson and Jessica's Desperate Plan to Win Him Back." My jaw dropped and I covered my face with my hands, peeking between my fingers.

Presley said in a knowing tone, "It was your steamy night, right?" I nodded and grinned from ear to ear. "I knew it!"

"What is this, Marisa?" Sasha held up an article showing a candid shot of Marisa dining with Jacob Reese, Sasha's recent ex-boyfriend.

"Please, it's the *Enquirer*," Marisa defended herself.

"It's a picture. You can't fake pictures!" Sasha said, skimming the accompanying article.

"I just stopped by his table to say hi. It was no big deal." Marisa hid her face behind another magazine.

"It says you left together," Sasha blurted, continuing to read.

"Oh, please, Sasha. We've been friends for how long?" Marisa said from behind the paper.

Presley held up another magazine, not making a comment. There was a double-page photo of Marisa sitting in the passenger seat of Jacob's car, trying to shield her face from the photographers with a scarf as Jacob held the collar of his jacket up in the same fashion. Both failed in their attempt to avoid the intrusive cameras. Sasha gasped.

Presley and I looked at each other. Trying to break the tension in the room, I held up a pictorial labeled "Say Cheese." It displayed various celebrities, highlighting their fat thighs, underarms and cellulite. "At least none of you are in this one!" Although they smiled, the tension remained. I decidedly pitied the girls. On second thought, this was nothing like my childhood. I couldn't imagine what it would feel like being famous, having the world watch my every move. It must be awful to have your physical and emotional scars pointed out for all the world to see, especially as an insecure teen. I thought back to my school days when the yearbooks would come out and everyone devoured the book, scanning for pictures and quotes of themselves. Biggest Flirt. Class Clown. Best Dressed. Imagine those books being released weekly, except the labels were Biggest Floosy, Stumbling Idiot, Worst Dressed. I couldn't handle that kind of pressure.

The door flew open and Bella pounced onto the bed. "Girls! Having a party without me?" She flailed her arms and legs to push the tabloids off the bed in disgust. "What is this crap? Trust me, do not read this poison!"

The girls hugged Bella and greeted her with adoring eyes. Bella reveled in their adoration and it was made clear why she would spend time with them. They idolized her.

"What's new with you?" Sasha asked Bella. "I hear you just got in from good times in London."

"Lucy and I both! What are you guys doing in here? You know, there are like fifty people in your house, right?"

"Yeah, it's cool. We were just hanging out. Do you have anything? We were going to make a call."

Bella opened her clutch, removing two small plastic bags. "Sure do!"

"Great!" Presley beamed.

Marisa put an issue of *Dazzle* in the center of the bed. The cover was a close beauty shot of Brooke Sands, Marisa's reported archenemy. Bella dumped two piles of powder onto Brooke's face. Sasha took a black American Express from her pocket and cut the two piles into lines.

The zigzags of drugs over Brooke's smiley mug was so wrong for so many reasons, and metaphorically said a thousand words about the drama, the distaste and the way things were. I couldn't help but take the camera out of my bag. This sent the girls into an absolute frenzy. "What are you doing with that?" Marisa shrieked as they all squirmed as if I took out a cobra snake.

"Oh, no—I wanted to shoot the magazine cover . . . Not

any of you! I just thought . . . with the lines . . . on Brooke's . . ." Shit. What was I thinking?

Bella intervened. "It's cool girls! She's a photographer and she likes to document stuff. She won't put us in any of the shots!"

They all sighed in relief and let me take the twisted photo. I made a point to let them know I had put the camera away afterward.

Lacy referenced the powder and asked, "Why are these different colors?"

Bella explained. "That's because this one is the usual but this is something special I got from a friend. It's *waaay* better. Try it!"

"No!" I cried out. "It's not what you think. It's glass . . . Crystal."

"I've never tried it . . . I've always wondered what it was like." Marisa shrugged.

"Oh, I have. It's great. I didn't eat or sleep for three days!" Sasha said, going in for the kill.

Bella threw her hands up, looking at me apologetically. I shook my head, watching Marisa take a second line. Marisa's eyes immediately watered as she cupped her hands to her nose. "Fuck! That stings!"

"You get used to it after a few," Sasha assured her. Presley did a line, handing a rolled-up bill to me.

"No, thanks. Not tonight." I said it and I meant it.

"Seriously?" Bella questioned. I nodded, watching the others in dismay.

Witnessing the girls ingest glorified Ajax reminded me of

the times in high school when the populars were barfing up Budweiser as I drove them home. Neither group looked so cool to me at either point. It turned me off from wanting to have anything to do with what they were doing.

The door burst open and Diane Hart, Sasha's mother, entered the room in a silky robe with a sleeping mask on top of her head.

"Hey, Mom," greeted Sasha. I panicked. Surely nineteen-year-old Sasha would be in hot water for the crack buffet sitting in the middle of her childhood bed.

"Honey, will you make sure that everyone's gone by four? I have that thing in the morning." Diane kissed her daughter on the head before sticking a finger into the pile and rubbing it on her gums. On her way out, she added, "Oh, Sash, someone threw up by your door!"

Jumping to the scene, Sasha confirmed that someone indeed had puked on the floor. She dashed out of view and returned to report, "We're out of paper towels! Gross!"

"Here . . ." Marisa held up an obnoxious Christian Audigier T-shirt retrieved from the floor.

"Yeah, use that. *So* a hundred years ago," Bella agreed.

Sasha opened a dresser drawer, removing three shirts of the same brand. She proceeded to mop up the pungent vomit. "I knew I kept these around for a reason."

My cell phone buzzed. I flipped it open and smiled. Wish you were here . . . JP

Bella grabbed the phone, read the message and rolled her eyes. She handed the phone back to me.

"Oh, please. He's only saying that because you haven't fucked him yet."

"You haven't fucked him yet?" Presley said in shock.

"You guys . . . stop. Bella, who's to say that he doesn't like me too?"

Presley folded her hands under her chin. "Maybe he's crushing on her!"

Bella leaned down and did a line. She made a painful expression that the girls mimicked, feeling her pain. "Whatever. It's been my experience that men are all the same. But you girls are still young. Guess you'll have to find out on your own."

Presley held her nose. "It smells like fucking puke in here."

Handing her a rolled-up bill, Bella agreed. "Yeah, let's get out of here. Your place?"

Presley nodded, going in for one last line. I felt relieved the attention had shifted away from me and offered to drive. I carefully coasted Presley's sports car through the winding canyon. Bella dipped her nail into a baggie and did a bump. "This one has a chemical taste." Presley, in the backseat, did a bump and agreed. She climbed forward onto the console and pressed the button that opened the sunroof. She then put her knee on the console and stuck half her body out of the sunroof. She reached down and opened the little baggie.

"What are you doing, Pres?" I said in a slight panic. I steered the car with one hand, holding tightly to Presley's knee with my other.

Bella, looking up at our lunatic friend, asked, "What the hell, Presley?"

Presley raised her arms, exposing the open bag to the warm breeze. "It's snowing in LA! Woooohoooo! Yeaaah, baby!" Bella and I glanced into the sideview mirrors to see white powder flutter into the streets. We looked at each other with wide eyes and open mouths. Together we pulled Presley back into the car and she plopped down into the backseat, laughing hysterically.

"You are one crazy bitch!" Bella shouted. At last, we came to a stop in Presley's driveway.

Bella held her pinky in my face. I'd had enough with the pressure. "I'm just not into it tonight. A little burnt out, to be honest."

"Lucy, what is with you? You haven't been yourself since . . . him."

"Oh, come on! In forty-eight hours? You know that's not true," I teased her. She flipped her lip at me like a little girl. Presley tickled me behind my neck and they both poked and prodded me until I laughed. I was starting to feel like an outsider again and here they were inviting me in. Not wanting to be on the other side of the fence, I succumbed to the peer pressure yet again. I took a bump from Bella's nail. Instantly, my shoulder muscles wildly contracted and my eyes went into a spasm. The worst burning sensation I could have imagined spread across my face, causing tears to pour from my scorching eyes. "*Bella!* What the *fuck!*"

"Ooops, sorry! Wrong baggie—my bad!" Bella barely reacted.

She and Presley exited the car and headed to the house. I was in complete disbelief. I didn't want to believe my friend would purposely trick me like that. It must have been an accident. It had to be an accident. As I stepped out, I wiped away the burning tears with the back of my hand and followed them inside.

chapter twenty-five

Fish out of Sparkling Water

The thought of leaving LA for the weekend made me nervous. So did flying commercial. I'd grown accustomed to the lifestyles of my celebrity friends. It had been well over a year since I'd been home, and I was looking forward to being in a safe, mellow environment. But at the same time, I wasn't sure how things would go with my parents. There had been a strange disconnect between us ever since they visited. I knew that they thought my job with Bella was a joke and I was certain that they would eventually question my future plans. As the plane taxied to the gate, I zipped back into a pair of suede Marc Jacobs boots and adjusted my dress. I stared out the window at the hazy mist. The luscious green foliage against the ice gray sky reminded me why Seattle was called the Emerald City. In baggage claim, I immediately spotted my parents. My mother's eyes were tearful as she clapped and waved. My father grinned, holding out his arms. Maybe this wouldn't be so bad. I dropped my borrowed Balenciaga bag and hugged them both.

Touching my sleeve, my mom remarked, "That's quite an outfit, Luce!"

"Bella lets me borrow her stuff. She's like a big sister with really great clothes!"

My dad patted me on top of the head the same way he had when I was a little kid. "Your hair has gotten so long. Is that a sweater or a dress?" He pointed at my short hemline.

"Oh, Dad, these are extensions!" I explained. "And it's Burberry! Well, it's a tunic—which is somewhere in between a dress and a . . . oh, I don't know." What did it matter? "I'm so happy to be home!" I embraced them both in one hug. Over my parents' shoulders, I saw Julie and her mother exiting the airport, hand in hand. If she was on my plane, I hadn't seen her. I hadn't thought about Julie in a while, nor had we spoken since the "cheesecake incident."

"I checked a bag," I said, walking in the opposite direction.

My dad teased, "For a three-day trip? Luce, after your recent travels, you still haven't learned to pack light?" He poked and tickled at my sides as usual.

"Yeah, Dad. Some things never change!" After a long drive out of the city, we arrived at home. I took my belongings to my childhood bedroom, which was now the guest room. Sitting on the edge of my old bed, I looked around. My colorful comforter had been replaced with a higher thread count solid wine-colored one. The butterflies that I had painted across the ceiling had been covered up. It really wasn't my room anymore. Although it was only two o'clock in the afternoon, the gray skies made it feel near evening. I checked my cell phone and found zero missed calls or messages. Restless, I ventured downstairs to see what my mother was up to in the kitchen. She was chopping vegetables at the granite island. There were enormous mounds of raw onions, carrots, leeks and potatoes piled high on the counter.

"Hey, Mom . . . Whatcha up to?"

"Just getting ready for Thanksgiving a day early, same as every year."

"Which troops did you invite to dinner?" I snuck a couple of carrot slices from the pile.

"Very funny. The Drixons, the Reimers and the McKennas are all coming over. I'd appreciate it if you were on your best behavior."

"Thanks. I'll try not to play with my food."

"Very funny. Refill my water?" She gestured in the direction of her glass.

"Sure." I placed the glass under the dispenser on the fridge. "What the hell is this?" The refrigerator was covered in tabloid pictures of Bella, Presley, Jax and Kelly Osbourne.

"They're pictures of you." Mom walked over, pointing to each photo with her cutting knife. "These are from London, I found them in OK! Magazine . . . This is from the World Music Awards, downloaded from online . . . and these are of you shopping in LA . . . I think." The images were cropped to show the celebrities, with only a glimpse of my eyebrow or elbow in each photo.

"Mom, these aren't pictures of me. You can hardly see me in any of these. And this one isn't even me!"

"Sure it is."

"Uh, no. I've never met Kelly Osbourne in my life!"

"Oh." She removed the photo from the fridge, tossing it into the trash. "Well, since you don't send pictures and hardly ever call, this is all I have to work with." She continued chopping vegetables.

"Mom, stop. You know how much I work . . ."

She didn't say anything, but from the corner of my eye I caught her raise an eyebrow and slightly smile. I knew her well enough to know that she was holding back from making a sarcastic quip about what I consider "work." Rather than let it go there, I held back as well. "What can I do to help?" I stole another handful of carrot slices.

"Actually, would you mind going to the pumpkin patch to get a few miniatures for the table?"

"Sure." I figured, anything to avoid the pink elephant in the room that represents my life and where it's going. Luckily, that conversation had yet to surface.

I drove my parents' minivan to the pumpkin patch about ten minutes away. The muddy sky was getting darker, almost guaranteeing a storm. Stepping into the chilly air, I wrapped my arms around myself to keep warm. The patch was dotted with plump orange pumpkins and stacks of hay. A large tin shed stood between the parking lot and a growing area as big as a football field. A cashier attended to several customers. As I strolled the dirt, a thunderous pounding sounded from above and the drizzle became a downpour. I took my time selecting an assortment of pumpkins and other squash, thinking they'd make a great centerpiece.

"Lucy?"

"Katelin? Wow, it's been forever!" Katelin Day and I had

been neighbors since elementary school. I noted that she was wearing our high school track team sweatshirt and the snap-away Adidas pants everyone was obsessed with back then. *Nice outfit,* I sarcastically told myself. Followed by a remorse-ful, *ugh I'm such a jerk!* We gave each other a hug.

"Let me take that from you," said Katelin, removing the basket of squash from my arm.

"You work here?" I asked, trying to sound impressed.

"Just helping out during the high season, not year round or anything."

I nodded my head approvingly, thinking to myself how working there must really suck.

Katelin asked, "Are you ready to check out?"

"I am. Thanks!"

"A lot of people from our class are meeting for drinks to-night. You should come! I could pick you up!"

"Oh, yeah? When? It would be really cool to see everyone."

"Earl's Pub at eight."

"Eight? Why so early?" I snorted. "Everyone still goes to Earl's Pub every week?"

"Is that early?" Katelin wondered aloud.

"Oh, I guess it isn't really. I'd love to go!"

"Sweet. Okay, Miss Butler, that will be eleven dollars." I handed over my debit card.

"Sorry. We only take cash." I felt like an idiot. Of course they only take cash! Their register is a shoebox, for crying out loud! "Don't worry about it! Pay me back tonight!"

"Really? Thank you so much, Katelin. I'm glad we ran into each other! See you later!" Taking the bag from my old friend and running in the rain back to my parents' van, I looked down at my muddied suede boots. "Fuuuuuuck!" I screamed, then took my head out of my ass long enough to realize I had offended the family piling into the minivan parked next to me. "Sorry, I'm so sorry." Turning the heat on full blast, I steered out of the pebbled lot.

Later that evening, Katelin and I pulled up to the pub. I am not even going to try to put up a front. I wanted to impress them all. I, Lucy Butler, had changed big time, and for the better, in my opinion. I was no longer a wallflower in LA and I wouldn't be back at home, either. Katelin had confirmed earlier that several of the populars would be there and I wanted them to know and see for themselves that I was way cooler than they had ever dreamed of being themselves. I wore an olive cashmere sweater paired with sleek black leggings and Dior ankle boots adorned with chains and studs. As Hollywood standards go, my outfit was casual. But as far as this town's standards, well, let's just say I knew there wouldn't be a "who wore it best" competition at the end of the night.

"Lucy Butler! Get your butt over here!" I skipped over to a crowded area, feeling back at home in my old stomping ground. Most people were casually dressed in hooded sweatshirts or plain thermal tops and jeans. Several others wore skirt suits or blazers, presumably because they were coming straight from work. I shouted to the bartender, "Hey, Trevor! Can I get a round of tequila shots for everyone?" Putting my bank card down, I sat on a stool with my back to the bar.

"How is Hollywood? We've heard tons of rumors!" beamed Erin.

"Yeah! Do you really live with Isabella Blackstone?" shouted Tiffany.

"Are you friends with Presley Dalton and Sasha Hart?" Erin inquired.

A bill for thirty-six dollars was delivered to me. I was amazed at how inexpensive the drinks were. "I don't think this is right. For twelve shots?"

"Yup. That's right, thirty-six dollars," Trevor confirmed.

"In LA, this would be at least a hundred dollars! Awesome!" I signed the tab, calling out, "Can you keep my tab open and get us another round?"

Three girls in smart suits and sexy heels entered the bar. This time, I called out to them. "Natalia . . . Jenny . . . and Katie?"

"Lucy! Hi!" They welcomed me with hugs.

"Hey, Miss Hollywood! What a surprise! Oh my God—you have to tell us everything!" Natalia said, jumping up and down. "Julie only skimmed the surface!"

"Julie? Is she coming tonight?" I hadn't even considered the possibility! But why wouldn't she come? She had always been the queen bee of the cool girls.

"No, I wish! She said that she had other plans. So . . . spill your beans! What is Isabella Blackstone like?" The girls directed their undivided attention to me for the first time . . . ever!

"Let's see . . . what juicy bits can I tell you? Bella Blackstone is a total blast! And Presley Dalton too. They're pretty much my best friends." The girls nodded in fascination. "Sasha Hart and Marisa Daniels, total cokeheads." The girls stood awestruck and listened in fascination. I knew that I was gossiping and talking absolute nonsense, but it felt so good to be the cool girl that had everyone's attention. I continued with the bullshit. "Oh, and I'm sort of dating Jax Phoenix, but . . . that's a whole other story." A collective gasp came from not only the trio that I was speaking to, but several others behind me. I was on top of the world! Or . . . on top of Redmond, Washington, rather. "But enough about me! You are all so dressed up! Where are you coming from?"

Natalia removed a silk scarf from her neck and tied it to her Chanel bag. "Jennifer and I are working at Microsoft! Pretty par for the course around here, right? But we love it! Our boss is the absolute best and the company treats us like a big family, so it's been great!"

Katie hopped up on the bar stool next to me. "I'm still in med school but had an interview today for the surgical residency program, so I'm crossing my fingers! Trevor, I definitely need my usual tonight!"

I was genuinely impressed and, even more so, intimidated. They were exactly who my parents had wished I would become. "Wow—congratulations, that is great . . ."

"Please, all congrats go to our future lawyer over here!" Katie reached over me and pinched Katelin's arm. Katelin smiled coyly and thanked Katie.

"Lawyer? What were you doing at the patch earlier?" I was so confused.

"My brother bought the farm last year, and with the baby and everything, they needed some extra hands over the holiday . . ."

"Your brother had a baby?" How did I not know any of this was going on back home?

Natalia nearly choked up her martini. "You'll never believe with who!"

"Who?!"

"Abby Coleman!"

"No! Freaking! Way!" So apparently, the only girl geekier than I was in high school married the hottest jock turned pro-baseball player for the Seattle Mariners. The girls that I was hoping to impress were doing seriously well for themselves. I can't believe I thought that I'd outshine them by gossiping about who I was hanging out with. What if I had stayed in Seattle and went to a regular college and got a regular job? Would I be happier? Would I have remained a wallflower? I did the right thing, following my dreams—right? But those dreams turned out to be a nightmare, so . . . what was I going to do now? I didn't expect to be the one asking these questions this weekend. I was overwhelming myself. What was a girl to do?

Drink. A lot.

Three shots and three vodka tonics later, my mind and body succumbed to the effects of the liquor. I craved a line of blow. It was all I could think about but I didn't dare mention it to this crowd.

"So, what's the best part about living the dream out there?" Natalia asked. I swung my fancy boots up on an empty stool across from me. As a result of the alcohol consumption, the part of my brain that filtered what I thought and kept it from spewing out of my mouth failed me miserably.

"It's not boring . . . or raining . . . and it's never the same shit, different day . . . not a mundane day-to-day sort of life." The girls gave each other side eyes.

"I'm not bored," quipped Tiffany.

"Please! Nothing ever changes! Look . . ." I pointed to the ample bouncer at the front door. "Same guy since high school."

"That's my cousin," Erin pointed out.

"Of *course* he is! Fuck, don't you guys ever wonder what else is out there? I mean, really . . ." Swinging my legs down, I stood up, bumping into an innocent bystander. His pitcher of Bud Light splashed side to side, dousing my sweater, running down my leg and into my boot.

"Damn it! What the hell!" I wrung out my sweater, grunting in frustration.

"Lucy, relax. It was an accident," he said.

"Do I know you?" I said, without as much as glancing up.

"We were lab partners for two years, bitch."

"This is a Lucien sweater! It was, like, two thousand dollars! And it was a gift. Wait, did he just call me a bitch?" I looked up at the girls, unaware that I was causing a scene. "I mean, I would relax if I was wearing fucking . . . Crocs. I could hose them off in the toilet or something." I was too far gone to see that nobody else was talking, yet I kept rambling. My head spun uncontrollably. About to lose my balance, I started to fall but caught myself in time. As I rested my arms on the seat of a bar stool, I looked down at the floor. Out of the corner of my eye, I confirmed that Erin was wearing . . . bright . . . pink . . . Crocs. "Oh shit," I said out loud.

Katelin stepped forward and discreetly told me, "I think I should take you home."

"That would be nice. Too bad it's like a thirty-hour drive."

chapter twenty-six

Thanks for Giving. Now Leave.

I hid under the covers of my parents' guest room bed. I was mortified at the way I had behaved the night before. What had gotten into me? When did I become such a . . . bitch? Seeing what my life could have been sent me into a tailspin. There was a knock at my door. "Hey, Lucy . . . It's Katelin. Your mom let me up. Can I come in?"

"Sure!" I sat up. Katelin entered the room holding my Dior boots. "You left these in my car. I wasn't sure when you were leaving . . . so . . ." She put the boots down on the floor and solemnly started out the bedroom door.

"Katelin, I'm so sorry. I don't know what came over me. It's so cliché to blame everything on the alcohol but . . . I was really drunk."

"It's okay. I would imagine living your lifestyle would change anyone."

"No, I haven't changed. I'm still the same person. I'm just . . . different, I guess."

"Different—changed—same thing. Don't worry about it. Everyone will get over it."

"But I won't. I really messed up."

Katelin forced a grin. "I have to help my mom with Thanksgiving stuff. It was good seeing you. Best of luck, Lucy."

"Bye, Katelin."

I pulled the covers back over my head and cried. The way that she said "best of luck" cemented the fact that she hoped to never see me again. Who could blame her? Even I couldn't understand why I acted the way I did. I didn't feel above anyone, but I did feel different. Major damage had been done and there was little I could do about it.

"Luce!" my mother shrieked from downstairs. "Come here, quick!" I made my way downstairs. My hangover headache flared. The house smelled like a delicious roasting turkey. My father was mashing potatoes as my mother watched *Access Hollywood* in the connected den.

"What is it?" I asked, sitting down next to my mom.

"Isabella . . . Something about her newest love interest or something . . ."

"No, Bella isn't dating anyone. It's a false report." I had just gotten up when my mother pointed at the television. Pictures of Bella and Mot Callahan flashed across the screen. Photos showed them frolicking in the ocean and kissing. The reporter narrated the montage. "Hurricanes Isabella Blackstone and Mot Callahan of Phoenix Rising hit the Caribbean Islands this weekend. The two lovebirds were seen out at all hours, taking ocean dips as late—or as early—as 4:00 a.m." I was mortified that my mother was watching this.

The report ended with a photo of the two getting hot and heavy in an outdoor bar, Mot's hand grabbing Bella's breast. The reporter concluded, "Well, it might not be a typical Thanksgiving, but it looks like Mot Callahan has a lot to be thankful for."

"That is so tacky. Bill, don't you think that's so tacky?" my mother shrieked.

"It really is. That woman has problems," my dad agreed.

I got up and poured myself a cup of coffee. Why did they have to see that? Mom followed me into the kitchen. "Doesn't she have kids? Where are they?"

"I don't know, probably with their father. I'm not sure."

"She isn't a teenager. The way she runs around with those loser guys is just . . . sad."

"Mom, I don't want to talk about Bella." Actually, I wanted to talk *to* Bella.

My dad kept pressing. "What exactly are you doing for her anyway?"

Just to get them off my back, I exaggerated. "We have a few photo projects coming up when I get back."

My father continued, "We just wish you would have stuck it out with Stefano. That made much more sense."

"Good sense that we paid for," my mother added. I ignored my mother's comment in regard to my degree, which was now worthless in their eyes.

"Dad, I can't begin to explain how horrible that job was. It would really upset you both to know even half of it."

My mother kept on. "Your entire life, you are going to work with people you don't like. You need to learn how to take the good with the bad." There they went again. I wished I had the guts to tell my parents that "taking the bad" meant being verbally and physically abused, never having time to eat or sleep, and above all doing heaps of drugs twenty-four/seven.

"Well, that was then and this is now. Bella is really invested in helping me get started as a photographer. She's my best friend out there and has my best interests at heart."

"I thought Julie was your best friend," my mom said.

"That, I definitely don't want to talk about." I knew that was coming.

"Why would a thirty-eight-year-old woman want to be best friends with a twenty-three-year-old girl?"

"Mom, just . . . lay off me, okay? I don't expect you to understand what I've been going through. I can't make any smart decisions with you nitpicking at me all the time. It's like I can't even breathe!"

"We are just concerned about your future!"

"Well, so am I! Imagine what it's like to be me!" I stormed up the stairs. The whole scene reminded me of the conflicts I had had with my parents when I was an adolescent.

"Thanks for offering to help, Lucy! Don't worry . . . we've got it all under control!" Mom yelled after me. I slammed the bedroom door and flung myself down on the bed. I heard my father ask, "Why is she so angry?"

I tried Bella's phone several times. There was no answer. I just wanted to go home. But where was that, really?

chapter twenty-seven

Not All It's Cracked Up to Be

As far as reconnecting with friends and family was concerned, Thanksgiving had been anything but successful. My parents and I set our different opinions aside, putting on a happy front for their guests. All through dinner, they bragged about their daughter's fabulous position as a personal photographer for the unbelievable Isabella Blackstone. My mother even showed several guests tabloid pictures of us together. I smiled, playing along, exuding a "life is peachy" image for the sake of my parents' reputation. After Thanksgiving, I was excited to return to LA so I could really roll up my sleeves on this photography business and show them all.

The first time I saw Bella was when we attended the Kick It charity event in Beverly Hills. I waited patiently at the end of the red carpet while she spoke to the media, posing for the cameras as giant spotlights swayed in the sky.

"Isabella! Isabella!" the media shouted for her attention. A few photographers, attempting to get Bella's reaction on camera, made pointed comments about her recent rendez-vous with Mot. Bella expertly ignored them as she slowly made her way down the red carpet. Then I heard them scream-ing "Denise, Denise!" as Denise Richards followed in Bella's footsteps. The same ruthless media taunted Denise with in-sensitive questions regarding her ex-husband's recent antics. She smiled through it like a pro. Bella and I walked onto the swank rooftop of the SLS Hotel, which had been decorated to look like a dance club circa 1980. Cocktail waitresses and bus-boys were outfitted to look like vintage renditions of Cyndi Lauper and Corey Feldman. The music of Duran Duran was blasting from speakers that had been fashioned to look like giant boom boxes. A look-alike Breakfast Club member pre-sented a tray of colorful cocktails. He asked, "Martini, ladies?"

"Sure!" we replied.

We took our drinks for a walk along an impressive wall of avant-garde-style photographs of shoes. One looked like a mountain range in the Mohave desert but in fact it was a macro shot of the bottom of a pair of dirty sneakers. Another, an image of crystal-encrusted Louboutins hanging across a tele-phone wire in the ghetto.

A plump woman with a jet black bob and leather pants cut us off as we moved from one framed photo to the next and offered a hand to Bella. "Hi! Thank you so much for coming! I'm Zee Zee Black. I own the Black Horn Gallery where all of these amazing photographs come from!"

Bella half shook Zee Zee's hand, then introduced us. "Well,

you should meet Lucy Butler. She's an incredible photographer."

I offered Zee Zee my hand, congenially seeking information. "Nice to meet you. So tell us about this charity event—it's called Kick It?"

"Yes . . . We are bringing awareness to a nonprofit called Soles for Souls. They deliver donated shoes to third-world countries."

"That's great! So, are you raising money tonight or . . . ?" I looked around, mentally calculating the cost of the liquor, elaborate sets and hired help.

"Oh no. Tonight we are raising awareness," she politely informed.

"Raising awareness by . . ." I thought back to the press carpet. Nobody had pressed Bella about her vast knowledge of the Soles for Souls Foundation. Instead, they had only hounded her for gossip.

"Kicking it!" Zee Zee half turned, plucking a cocktail from a neighboring waiter's tray. "Have a great time, ladies!"

I turned to Bella. "They've got to be kidding."

Two muscled arms embraced Bella from behind. She turned to see Danny Danson, heir to his grandfather's oil fortune. "I got a room. We are getting the fuck out of this freak show. Room 3936, if you're down." He disappeared as fast as he had appeared, followed by five or six other unaware rich kids.

"I don't even know that guy. Let's go find a real party. This is lame," Bella said.

On our way out of the lobby, I spotted Presley waiting for

the elevator. "Pres!" The elevators opened and Presley stepped in, holding the door open.

"What are you chicks doing? Come to a party with us!" "Us" referred to Sasha Hart and Marisa Daniels. Naturally, Bella and I were in.

We stood in front of room 3936 and waited. Danny Danson threw open the door. He was wearing a robe and slippers. "I knew you'd come up! Come on in, bitches!" He kissed Presley, Sasha, Marisa and Bella, ignoring me—presumably because I wasn't famous and therefore did not matter. Walking into the master suite, he made room for the celebrities by asking other nonfamous guests to make room for the guests that "mattered." "Check this out." Danny took a remote from the pocket of his robe and, with the touch of a few buttons, closed the drapes and dimmed the lights. "Bitches, want to smoke or what?"

"Of course! DD, you always have the best shit," Presley purred.

Marisa got up from the bed. "No, thanks, I'm not into it tonight . . ." She walked out and closed the door behind her, leaving the room in total darkness.

I hadn't smoked weed since high school. It just made me lazy and stupid and I didn't see the point. "I'm not into it tonight either . . ."

"You won't smoke? You do everything else," Presley pointed out.

"Come on, not everything . . . I'm going to sit this one out."

Bella snorted, which I interpreted as a scoff at me. I didn't understand why she got so upset when I didn't participate. The room lit up with the glow from a lighter as Danny took a hit from a pipe. He passed it to Sasha, who took an equally large hit. She passed it to Bella, then Bella to Presley, who skipped me and handed it off to Danny. As Danny took another hit, Presley put an arm around me and said, "Are you sure? Not even just this once? It's amazing. How I feel right now . . . trust me, you want to feel like this." I could feel the smoke from her mouth waver around my face.

"Thanks, but I'm trying to chill on the partying."

Bella crawled through the group and sat on my other side. "Luce, it's not that big a deal.. Try it. You'll like it!" It was like the cartoon where there was an angel and a devil on each shoulder, except both of mine were carrying pitchforks.

"You guys . . . I've smoked weed before, I'm just not into it. But I have to say . . . your weed . . . it smells funny. Like . . . eggs." Everyone howled in laughter. Danny clapped his hands and Presley fell over sideways, the pipe in her hand. "What? What's so funny?"

Covering her face with a pillow, Bella spoke into it. "It's not weed!" They continued laughing as I felt progressively left out of the inner circle.

"Well, what is it then?"

"Crack!" Presley and Sasha cried out in unison.

I could barely think straight and I was sober. I had never in my wildest thoughts imagined myself in the same room as crack. I knew I should get out of there immediately, but I couldn't leave Bella, especially in this state. Holy shit. Crack. Bella was smoking crack. The teen idols were smoking crack. I didn't know what to expect. Would they all trip out and go crazy? Was it dangerous for me to stay there? I'd have to wait it out. I just couldn't leave her there.

An hour later, the group lay scattered about, their dilated pupils all transfixed by a candle in the center of the room. I sat erect in absolute shock. These people were admired and celebrated for their decadent lives and impeccable style, yet here they were acting like common street junkies.

Presley mumbled, "What's going on with you and Jax?" I was surprised Presley could even speak.

"We're spending New Year's Eve in Vegas. You coming?"

"Can't. I'm hosting a party in Malibu."

Bella moaned. "Cancel?"

"They already paid me two hundred grand. I'll get sued."

"Bummer." Bella reached up to her nose to scratch an itch but her motor skills failed. Instead her hand flopped across her face. "Lucy, you didn't tell me Jax was coming with us."

I had been dreading telling Bella that my New Year's plans included Jax. "He's just meeting us there."

"Is Mot coming?"

"Maybe." I had asked Jax but he'd reacted oddly, so I decided not to push it.

Sasha only managed to get a few words out. "Lucy . . . Jax . . . New Year's . . . kiss."

Bella squashed the fantasy. "Yeah, if he even shows up."

Presley wiped at a drip of drool coming from the corner of her mouth before putting a hand on Bella's ankle, teasing, "So bitter . . ." The wasted girls lay wilted around the room like worthless carrion, while I wondered what I was doing there in the first place.

chapter twenty-eight

...4...3...2...1...Zero.

"That thing makes me nervous." I couldn't step anywhere near the glass-encased pool that extended from our high-rise at the Palms Hotel. It dropped off the edge into space, dangling over all of Las Vegas.

Bella smiled wickedly. "Really?" She swam to the very edge just to taunt me.

"Does this make you nervous?" Bella jumped and splashed as I begged her to stop.

There was a knock at the door. "Hopefully, this is the Nevada psych ward coming to take you away!" I opened the door. An enormous bouquet of white roses blocked my view. James—here? Could it be? How would he know where to find me?

A British accent announced, "Special delivery for a special girl!"

Shoving the flowers aside, I threw myself at Jax. "You're here!"

He carried me like a new bride into the suite toward the pool. "Of course I'm here. I said I would be!" He set me down and we held hands. "Happy New Year, Bella. Looking beautiful as always." Bella swam up to us, standing on the steps. She tugged at the minuscule bikini and wrung her hair out over her breasts. If it had been any less desperate looking, I might have been jealous. "Hi, Jax. Is Mot coming in? Or . . . ?" She excitedly glanced into the foyer.

Jax grinned, clenching his teeth together. "Yeah, Mot's not going to make it. After his wife got wind of those Caribbean pictures, she put his ass under lock and key."

Bella and I glared at Jax. *"Wife?"* we both questioned in disbelief.

Jax nodded his head. "You didn't know?" He turned to me. "Well, no worries, darling. I definitely am not married." Taking my face into his hands, he planted a kiss on my lips. "Although it is Vegas . . . and you never know, do you?" He winked at Bella. "I'm off to hit the tables with the guys. I'll meet up with you ladies tonight and we'll all go out together." I stared at him with adoration, nodding yes. Bella waved good-bye before falling backward into the pool.

By ten o'clock, we were set to go. After spending nearly two hours getting ready, Bella and I were in full party mode. "I've had more hands on me this week than this dress will in a lifetime!" Bella boasted in regards to the impossibly tight and impossible to find Tom Ford for Gucci cutout dress. She snorted a line of cocaine from the bar before leaving the room. I picked up the straw and dipped down in a zebra-printed

Giambattista Valli dress. I threw my hips from side to side and let the ostrich feathers on the skirt flutter back and forth. I was on cloud nine, feeling like I had it all—the budding career and the blossoming romance!

When we got to the club, the party was in full swing. The place was so ridiculously packed that I couldn't even imagine going there if one was not VIP, which luckily—obviously—we were. We were escorted to a private area overlooking everyone else. We even had our own bar. Security was extremely tight. I observed a man offer a bouncer five hundred-dollar bills to have access. Even so, the guy and his buddy were soon escorted back down to floor level. Jax handed each of us a flute of champagne and we all three toasted each other a happy new year.

"Let's go to Britney's table!" Bella yelled over the music.

"Cheers!" I shouted into Bella's ear while holding up my drink.

"Yeah, Spears!" Bella shouted back, leaving me with my drink in the air.

We approached Britney's table, clinking our glasses to hers. "Happy New Year's!" she yelled from atop the table. Paris Hilton joined Britney on the table. Usher stuffed a couple hundred-dollar bills into Paris's corset and we all laughed. Bella jumped onto the table and I followed suit. A cocktail waitress handed everyone sparklers. The countdown began. I made my way to my man, who was at an adjacent table with his band.

We leaned into each other, my arms around his neck and his around my waist. The crowd of thousands began to shout out the countdown. "Ten . . . nine . . . eight . . . seven . . . six . . ."

We touched lips. "Five . . . four . . . three . . . two . . . One." The crowd exploded, *"Happy New Year!"* Heaps of confetti rained down. Sparklers fizzed and flickered all around. The spectacle was pure magic. The kiss was spectacular. Jax bit into a tiny something and chased it with a drink. He then popped the other half into his mouth, resumed kissing me and pushed it past my lips with his tongue. I accepted it but did not swallow. "Ecstasy," he explained as he took my hand and tipped my flute to my lips. Out of my control, the pill washed down with the bubbly. I had never done Ecstasy before. I was nervous, not knowing what to expect. It's supposed to be a sexy drug—would I be more inclined to have sex with Jax? Am I ready to have sex with Jax? I felt safe being with him and knew that he wouldn't let anything bad happen to me. He kissed my neck. With each passing minute, I gained interest in the hypnotizing display of flames from the sparklers and glitter falling from above. In time, all of my senses were hypersensitive. It felt like I was floating and swimming in euphoria.

We all returned to the hotel. Many of the celebrities had suites near Bella's. The entire floor quickly became a rowdy, chaotic party. Everything was a blur. I remember spinning up and down the hallway, in and out of rooms. Unsure of my whereabouts and all alone, I recall resting against a wall in hopes that I would stop spinning. My body slid down the wall. I faded in and out . . . in . . . and then . . . out.

chapter twenty-nine

Fantasy Suite, Not So Sweet

Hours before, the halls of the top floor became silent as the partygoers filed back to their own rooms or, of course, the rooms of others. Since then, I remained in the hallway. I had passed out up against the textured wallpaper. I slowly awoke, opening my eyes before sitting upright. I was so groggy. I picked off long curls of ribbon and pieces of confetti from my dress. I looked up and down the sunlit hallway, realizing it was already New Year's Day. But, where was I? I was too groggy to be frightened. It felt like a dream. Gazing up at the door behind me, I read *Penthouse Fantasy Suite*. With a sigh of relief, I pulled myself to my feet and took the key card from the top of my dress. A green light granted me entrance.

The living room and bar area were silent and empty. The hotel phone rang and I heard Bella talking from the master bedroom. I quietly picked up the phone to eavesdrop. "Hello,

Miss Flintstone. The kitchen is running slightly behind schedule. Your breakfast will arrive in approximately twenty minutes. We appreciate your patience." Okay, I had twenty minutes to shower and tidy the suite before breakfast arrived. I collected at least ten empty bottles of Cristal and equal amounts of Dom Perignon and put them in the foyer. I tossed the pillows back onto the oversized couch and flushed away countless cigarette butts left in the ashtrays. Done tidying, I took a much-needed shower and got dressed.

Breakfast was delivered by an eager hotel employee. Hopeful to see someone famous, he looked past me, his eyes darting around the room. "She's asleep. Sorry, it's just me." The employee blushed and smiled, handing over the bill. I signed it and returned it to him. When I turned around, I knew that the employee wasn't looking for Bella—he was checking out the devastated hotel room. I don't know how I'd overlooked the broken furniture, sideways paintings and F-5 tornado–status damage. There was no way to describe the catastrophic mess that was made, which I figured one day I would try to do. So, naturally, I took pictures.

On the cart, the giant plates were covered with large silver lids but the pungent smell of eggs with cheese and bacon wafted through. It didn't cross my mind to question who had ordered the food, given the fact that I had never seen Bella eat a proper meal. I pushed the door open with the cart. The bedroom was also a disaster. The curtains were drawn to conceal the daylight, so I could barely see the comforter and pillows in a crumpled mess in one corner. Clothes were scattered everywhere and a bra was hanging from the chandelier. Empty bottles of champagne lay about the floor. I pushed my way into the room, the cart acting like a sort of bulldozer, clearing the way. Bella was sitting on a bare mattress with her back to me, rocking back and forth and tipping a bottle to her mouth. Once my eyes adjusted to the dimness, I realized that Bella was in the midst of a sexual encounter! A man let out a moan as the star kept rocking back and forth, up and down. I attempted to walk backward in a discreet way, hoping I could retreat from the bedroom undetected. As I slowly crept backward, I grabbed the giant door. The hinge let out an alarming sound. I closed my eyes tight as if that would make me invisible. When I opened my eyes, I saw Isabella staring right at me from over her shoulder. Not as my friend, who I'd been spending time with, but as the movie star, who seemed larger than life. She said, "Lucy, don't be shy. Come in!" Before I could respond, Bella's partner put his hands around her tiny waist, pulling her to the side just enough to reveal his face. Jax looked straight into my eyes, flashing the grin that had previously melted me every time. Only this time, his smile instigated a terrible dropping feeling in my stomach—the kind you get during the descent on a roller coaster. Instead of acting guilty or shameful, Jax reached out his hand and invited me to come closer. I felt as though my world had crashed into a million filthy little pieces. A knot the size of my fist was forming in my throat. I was too shocked to cry and refused to let them see me get choked up.

I somehow was able to say, "Actually, I'm not feeling so well . . . from last night and . . . um . . . yeah. I think I'm going to fly home early." My face was toward the naked duo but my eyes focused on a faint blue flower print on the mattress. I knew that if I dared to look either in the eye, there was no way I could keep myself from losing it.

"That's cool. Pick me up Wednesday morning from the airport and we can catch up then." She acted as if I walked in on them playing Scrabble.

"Okay, well . . . have . . . fun." I closed the door. My heart was overloaded with sadness. I picked up my small suitcase and walked around the room, scooping up my few belongings. I quickly gathered my things and left the suite. Once out in the hallway, I fell backward again into the same wall, slamming my head against it before sliding down. Folding my knees in and hugging them tightly, my mind raced. What *was* that? One thing I was certain of: *I'm getting the hell out of here.*

Thankfully, my parents had not cancelled their "emergency only" credit card and I was able to charge a return flight to Los Angeles. I'd figure out a story to tell them later and eventually pay them back. Knowing that I planned on further lying to them and being further in debt to them financially made me feel even lower then I already was. At the airport, I stared into space, repeating in my mind every detail of what had just happened. I played and replayed alternative ways I could have handled the situation. I could have picked up a bottle and thrown it at them. I could have screamed and cried. I could have let them know that I quit both of them, then and there.

I pulled the hood of my sweater as far as it would stretch over my face, which was shielded by dark sunglasses à la the Unabomber. The next available flight was at 7:15 and I had no choice but to wait out the five hours. Hundreds of people buzzed by but I took no notice to any of them, nor did they to me as I slouched miserably in a corner seat. When I arrived in LA, like a "normal" person, I waited in line for a taxi. It was a hard jolt back to reality. Climbing into the back of a cab, I leaned against my luggage as the car crawled into the city. A large billboard for an airline caught my attention. I stared at the slogan, *Go to a place that makes you happy.* I wondered where that place was. When was the last time that I felt totally comfortable, safe and . . . happy?

"Driver, actually I've changed my mind. I'm not going to that address. Please get off at the next exit." The yellow cab pulled up to the tiny complex with the bean-shaped pool. I considered a few clever greetings I could use on my true friends. I tried to think of the best way to apologize for my behavior and for the fact that I hadn't spoken to them in over three months.

I passed through the always open gate, dragging my bag behind. Julie's familiar laugh bellowed through the outside corridor. Before knocking, I peered into the window. There was a dinner party taking place. They were all howling over a story Sebastian was animatedly telling. I didn't recognize some of the new faces. They were drinking wine and eating in the candlelit dining room. Julie got up to change a song on the stereo. As she moved closer to the window, I backed up, stepping into the dark. She didn't see me and returned to the table. She sat down on the lap of a handsome guy, kissing him softly on the lips. He mouthed the words "Love you" to her and she did the same! Julie had always told me about all of her boyfriends! Who was this guy? I stared at the warm and intimate scene, realizing I no longer had a place there. I've never felt lonelier.

I picked up my bag and decided to walk home. Strolling Sunset Boulevard proved to be enlightening. I watched hopeful throngs of people desperately waiting to get inside Hidden. Why? I wanted to scream out at them across the boulevard, "You're waiting to get into a room to sit next to the people you are standing next to outside!" I watched as a celebrity was rushed inside without waiting in line. Why? The people waiting in line were visibly frustrated. Meanwhile, there was an almost vacant lounge with a similar menu twenty yards away. It made no sense.

I continued down the boulevard that once seemed so exciting and attractive. Now it felt seedy and unappealing. Like a zombie, I dragged on toward my apartment. Once inside, I stared at my phone. It wasn't ringing, and there were zero unread messages.

The solitude made me uncomfortable and I felt the need to self-validate. Okay, so four people aren't talking to me. Who needs them? They aren't my only friends! I called Presley. After several rings, she answered, "Hey, girl! What's up?" In the background, I could hear loud voices and music.

"Hey! I was just calling to see how your New Year's was."

"Oh, so sweet! It was cool. From what I can remember, you know! Are you with B? You girlies should come out. Everyone is here!"

"No, she's still out of town. I'm thinking of going out though. My New Year's was okay, mostly just the—"

"Hey, doll. It's really loud in here! I've got to jet. You bitches call me this week! Love you lots, babe!"

I decided that maybe sending a text was the way to go. Everyone was probably out and unable to talk. I sent a text to Sasha: Hey, Sasha! What's going on tonight? Just got in from Vegas! Sasha answered: R U and B up 2 party? I replied: Just me! I'm down 4 sure! Sasha didn't respond. I tucked the phone under a pillow and lay on my bed. It didn't take a genius to realize that I was completely unwanted on my own. To them, I was "Bella's friend." Who I was as an individual would never be enough for them because there was nothing the others could gain from me. I had never felt so alone as I cried in the dark. I thought, Bella may be a shitty friend, but now she is my only friend. Maybe, when she sobers up, she'll feel horrible about what happened. Maybe, in her own way, she was just protecting me from making a mistake with Jax. I was sure that when I picked her up from the airport, she'd have a reasonable explanation for everything.

chapter thirty

New Year, Nothing New

It was time to pick Bella up from the Vegas trip. A green light invited me to access the beautiful canyon. Turning up the music, I enjoyed the relaxing drive in her Mercedes convertible. The wind kicked up my hair and the warm sun felt comforting on my skin. Gotta love winter in Southern California.

Upon arrival at the private aviation lot, the large wrought-iron gates parted like the gates to heaven. Paparazzi and on-lookers hoping to get a glimpse of something spectacular lined the perimeters, scrambling for a premier spot for star-gazing. They paid me no mind. A small Learjet appeared and landed just as the convertible crawled up next to it, the car's door parallel to that of the plane. The door of the plane slowly fell out, and Bella emerged. Adorned in one of her signature billowing oversized hats and dramatic sunglasses, she blew her signature three kisses to the mesmerized crowd. I rolled my eyes, still feeling slightly sour. As the photogs set off a shooting frenzy, the flight crew packed her multiple pieces of designer luggage into the trunk of the car. Bella took the pilot's hand and gracefully entered the passenger side. I couldn't help but wonder if her "act" was also intended for me. We barely greeted each other beyond polite half-smiles.

After several stoplights, it was Bella who broke the silence. "It was the Ecstasy. I would never intentionally hurt you." She convincingly went on. "Men are just . . . bad habits, Lucy. And I am thinking, why don't we kick all of our bad habits starting today? New year, new us!"

I looked at Bella through watery eyes. *"All bad habits?"* I had been thinking the same.

"And I also was thinking . . . we should have a nice, quiet dinner tonight and go over what you've shot so far, start to plan for the exhibit."

"Really?" I thought about how much we'd both been through lately. Maybe we could get past it.

"Yeah, really." We were back on and so was the plan! I was relieved.

"Mommy! Mommy! Mommy!" The twins sprinted through the house, jumping all over Bella as she dropped to her knees, smothering them in kisses. She hadn't seen them in weeks and, as far as I knew, hadn't called them either. They hugged Bella tightly. Although I had spent a great deal of time with their mother, I had hardly seen them.

An elderly woman made her way down the hall. Wiping

off their hands with a washcloth, she said, "Welcome back, Miss Bella."

"Thank you, Maria. You know what? I'm staying home all week so I'll take the girls from here! Why don't you take a paid vacation and do something special for yourself?"

Maria looked at Bella in disbelief and what I interpreted as concern. "Are you sure, miss?"

"Yes! Please, I'm their mother! I'll take it from here. Thank you!" Bella counted out several hundred-dollar bills and stuffed them into Maria's apron.

Later that evening, I relaxed in an overstuffed chair dressed in denim cutoffs and a T-shirt, flipping through the latest issue of *Vogue*. Bella came in, falling back on the adjacent chair. She yawned. "I forgot how exhausting those two are. They finally fell asleep . . ." Turning over to her side, she asked, "So . . . what do you want for dinner? Italian . . . French . . . Sushi?"

"Neither of us can cook any of that stuff." I laughed.

"Oh please, like I was suggesting manual labor! We're going out!"

"We can't . . . You sent Maria home."

"The girls are asleep. They don't need anyone to watch them snore and slobber on my Egyptian cotton." I was unsure whether or not Bella was joking.

"You're kidding, right?"

"Sushi sounds perfect. Let's go to Soy!" Bella stood up, holding her hand out to me. "Come on. Let's go upstairs and get pretty!"

I reluctantly stood up. "B, we can't leave the girls here alone. It's not right. Let's just order in and have our meeting here."

"I appreciate your concern over my children, but they are mine. You worry about me. I'll worry about them." As I followed her up the stairs, I thought about what she'd just said. *You worry about me. I'll worry about them.* Was I supposed to worry about Bella? Who was going to worry about me?

As expected, Soy was packed. After an attack of flashbulbs, we were escorted inside to a small table in the back. Bella ordered a bottle of top-shelf sake and an order of edamame. We raised the tiny cups and clinked them together as Bella toasted, "To us!"

Surprisingly, Bella got straight down to business. "So, there are probably a few good shots but we definitely need to bust out some more to bring everything full circle." It was as if she was talking just to have something to say. We had never discussed a vision or specific plan. I'd been shooting all along, but just in general, without direction. I was taking pictures of everything that I could, hoping that at some point the theme would just surface.

"I'm not sure what you mean. What I'd like to do is to paint a picture of your reality through portraits, some staged and others candid. But also close-ups on things that would fascinate people. Maybe the stacks and stacks of fan mail in the garage. To the average person that would be mind-boggling. Or maybe turning the camera on the paparazzi? That might be too cliché, I don't know. But my point is, I want to show people the real you in a beautiful, artistic way, rather than calculated images that they would expect to see." I mentally ran through the shots that I'd taken of her over the past month. They were all very staged and typical movie star fantasy photos. Not at all what I'd hoped for. I wanted to show realness. I didn't want to be the type of photographer who created a false reality people felt they couldn't live up to.

"Okay, so we need to show more of my real life." I nodded, thinking she'd understood. "We could show me as a mother, in bed with the kids reading a book at night. That's unexpected. Or a really cute apron in the kitchen type of thing?"

Excuse me? How could I tell Bella that this was not her reality at all? Tucking her kids into bed at night? Reality check: Your babies are forty-five minutes away and home alone right now. And we are forty-five minutes away because you don't know how to cook anything but crack. I bit into an edamame bean and mentally crafted my response carefully.

During this contemplation, Rex Serravezza—a genuine rock star since the early nineties—stumbled to the table. He scooped his arms around Bella from behind and lifted her out of the chair. Had he done it to any other woman in the world, they probably would have cried for help. But not Bella; she loved being out of control and taken for a ride, literally. I followed them to a secluded room in the back. A rowdy rock-and-roll crowd had secured the cavernous private room. Bella sat on Rex's lap and together they did a shot of sake. I shifted in a chair that was secluded from the rest. I felt out of place watching Bella and Rex flirt in their own world. There was no one for me to talk to. Everybody was deep in their own conversations or too busy getting shit-faced off four-hundred-dollar bottles of sake. What about our important discussion? It was quite some time before Bella peeled herself off Rex's pleather pants and motioned for me to follow her to the restroom. I knew what that meant.

"Did he give you that?" I asked, pointing to a bag in Bella's hand.

"Shhh." Dipping her pinky into the bag, she offered a full nail to me. "Here."

"What about the 'new year, new us'?" I crossed my arms, backing away from Bella.

She took the bump and opened the door. Before she exited the restroom, she added, "Starting tomorrow. Don't be such a killjoy, Luce. I'm getting tired of you tossing a wet blanket onto everything."

She forced the tiny white plastic bag into my hand before leaving me alone in the restroom. I held the bag up in the fluorescent bathroom lights and crushed the soft white rocks between my thumbs. I swung the door open in a vacant stall and chucked the baggie into a toilet while simultaneously flushing with my foot. I couldn't get rid of it fast enough. I glanced at my phone for the first time all night. It was nearly two in the morning. On a Monday. I returned to the private room where I found Bella draped over two other has-been rockers. They were all entangled, taking shots. I could tell that Bella was wasted.

"We should get back to the house, Bella." She pretended not to hear me. "The girls will wake up in a few hours for school . . . and someone should be there."

Bella shot a cruel look at me and snapped, "If you are so fucking concerned, then you go. Take the car."

She reached into her evening bag and pulled out a valet ticket and a wad of cash before rudely throwing it in my direction. Money fluttered about. The rockers jeered and laughed at me. Humiliated, I picked up the ticket and headed out the door in disgust.

The sound of the alarm clock in Bella's guest room woke me up. It was six in the morning. Although I had heard Bella come in a few hours before, I was pretty sure she wasn't getting up to take care of the tots, hence my setting an alarm.

I stretched in the morning light, then jumped out of bed and pulled my hair back in a ponytail, securing it with an Hermès scarf I found lying on the dresser. I heard the girls giggling and running around upstairs. I had changed back into my cutoffs and T-shirt before I went to bed, so I was all ready to go. I rounded the corner to help the twins get ready for the day.

I was stopped in my tracks by a frightening sight. There, at the base of the stairs, lay Bella, still in the purple Bottega Veneta genie pants and asymmetrical brown leather jacket from the previous night. Her head and arms rested on the first two steps. I rushed to her side. "Bella!" I frantically called out. Panicked, I gently put my fingers to Bella's neck, feeling for a pulse. I felt nothing. I moved my fingers closer to Bella's ear. Still nothing. Bella pulled her head away, moaning, "Don't touch . . . go away." Two lines of powder were on the step, inches from Bella's face. I could hear the children beginning their descent downstairs. I jolted upward, thinking fast. Hooking my arms through Bella's, I dragged her around the stairwell. I opened the door to the closet under the stairs and left her on the floor. My heart was pounding as I closed the closet door with her inside. I swept up the powder residue from the stairs just before greeting the unsuspecting children.

"Hey kids!" Backpacks on, ready to go, the girls looked around.

"Where's Mommy?"

"She had a meeting this morning! I'm going to take you to school!"

Clearly disappointed, the girls asked, "Who's going to make our breakfast? Maria always makes us smiley waffles."

"Well, your mom thought it would be special if we went to the McDonald's drive-through today." The twins gave each other looks of puzzlement that quickly turned into smiles.

"Alright! You ladies get in the Range Rover. I'll be right out!" I scrubbed my hands in the bathroom and quickly left to shuttle the girls to school.

Returning from delivering the twins to safety, I raced to Bella's house. I ran up the driveway at a full sprint, not knowing what to expect when I entered the foyer. The closet door was open. I tiptoed around the downstairs, desperate to find Bella, but for some reason feeling cautious. I sensed trouble. I peeked into every room and down each hallway.

"What was I doing in the closet?"

I jerked back, clutching my chest in relief. "Oh my God . . . You're okay! Thank goodness, Bella! I thought . . . well, never mind what I thought. I am so glad you are alright!" I was overwhelmed by tears as I threw myself onto Bella. Bella, not being much of a hugger herself, did her best and lightly patted my back.

I joined Bella where she sat on the arm of an overstuffed chair.

"Where are the girls?" Her voice was husky, her face mascara-smudged. I had never seen anyone look so disarrayed. It was unnerving.

"At school," I responded gently.

Bella nodded before unleashing an outpouring of tears. I consoled her by rubbing her back.

My mind was spinning. The whole scene felt way beyond my maturity level and emotional capabilities. When did things take such a drastic turn? Again! How did I get to this place? I looked at Bella—more than fifteen years my senior—and realized that she wasn't larger than life at all. I didn't look up to her, I didn't want to be her, I wasn't even sure if I would be her friend under any other circumstances.

"Whew! Sorry about that, Luce!" Bella pressed her manicured hands into her cheeks in an attempt to pull herself together. She grinned her super famous smile and even forced a laugh, but her eyes looked miserable. She couldn't fool me anymore. "What's on the agenda today? I just need to wash up and . . . I just need to . . . you know . . ." She struggled to find the right words that could turn it all around. I clenched my teeth and focused on my hands as I picked at my cuticles. "We can do a photo shoot today! What do you want to shoot? We can go to the beach, or . . ."

That was enough to pull me out of silence. "Bella." Our eyes locked, both weary and exhausted. "There isn't ever going to be a gallery show. Let's just be honest."

"Of course there will be a show! Lucy—you are a photographer! A great photographer!" Bella put on her best act.

"Bella, you've never seen my work. Your support means so much and I am so thankful that you believe in me, but as kind as it is, it might be holding me back more than anything."

"What are you saying? You want me to look at your port-folio? Let's go get it!" Bella impulsively urged. She picked up a shoe by it's strap from beside her with her left hand and reached out to me with her right.

Looking up at Bella, I thought back to the time when I was at Stefano's house and he offered me coke, when Jax pulled me back into the limo away from my waiting friends, and how I so eagerly went along with everything Bella told me to do without question. I could no longer ignore that all of these circumstances were crossroads where I could go left or right and I consistently chose to go along for the ride, not examin-ing my options at all but letting others choose for me. Through all of it there had been a small voice inside telling me that this was not what I wanted or needed. Yet I kept going with it because the intoxicating high of being somewhere everyone else wanted to be was too addicting. I had to start living my life with intention again.

I took Bella's free hand in both of mine and held it close to my heart. "I can't do this . . . It's not who I am." I concluded that I had become a paid companion, lured by the promise of my dream career. Pathetic on both accounts.

Bella dropped the fringed heel and put her hand over mine. "No, Lucy. Please don't . . . You're my friend . . ."

"And I always will be." I felt a massive weight had been lifted from my shoulders. Part of me couldn't believe what I was saying, but deep down I knew that it was the right thing.

Bella removed her hands, straightened up and smoothed out her dress as if she were about to walk a red carpet, un-aware that she appeared as if she had just walked through the Red Sea. "Okay. If that is how you feel, then do what you need to do. Let's get together this week for dinner or drinks or something," she said as she turned her back, but not before I saw a single tear fall down her cheek. With one strappy heel on her right foot, she hobbled out of the living room and up the stairs.

Once again, I collected my belongings and showed myself out. At the base of the driveway, I put my Jeep in neutral. I rested my chin over the steering wheel and took a long look at the gargantuan estate. I knew that this would likely be the last time that I ever saw the house, and possibly Bella as well.

I sped down the Pacific Coast Highway, letting the salty air tear through my Jeep. The farther away I drove, the more liberated I felt. Feeling dramatic, I wiggled my wrists free of the bracelets that as of late felt more like handcuffs, flinging them up toward the hilled side of the highway. This "stuff" didn't mean anything to me anymore! While maintaining a speed of sixty and with one hand on the wheel, the other untied the Hermès silk scarf free from my hair as I raised it toward the open roof and released it too. The rearview mirror reflected the once-coveted item as it fluttered like a butterfly into obscurity. The release of each material item pushed me a little closer to feeling myself again. I ejected a Phoenix Rising CD from the stereo and Frisbee-tossed it toward the beach. I took in a deep breath of ocean air and loudly exhaled.

I headed straight to my first apartment. It had been so long. I could only pray my friends would have me back. Showing up and begging was my only hope. I stood before the front door in plain denim shorts and a label-less white T-shirt— looking and feeling like myself again. I began knocking frantically until Julie opened the door. Sebastian stared from behind her. They looked at me standing there, my eyes still red and swollen.

"I'm sorry . . . please . . . I'm so sorry," I pleaded as I collapsed into tears. They took turns looking at each other with uncertainty. "There is no excuse for my behavior but I can promise you that I will never let you down like that ever again. I promise. Please forgive me?" Just as I was about to give up hope and turn around, my friends reached out and took me back. I sobbed in relief as I clung to their arms.

chapter thirty-one

One Year Later

"What did I tell you? This crowd would come to the opening of an envelope," Zee Zee Black chortled over my shoulder while expertly adjusting the position of an easel.

The Black Horn Gallery was the talk of the town. Multiple klieg lights swiveled outside, their come-hither movements attracting throngs of people. Presley Dalton and a sculptured male model made their way down the crimson carpet as the media went wild. Limo after limo pulled up to the entrance as one glam gam after another exited a car and strutted to the entrance.

Outside, an entertainment reporter interviewed Sasha Hart about her latest drug scandal. Sasha unconvincingly defended herself—" . . . I mean, I've never even seen a drug in my whole life, except of course in movies and stuff. I have faith that whoever hid a video camera in my dressing room and tried to set me up and blackmail me will be found and brought to justice."

Jax Phoenix hurried down the press path without stopping while flashing a peace sign. Behind him trailed Mot Callahan and Paul Pardee. The press only called for Jax. Mot flicked his cigarette to the side, nudging his bandmate. They gave each other a *here we go again* look and headed to the entrance.

"Like moths to a flame!" Julie giggled as I hiked up the roped-off curved stairs to meet her on the off-limits second floor. "Lucy, are you seeing this right now?" I joined Julie and Sebastian on the balcony overlooking the interior of the gallery. To say that my stomach was upside down would be the understatement of the century.

On the main floor, two fashionable women cocked their heads while standing in front of a five-foot-wide silver print. "Is that . . . Brooke Sands?" one woman asked the other. An enlarged cover of *Dazzle*, covered in a dozen lines of powdery substance and a rolled one-hundred dollar bill, was largely displayed before them. The face of the starlet was barely legible. Sasha Hart, recognizing the origins of the photo, let out a gasp, causing the women to avert their attention to her. Sasha took a swift step backward and, with a nervous laugh, disappeared into the crowd.

The posh groups meandered their way through the rooms, beginning to make sense of the exhibit entitled "Over-Exposed." The collection showcased my behind-the-scenes photo essays in which none of the images revealed the faces or named who was who. That was left to the imagination of the viewer. It was a difficult decision to make, whether or not to use the images to launch my career. But as long as it remained that nobody would know the true identity of the people in the pictures, no harm would be done. As Bella would say, if you're going to step on people to reach the top, you might as well wear stilettos. And the ones I wore that night were gorgeous—I got them on sale.

One of the critics' favorites was a photo snapped over the shoulder of an anonymous celeb (cough, Presley) when I had turned the cameras on the paparazzi. The crowds of men and women were crushing in all around us, several elbowing others in the face and violently—desperately—fighting for the best shot. It was disgusting and scary. And it sold for close to five figures!

Another shot garnering attention was an image of a hotel penthouse, post party. Everyone had heard rumored hotel-trashing stories, but until now they could only imagine what that entailed. The empty Fantasy Suite and its usually impeccable gold and white interior was barely recognizable. "How do you break a chair . . . in half?" one magazine editor asked. "Is that a chandelier . . . in the sink?" said another astounded viewer. My heart broke every time I looked at that photo. I remember signing for breakfast that morning, thinking that life couldn't get any better. Then the rug got pulled out from under me and I thought in the same minute that life couldn't get any worse. I hoped to never have sixty seconds like that ever again in this lifetime.

"Julie, I couldn't have done it without you," I whispered to my friend.

"Are you kidding?" Julie whispered back. "All that I did was carry some stuff and—"

"No—all of it. The past year, the past decade, really. No matter what mess I made, you remained my friend, and I don't know how I will ever begin to thank you enough for putting up with all"—I waved my free hand around the gallery— "this."

Julie stopped my hand and held it in hers. "Lucy! That's what friends are for. And when I become a hard-partying movie star who sleeps her way through Tinseltown, I shall expect the same . . . Deal?"

We shook hands. "Deal."

"Oh! Lucy! Oh my God! He came!!" she shrieked.

"Who? What?" I matched her excitement.

Sebastian quickly clapped a hand over each of our mouths before dragging us all down to the floor. I blew the scarf tied around his wrist out of my mouth. We slowly rose back up, first only exposing our eyes—carefully assuring that nobody had spotted us. Still quieted by Sebastian's hand, Julie pointed and moved her finger along the halls of the gallery. We followed her finger until we saw him.

Stefano flew from one side of the gallery to another and back again like a pinball, the latest assistant frantically trailing him along the way, trying not to be snapped by his boss's cape every time he shifted direction. "How much is this? I want to buy it off the wall right fucking now! Off the wall! *Now!* And the two in the back as well!" he exploded at a caterer passing out charcuteries. The young man shrugged and briefly explained that he didn't work for the gallery before glancing up at the print in question. The photo was of an enraged man in motion, blurred beyond recognition, kicking a tripod and sending a camera into flight toward a set of models who were fleeing the set, horrified for their lives. The caterer looked at Stefano, then back at the image, back at Stefano—clearly recognizing that he was the man in the photo. Each time the boy averted his eyes back to Stefano, Lepres' face got redder and his fists got tighter. The caterer's shoulders were shaking in laughter as he walked away. I had to admit, that felt really good! It was my way of holding a big fat honest mirror in front of Stefano. It was also my way of metaphorically high-fiving his face.

After another celebratory toast with Sebastian and Julie, I slowly walked along the balcony alone, looking down at the scene below. I could hardly believe what I had managed to accomplish and everything I had been through. I checked on my parents, who were sipping cocktails in a corner and whispering. I knew that my mom was giving my dad a list of who's-who, and I knew that she was enjoying every minute of it. I smiled to myself, knowing that I had finally done them proud. Jax paused at the door and, as if by instinct, he looked up and our eyes met. He gave me a nod and a flirtatious wink before turning around and continuing his exit.

Two arms wrapped around me from behind. I turned and kissed James on the lips. Yes, that's right, James Braves was my boyfriend.

"Okay, Miss Butler . . . Now that you are a photography superstar, what will be your next move?" he pressed.

"Oh, so now you're back to being my guidance counselor? I like how that works," I teased, kissing him again. Julie popped open another champagne bottle as Sebastian shot off a mini confetti cannon, sending a glittery explosion of sparkles over our heads. I gave Sebastian a pointed stare. I didn't want to make a mess at my first showing. "Confetti? Really?"

"We're celebrating," he playfully whined.

"Someone major is making their way in," James alerted. A lightning storm of flashes was followed by shouting as a small mob made its way inside.

After a grand entrance, Bella breezed in and headed straight to a wall just below us where an enormous screen print of a paycheck was displayed. She had written it to me in the early days. Our names had been blacked out but in the notes section, it clearly read: *Friendship*. She stood in front of the enlarged check, her eyes widening in surprise. A trio of onlookers commented on the desperation represented in the image. At the time I assumed it had been written as a joke. Now I knew there had been some truth behind it. I was never supposed to be Bella's personal photographer protégé. I was her paid friend.

"Excuse me, Miss Blackstone. My name is Cristof Phillipe, of *American Photo*, and I am wondering if I can quote you for an article that we are doing on the exhibit?" A smart-looking man with a tape recorder eagerly hoped for a positive response.

"Sure," Bella obliged. I took a dry gulp.

He readily stepped in front of her and pressed record. "A majority of the focus here is the darker side of Hollywood—images suggesting the existence of a whole subculture much seedier than that which is documented constantly in the tabloids . . . Would you agree?"

Bella put on her brightest demeanor. "I myself am just shocked, of course. I have never really known any of this to exist in the business. You hear stories, but to see it firsthand . . ." Her eyes drifted to the familiar *Dazzle* magazine cover. She maintained her act.

He continued, "How long have you been a fan of Lucy Butler's work?"

Bella briefly glanced up at the check. She released a small but sincere smile and responded, "This is my first time seeing Lucy Butler's work but I have always suspected that she was a talented artist." It was the most honest thing that I'd ever heard her say. Sounds cheesy, but I was actually proud of her.

"So you'd heard about her work previously?"

Her slight smile grew. "She's a friend."

Presley Dalton, Sasha Hart and a cluster of other young darlings caught Bella's eye as they whirred past her to make their exit. Bella excused herself from the reporter and quickly trailed the girls. The double doors closed after the girls left and swung back open for Bella, unleashing an electrifying sea of flashbulbs and commotion. As she paused in the doorway to deliver an expert pose, she pushed her left shoulder forward and flicked off a tiny piece of glitter.

acknowledgments

This book was a true labor of love. It would not exist if it weren't for my incredible, unwavering friends who supported me not only mentally and spiritually, but lent me their computers when mine broke down, printed my edits at their jobs—forever anonymous!—opened the door to their guest rooms when I needed a reprieve and encouraged me to keep going for it when it seemed like things were never going to happen. I am forever grateful to you. A special word to Adam, Amalia, Ashley, Debbie, Deena, Julie, Lindsey, Rebecca, Samantha and Valerie: This book is dedicated to all of you.

To my parents, Robert and Susan; my sister, Jennifer; as well as my entire extended family: Thank you for giving me a life so good that it didn't inspire my first book to be in the self-help section. Second, maybe. I'd be lost without you and I love you very much.

My literary agent, Kirsten Neuhaus is more than just that. She not only believed in me from the start, but she held my hand through the entire process. Kirsten was unbelievably patient with me, the greenest of all writers—as she had to explain all-things-author, starting with how to track changes (not kidding). I thank my lucky stars every day that I met you. On the same note, I couldn't have asked for a more marvelous editor than Denise Silvestro. Kirsten and I were hoping to find someone witty and fun who "got it"—and then you came along and made us do a happy dance. Many thanks to Lauren Driver who generously guided me to become a better writer and Meredith Giordan, who was so dependable and much appreciated. I am eternally thankful for such a wonderful team.

Robert Verdi, you made my vision come to life and dove into this project headfirst with good energy and heart. Julie Katzenberg, you are the glue that kept it all together and I salute you. I loved working with you both! Thank you for taking a chance with me!

And last but not least, the only real bitch in my life—Bella, my loving little lap dog.

about the stylist

Photo by Fadil Berisha

Robert Verdi is one of the most highly recognizable faces in the world of fashion today. Verdi is the go-to style guru for A-listers like Eva Longoria, Bethenny Frankel, Kathy Griffin, Hugh Jackman, Terrence Howard, and Kristen Wiig. Famous for his wit and wisdom, Verdi is a beloved style expert on screen and in the media on shows such as *She's Got the Look*, *Surprise by Design*, *Full Frontal Fashion*, *Fashion Police* and *E! Entertainment News Red Carpet*. Known for his trademark look of wearing sunglasses on the top of his head, Verdi recently launched his own collection of sunglasses on HSN.